D0534228

IN THE
SKIN
OF A
MONSTER

KATHRYN BARKER

ALLEN&UNWIN
SYDNEY · MELBOURNE · AUCKLAND · LONDON

First published by Allen & Unwin in 2015
Copyright © Kathryn Barker 2015

Allen & Unwin – Australia
83 Alexander Street, Crows Nest NSW 2065, Australia
Phone: (61 2) 8425 0100
Email: info@allenandunwin.com
Web: www.allenandunwin.com

Allen & Unwin – UK
c/o Murdoch Books, Erico House, 93–99 Upper Richmond Road,
London SW15 2TG, UK
Phone: (44 20) 8785 5995
Email: info@murdochbooks.co.uk
Web: www.allenandunwin.com

Murdoch Books is a wholly owned division of Allen & Unwin Pty Ltd

A Cataloguing-in-Publication entry is available from the National Library of Australia www.trove.nla.gov.au. A catalogue record for this book is available from the British Library

ISBN (AUS) 978 1 76011 171 7
ISBN (UK) 978 1 74336 782 7

Teachers' notes available from www.allenandunwin.com

Cover and text design by Design by Committee
Cover photo by Freeimages/StillSearc
Set in 10.5/15.5 Stempel Garamond by Midland Typesetters, Australia
Printed and bound in Australia by Griffin Press

10 9 8 7 6 5 4

For Mum and Dad, for everything.
And for Rob, Wyatt and Orson ...
for being my everything.

ALICE

The night before you shot up our school, I slept like a baby. So much for twins having some kind of mysterious connection. I was probably dreaming of fluffy bunnies, or something stupid, when you crept out of our bedroom and nicked Dad's gun.

The night before it all went to shit for the *second* time, three years later, I didn't sleep at all. I just lay there, grinding my teeth and wishing I hadn't chucked up the sleeping pill. Actually, that's an exaggeration – I must have dozed off a bit because I remember being woken in the morning by your sort-of-pet kookaburra. It still flew back for a laugh sometimes, even though nobody fed it anymore.

There was no point trying to sleep in with all that cackling, so I got up and got dressed. I put on jeans and a T-shirt, despite it being a school day. It didn't matter what I wore, because I was wagging, and it's not like I could ever wear a school dress again anyway. Trevor Campbell and his mum saw to that.

The day you shot up our school, Trevor used his mobile to take photos instead of calling the cops. Apparently the poor boy was in 'far too much shock' to dial 000, although he did seem to manage the camera function just fine. Most of the photos turned out blurry because Trevor was too far away (i.e. a nice safe distance), but he did fluke *one* killer shot.

Trevor's mum sold that photo to the tabloids and made enough money to move the whole family up to the Tweed. She probably should have held out for more, though, because these days that photo's practically an icon. Seriously, people crap on about it all the time. They especially like to say how 'profound' it is, on account of you wearing an innocent little school dress but aiming a gun. On account of you being 'just a girl' and 'just fourteen' and 'just so otherwise normal'. Not 'horrifying', not 'terrifying', merely *profound*. Boy, I can't stand 'profound'. If you ask me, it's just a word that adults use as an excuse to gawk at bad things. One thing's for sure – thanks to that 'profound' photo Trevor took, your face (and therefore my face) will always be associated with a frumpy brown school dress and, well, the obvious.

Anyway, three years later I was lacing up my sneakers and the kookaburra was building up to a very annoying crescendo, when all of a sudden Dad yelled, 'SHUT UP!'

That was unusual. Like, aliens-landing-on-your-lawn unusual. Dad hadn't raised his voice above a squeak in the whole time I'd been back from Merryview. He always pretended to be asleep until I'd left for the day. I guess that bird must have really been getting on his nerves for him to blow his cover like that. To be honest, the yelling kind of scared me. I think it must have rattled the bird a bit, too, because for a moment there was this intense silence, as if the three of us were in some weird father-daughter-kookaburra stand-off. Then, for no reason at all, everything went back to normal. The bird started to chuckle, Dad ignored it because he was pretending to sleep, and I pretended to go to school again.

That whole thing about Dad yelling isn't *significant*, by the way. It didn't play a part in what was about to go down, and the kookaburra isn't some lame metaphor either. I just remember it, that's all, even after everything that happened.

When I left the house I headed out of town along the old highway, just like every other morning. As I walked I counted my steps for something to do. It wasn't like when we were little and I had to touch the light switch an even number of times. It was voluntary, for the most part. I did it to keep myself occupied, you know? It always took me between 562 and 588 steps to get to the old highway. After that, it took another two hundred or so to reach the Giant Emu. The Emu closed down, by the way. Thanks to you, our town had a much bigger claim to fame, and the new breed of tourists didn't go in for gimmicks about 'eating Australia's coat of arms on a tasty burger'. I don't know why – maybe they didn't think it was respectful or something.

Once I'd passed the Giant Emu, I had this little habit of staring off into the bush while I focused on my counting. The game was to look anywhere except the old highway until the *Welcome to Collector* sign was safely behind me. The damn thing still said *Population 865* in big white letters. I guess people were a bit superstitious about updating it. Maybe they figured the little white numbers were like those little white crosses you see lining the highways, and removing them would be some kind of sacrilege. Parents of dead kids can get very touchy about that sort of thing. I'm not sure what the *real* population of Collector was that day. In addition to your seven, I know the town lost plenty more. People moved away. I suppose babies were born, but I never saw them. I never saw balloons tied to letterboxes anymore either. That might not mean anything. It's possible that there were still plenty of kids, with the regular number of birthday parties. Maybe it's just that, after what you did, the idea of advertising a happy gathering of kids seemed insensitive, or foolhardy. At any rate, I was seventy-three steps past that damnable sign – 1,348 steps from town – when I first heard the car. It might have been trailing me for a while, but I didn't notice because I was focusing on my headache. That was another trick of mine. I never took any water with me on my walks because the dehydration gave me a headache. It sounds a bit twisted, but I liked those headaches. It was the kind of pain you could really get a handle on, you know? By the time I heard it, the car was crawling along right behind me, keeping pace. I didn't actually turn around and check. There's a reason for that, but it's kind of complicated. The truth is, the first thing that popped into my head at that moment was this Oprah special I'd seen about perverts. She had some expert on who said that if you think you're being followed, the safest thing to do is turn around and say: 'Are you following me?' Apparently perverts are often cowards to boot, and that scares them right off. I guess I didn't turn around because scaring off that car wasn't exactly what I wanted.

I suppose that, on some level, I'd been waiting for something to happen. I'm not an idiot. I knew that a lot of townsfolk hung their grief on me. I could understand that. It was the whole 'identical' thing. It can't have been easy for those parents to see me cruising around with the exact same face as the girl who'd gunned down their kids. I knew that bad stuff would come of it. I also knew that walking along a deserted highway every day was probably tempting fate. I didn't have a specific death wish or anything – I just kind of … *knew*, and did nothing. That's the best I can explain it.

Sure enough, the car came to a stop and someone got out. Chances were, whoever it was, I knew them. Chances were I'd played netball in their team, or babysat their kids, or skated on their driveway. They wouldn't know *me*, though. I'd just be a version of *you* to them now. Whatever they had planned, they'd see you when they did it. Looking back, it can't have been more than a few seconds between that car door shutting and the craziness that happened next, but it felt like ages. I mostly thought about you, and then I thought about Dad. It occurred to me that if I died in some terrible fashion, he'd be respectable again. He could climb out of his no-man's-land of tainted grief, and join the ranks of 'legitimate victims'. The people who were inclined to give him sympathy wouldn't have to confine it to secret backyard mowing, or surreptitious food parcels. They could come out of the closet with it. And eventually I'd be accorded legitimate victim status too, and everyone would get around to feeling pretty awful about how I'd been treated just because of what you did. And then, right when I was in the middle of this nice little fantasy about me dying and everyone feeling massively guilty, that's when I saw her. She was standing over near a gum tree that was growing lopsided. At first I figured I must be seeing something that wasn't there, on account of the headache. Like a mirage of some sort, just not the usual kind. But it wasn't a mirage, not even a little bit. *It was you.*

You were all weirdly see-through, a cross between a generic TV ghost and Princess Leia doing her 'help me, Obi-Wan Kenobi' thing. I thought it was *me* for a second, that I was having some lame out-of-body experience. Isn't that ironic? All that whinging about people confusing the two of us, and even *I* did it. But the clothes were all wrong. You had this I'm-so-tough-singlet-and-camo-pants vibe happening, and I was still in my ordinary jeans and T-shirt. Looking back, I suppose I should have realised that the singlet-and-camo-pants ensemble wasn't right for you either. But there were a lot of misconceptions about the way you dressed. They got it wrong in both movies, although the second was the worst. They made you a clichéd 'loner' type in that one: black nail polish, too much eyeliner – you know, all the predictable rubbish. That was a real joke, considering how much care you took to look respectable. You always made such a fuss about dressing preppy, even though you hated all that shit. I guess it was this massive joke you had on everyone, but I still don't get it. This is all hindsight stuff, of course. When I saw that ghostly version of you standing out by the old highway I didn't take time out to notice fashion choices. I just kept walking towards you like a zombie.

You didn't see me. You were looking in the other direction, muttering to yourself like a crazy lady. It wasn't until I got close enough to hear what you were saying that it hit me. People always go on about eyes being 'windows to the soul', but I don't buy that. Teaching your eyes to lie isn't such a big thing, provided you've got some time on your hands. A person's voice, though – well, that's another story. There's always some inflection that totally busts you. When I heard your voice, that's what convinced me it was you. I know your voice better than anyone's. Hell, I *should* know it. Your voice is *my* voice, but with edge.

You weren't talking to yourself and you weren't talking to me either; you were talking to an imaginary friend. Like when we were little and you pretended to see fairies, just to shit me. Only, this wasn't exactly a fairy-style conversation. I mean, just picture it, okay? A ghost version of you, telling someone who wasn't even there to check a non-existent pie oven for food? I don't remember if I questioned my sanity right then, but I probably should have.

In typical fashion, I just stood there doing nothing. I didn't turn around to see whether the car had started creeping towards me again. I didn't call out your name. I didn't take any decisive action whatsoever. I just listened, like some kind of stunned mullet, while you bossed around thin air. And then you said, 'Let's go.'

You know how, looking back, you realise that your life could have been a whole other story if just one little thing had gone differently? Everyone in our town has played at that game, I'm sure of it. The 'what if I had done *this*, or hadn't done *that*' torture, where you tally up all the inane stuff that would have meant someone else's kid got shot instead of yours.

Well, things could have been very different if you hadn't said 'Let's go' right at that moment. You see, it made me panic. I had issues about you skipping out on me, funnily enough, and I wasn't about to let it happen a second time. I lunged forward and tried to grab that translucent version of you. The moment we touched – that's when it happened.

That was the precise moment it all went to shit, for the second time.

LUX

'Why don't you take the coat off?' whispers Ivan, loud enough for the others to hear.

Sweat is literally dripping off my nose and the trench coat's already suspicious.

'It's my lucky charm,' I lie, while giving him the finger.

Ivan knows damn well that taking the coat off would raise too many questions, and that I prefer to keep my secret. We've argued about it a lot over the years and more than usual lately. He wants me to take it off, especially now, given what's going down. He thinks it will give them hope. I think so too, which is precisely why I wear it.

At the moment 'them' is a little kid with no name, and a boy we're calling Boots, mainly because he has some. Boots looks to be in his early teens, which isn't much younger than he and the kid think I am. They'd be wrong about that. Me looking like an ordinary seventeen-year-old boy is about as deceptive as Ivan looking like a monster, but they'll work that out eventually, assuming they live long enough.

Ivan and I don't normally have a 'them'. We travel alone, for lots of very good reasons. But things have been different lately. Ever since we realised this place was doomed no matter what we did, he's been on this lost cause mission. I've decided to humour him, hence our two new companions ... whom I've possibly just gotten lost.

Shit. It used to be that I knew this place – every step from the dried-up creek bed to the creepy old boulder patch, and all the stuff in between. After more than three years stuck in the same stretch of outback, I *should* know it. Not now, though. Now there's just too much crap from all the nightmares that people in the *real* world keep having. It makes it difficult to navigate.

Normally I'd just use the Southern Cross to get my bearings, but I want to avoid looking to the heavens around Ivan. Given how things are panning out, I'm sure he'd read too much into it. People deal with the prospect of certain death in curious ways. In addition to his new 'save the kids' policy, Ivan's taken a fancy to religion. I'm trying not to encourage it.

Wait, I signal to Ivan in our private sign language. We're standing in some completely generic bedroom that's feminine, but not quite authentic. Something about the décor looks a bit porno, which probably means it was a boy who dreamt it. You get that a lot. Other than violent nightmares, sex dreams are the most popular thing in here, especially now that everything's gone to shit.

If it was just Ivan and me, I'd tell him straight up that I was lost, but Boots and the kid complicate matters. They're scared enough already and I don't want to push it. Scared kids are prone to tears and tanties, both of which are bad when lives depend on quiet.

I go to give Ivan the signal for *lost*, then realise we don't have one. In all these years, it's actually never come up. I suppose when all you ever do is track and kill monsters, you don't really have any destinations as such to misplace.

In the absence of 'lost' I just stand there like a fool, saying nothing.

Ivan responds by opening his jet-black eyes extra wide, which is as close as his non-human face gets to raising an eyebrow. It's a trick I taught him years ago, and have regretted ever since. Instead of giving his expression a much-needed cynical edge (which was my intention) it just makes him look like a dim-wit. Ivan thinks it's hilarious.

'Very sophisticated,' I whisper. 'You should use that exact expression every chance you get.'

Really? signs Ivan, looking genuinely pleased.

I shake my head, careful not to smile because I don't want to encourage him.

Then I tap my nose twice, which is one of my more *specialist* signs. It translates to, *Reverse psychology, you idiot.*

When Ivan finally gets it, he smacks his forehead in the universal gesture for *silly me* … only he does it with both hands instead of one. That's my fault. He thinks that two hands must mean *double silly me*, and I've never had the heart to correct him.

'This way,' I whisper, fighting the urge to chuckle. I think I'm leading us west, or at least that's the plan. We're going to make our final stand by the western border, because Ivan figures that's where the last of the survivors will gather. He's right, of course, but I've got my own reasons for being in no particular hurry to get there.

After about ten minutes of walking, Ivan points, ever so innocently, to an old road sign poking up through the rubble. Clearly he's known all along that I'm lost. I raise an eyebrow, just because I can, and head for the sign.

People in the real world don't dream of road signs much, so we don't get them in here very often. They're handy though, because before the gangs and warfare, the kids who lived in here used to write directions on them. *Real* directions. The kind that tell you how many steps to the nearest source of water, or where to find shelter. I check both sides of the old sign but there's just the skull and crossbones again, scrawled over the top of some cracked white letters that read *Welcome to Collector, Population 865*.

Collector used to be a bit of an obsession with me. I thought that if I could just understand the real-world town that mirrors this place, then maybe … Shit, I don't know *what* I thought. It's too late now, anyway. Collector might have 865 people left but, thanks to whatever happened there three years ago, *we* clearly don't.

I'm about to keep on walking when Ivan gestures *wait* with a silent flick of his left hand. He's being quiet because the no-name kid's asleep in his arms, and he's trying not to wake him. For no good reason that shits me, so I say 'Hold up' to Boots, louder than strictly necessary.

Ivan either misses my jibe or ignores it. He gives the breeze a long wet sniff. All I can smell is the sweat that's drenching my trench coat, but his nose is way more sensitive than a human's.

'We can sleep that way,' whispers Ivan, soft as his deep voice will let him.

Ivan's 'we' doesn't include me. Unlike everyone else in here I never sleep, and I hate faking it. I don't exactly have a choice in the matter, though. Boots has been with us two full days already. If I don't pretend to sleep soon, he'll start asking questions.

'All yours,' I say, with a flourish.

Ivan takes the lead and I fall back, glad of the privacy. We walk along in single file, picking a path through the junk. It's quiet except for a kookaburra chuckling to itself somewhere nearby. That laugh means we must be near the Edge, because birds never fly over this place. They keep well enough away, and so do the animals. Occasionally you'll see a roo or one of those giant snakes sunning itself off in the distance, but they never get too close. They just watch us for a while before disappearing back across the outback, to whatever else is out there.

I try to zone out, staring at Boots's back as we march along like soldiers. There are a few early-morning flies crawling across his T-shirt, but mostly they prefer the black warmth of his semi-automatic. The gun's too heavy for him but he insisted on bringing it. I guess it makes him feel safe, despite the fact that it's empty. I should probably do something about that, though finding ammunition's always a problem. The people in Collector might keep dreaming of guns, but they rarely bother with little practicalities like bullets, so we're always running low. Perhaps if …

'*Shit!*' I trip straight into Boots. We both fall forward, tumbling onto a rusted-out Holden that some revhead no doubt dreamt up a while back.

'Sorry,' I groan, but that's as far as I get before Ivan sweeps down and pulls us both to our feet with one arm. The little no-name kid, still asleep on his chest, doesn't even stir.

'Are you okay?' Ivan whispers. His wet black eyes scan us for any obvious damage.

'We're fine,' says Boots, not reacting at all to being touched by Ivan's sticky skin, which is impressive.

'You're *sure* you're okay?' says Ivan, giving me one of his mother-hen looks.

'I'll let you know if I need you to carry me,' I deadpan, but it's the wrong answer. Sarcasm doesn't translate well with Ivan. He just nods earnestly, and keeps on walking. I leave a decent tripping buffer between Boots and me, then I fall in behind.

I'm not normally clumsy. My coordination's off because my left eye's temporarily useless. Ivan's still a bit pissed at me for that, and I deserve it. Yesterday when he was carefully dragging his claw down my cheek to give me a fresh scar, I deliberately jerked my head forward. I shouldn't have done it, especially since he was doing me a favour.

Ivan yelped so loud when he saw the split to my iris that he almost woke Boots and gave the game away. Poor Ivan; he really hates doing me damage. Luckily for me, he hates seeing me do it to myself even more.

I used to tell Ivan the cuts were to discourage all the female attention – he couldn't deny it was an issue. It's insane how quickly girls decide they're in love when you look like I do. That excuse doesn't really hold now, though, when almost everyone in here is dead, girls included. Lately I've been hinting to Ivan that the scars have always really been about believability. Looking too pristine in this hellhole would be suspicious, and if the cuts heal too quickly people will notice. Total bullshit, of course, but he's a good enough friend not to call me on it.

Apparently not a good enough friend to spare my *senses*, though. I don't know where he's leading us, but the stench is getting unbearable. It's the smell of decay, sure, but not the usual human variety. This is something else altogether. I'm about to object, when we turn a corner and there it is – the source of the smell that's got us all gagging. It's Sea World, or at least that's what the sign says. This particular aquatic wonderland is little more than a few squashed Coke cans floating in pools of sludge.

Judging by the faded paint and general decay, this is probably one of the old dreams, from back when kids imagined cutesy stuff instead of guns and death and monsters. The sludge is no doubt hiding some adorable sea creature left to fester, which would explain the smell. Adorable is all well and good when Mummy's there to feed it, but there are no mummies here. Not for long, anyway – adults fare rather *badly* in this place: they rarely adapt.

Ivan lowers the no-name kid to the ground and I realise this is it, this is his genius place to rest.

'You've got to be kidding,' I say, very much hoping that yes, he really is kidding.

Smell will hide child's scent, he signs back, not kidding one bit.

Having such a little kid with us is dangerous, sure, but it's pretty unlikely anything will be on the prowl during daylight hours. That's when the monsters sleep, so we should be okay. Finding a place that will mask the kid's scent is a sensible precaution, but bedding down with rotting dolphin? Definite overkill.

Just as I'm trying to remember the hand signal for *paranoid*, Ivan tenses. We've been hunting monsters together for over three years, him and me. Tensing is all it takes. I grab my gun, which *does* have bullets, and shove Boots and the kid behind me.

Surrounded – three – human, Ivan's hands tell me in a blur.

Shit. We've stumbled across a gang, which is either bad or very bad.

If it was just Ivan and me we'd fight if we had to, but there's Boots and the no-name kid to think of. Ivan will be distracted trying to defend them, and he might be tough but he's not indestructible. We'll have to try and talk our way out of it, and by 'we' I mean 'me'. In these circumstances I always do the talking. People are prejudiced, especially under pressure. Given the choice between someone who looks human and someone who looks like a monster, they prefer to assume that the human's in charge.

Two members of the gang step out of hiding. There's a dark-haired boy wearing a faded Superman T-shirt. He looks about seventeen. Next is a blonde girl, maybe a year younger. Not exactly your typical threat, although both of them *do* have guns pointed straight at us.

'Greetings,' I say, lowering my weapon and flashing what I hope is a passable version of 'friendly smile'.

I look from Superman to the blonde, but neither of them seems to be in charge, and you can always tell. Sure enough, Superman flicks a giveaway glance at a decrepit ticket booth. And from behind it, out steps the third so-called human that Ivan caught scent of.

She isn't wearing that ugly brown school dress this time, but I'd know that face anywhere.

I glance back at her two gang members. Both of them are still watching Ivan as though *he's* the one to be scared of. Clearly neither of them have a clue who – or what – their leader is. They don't recognise her face. They must have heard the stories, though. *Everyone's* heard the stories.

Apparently not, judging by the trust in their faces, and Boots and our no-name kid seem equally oblivious. Ivan and I are probably the only ones *left* to recognise her.

'What are you doing here?' she says. She doesn't know who I am, but then again why would she? None of the other versions of her had.

'We've been heading west,' I say, not even bothering to lie. I figure she isn't going to live long enough for the truth to be a problem.

'The monsters are closing in,' I add, which is meant to be ironic, considering she's a monster herself in every way that counts. I'm hoping for a reaction. Something a bit defensive perhaps? I'm disappointed. She doesn't even flinch.

'Is it just the four of you?' she asks, ignoring what I just said about monsters, as though it has nothing to do with her.

Her question about the size of our gang is obviously tactical. She wants to know whether they can overpower us if it becomes necessary, or convenient, or, knowing her, *fun*.

'Yes, it's just us,' I say, trying to sound worried without overdoing it. I slowly lower my gun to the ground and put my hands in the air. It looks like I'm making the universal gesture of surrender, but looks are usually deceiving. Ivan will have understood my true meaning, the almost imperceptible flicks of my left hand that spelled out *on my mark*.

Ivan and I have fought together so many times that I don't have to tell him to protect Boots and no-name while I draw the fire. As far as tactics go, this one's definitely not his favourite. The sentimental beast really does hate seeing me get hurt. He'll do it, though. He always does what I ask when it comes right down to it. Besides, he's a sucker for saving helpless kids, and our two companions certainly qualify.

The trick is to create a bit of distance, so that Ivan and the others won't be hit by any stray bullets.

The gun on the ground gives me the perfect excuse to shuffle forward, under the pretence of moving away from my weapon. Three, maybe four steps and I'll grab the knife that's strapped to my arm and make my play. Her entourage will probably land a few good shots, and every bullet will hurt like a bastard, but I can manage that. When it comes to killing this particular monster, I'm *extremely* motivated.

Later we'll make up some bullshit story for Boots and no-name about how the bullets miraculously missed all my vital organs. I'll have to crack out the 'I can't believe I'm alive' routine again – always humiliating – but it's a small price to pay.

'I'm Lux,' I say, to keep her distracted. It's true in a way. I saw the name on a box of washing detergent that some bored house-wife dreamt up, and figured it was suitably depressing. It's better than Omo at least, which was my other ready option.

'I'm Kell,' she says, but that's not her *real* name. After so many years – after killing so many versions of this school-girl monster – I know what her name is. Maybe she doesn't. Maybe she's forgotten it, like most people do in here, or maybe she's lying. Either way, it's irrelevant.

I risk a quick glance at Ivan. Between us, we've killed all kinds of dreamt-up monsters, but she's always the worst. Sure enough, hot spit is frothing in his mouth. Ivan hates this school-girl monster almost as much as I do. She's what you might call a *shared interest*.

Just one, maybe two more steps and we're there. Given Ivan's speed, that should be enough for him to swoop Boots and no-name away to safety while I do the honours. I'm just about to give the signal, when there's movement behind me, and Ivan's suddenly right by my side, grabbing my arm.

Our sign language is fairly rich with expletives, but I settle for a simple *What the …?* expression instead. It's wasted. Ivan isn't looking at me; he's staring at the girl with a look of surprise that leaves mine for dead. I follow his gaze and …

The pendant that's hanging around her neck doesn't have all the scratches and dents from three years of hand-to-hand combat, but there's no mistaking it. Even from this distance, and despite my banged-up eye, I can tell that it's mine.

My first thought is that she's stolen it. Somehow, impossibly, the little sneak has managed to nick it right out from under me. I'm just about to reach for my neck and check if it really is gone when I stop myself. Probably not the *best* plan, considering our little stand-off. Any sudden move from me and her entourage will assume I'm going for a gun. No prizes for guessing where *that* would lead us.

No, she hasn't stolen my pendant. I can still feel it resting against my chest, just like always. Somehow she's acquired her very own copy. *Someone must have dreamt it up, again.* In all these years, that's never happened. There's never been a copy, only mine. I hate that she has it. The pendant's from the nightmare that landed me here in the first place. The only place it belongs is hanging around my neck, like a noose.

But her wearing my pendant is a nasty coincidence – it doesn't change a thing. She's still just another version of the school-girl monster, and she still has to die. Let's try this again, shall we?

On my mark, I signal to Ivan, for the second time.

But Ivan doesn't move back towards Boots and no-name, ready to protect them. Instead, he grips my arm even tighter, until his claws pierce my trench coat and dig into the skin. Ivan's never laid a hand on me – not unless I begged him to, for the scars, and even then he only did it under protest. For such a built-to-kill beast he's surprising like that, which is why the grip has me thrown. And then I make the connection. Or rather, I realise that *Ivan* has made the connection.

I should have told him. I should have told him right from the start. That would have been the decent thing to do. I didn't say a bloody word, though, and now he must have worked it out. Seeing Kell standing in front of us with my pendant around her neck, he must have put it together. *Shit.* He's finally twigged that the girl from the nightmare that created me wasn't just anyone, like I led him to believe – she was a school-girl monster. The very same thing that we hunt and so desperately hate. But has he realised about the timing? That my nightmare is where it all began? That the very first version of the school-girl monster to ever show up in here *arrived with me?*

I open my mouth to try and explain, but his claws clench even tighter. I can feel blood trickling down my arm, not that the others will have noticed. My trench coat is black and it hides a lot, which is precisely why I wear it. Besides, Ivan and I have practice at discretion. To everyone else it will look like he's holding my arm in a protective gesture, which is worse than ironic.

All I can do is stand here and wait for whatever comes next. Ivan can't kill me, but he can sure as shit *hurt* me, and if that's what he wants, then so be it. I won't fight him. Whatever I have coming my way, I deserve it.

I brace for the blow, but Ivan does nothing. He just stands there in silence, clenching my arm like a vice. Then he does the unthinkable. He turns to Kell – the girl who's nothing more than another version of the monster we've been hunting all these years – and says, 'We want to join your gang.'

After all I've seen in this nightmare place it's fairly hard to shock me, but apparently not impossible. Ivan asking to join Kell's gang sure does the trick.

'Of course you're not joining our gang!' blurts out the boy in the Superman T-shirt.

Shit, shit, shit. It doesn't seem like the Superman boy *meant* to challenge her authority, but that's exactly what he's just done. Damn fool.

Kell doesn't even flinch, but she's clearly pissed at the boy for speaking on her behalf. 'Alright,' she says eventually, with a smile that doesn't make it past her lips. 'You can travel with *my* gang.'

The Superman boy blushes all over.

Ivan and I have never joined a gang before. Boots and no-name constitute a crowd for us. I'm beyond confused, and I'm not the only one.

'Not the little one, though. He'll attract the monsters.' Kell directs the comment to both Ivan and me, clearly not sure anymore exactly who's in charge.

Finally, something to put an end to this madness. Even though she's right – the no-name kid *is* too young – Ivan will never just abandon him. Whatever he hoped to achieve by joining her gang, he won't go through with it now.

Sure enough Ivan lets go of my arm and walks over to little no-name. He crouches down and talks quietly, so that only the kid and Boots can hear him. He'll be giving reassurances until the moment's right to sweep them up and away to safety. I'm watching him intently, waiting for the signal to attack.

Only, something's not right, because no-name doesn't look reassured. He just keeps shaking his head and crying. The kid's scared, clearly, but Ivan still hasn't given me the signal. And then the unthinkable happens, *Ivan hisses at the kid.*

Even from this distance I can see that it's a proper, run-for-your-life kind of hiss. And the kid does exactly that. He drops his teddy and sprints in the other direction. It's an understandable reaction – Ivan can look bloody terrifying when he has to. I wait for some kind of signal to explain what's going on, but it doesn't come. The kid's gone, and Ivan isn't doing a thing about it.

Ivan and I have been friends for almost the whole time I've been in here and I've never seen him scare a child on purpose. Or abandon one, for that matter. In fact, Ivan's just about the biggest softie you'll ever meet.

Explain-explain-explain, I signal with urgent flicks of my wrist, over and over again, until it probably looks like I'm twitching. It's no use. Ivan won't look in my direction.

He's just standing there as if he couldn't care less what just happened with no-name. Well, the others might buy it, but I don't. Ivan's eyes are always wet. Not *that* wet, though. Those are tears, or as close as his body will come at them. So why do it then? Why give up no-name?

I look at Kell, her finger resting on the trigger of her gun, and see that she's just as surprised as I am. She must have been betting that we'd leave or fight rather than abandon one of our own. In retrospect, she probably had *no intention* of letting us join her gang. She's stuck now, though. If she tries to turf us out at this point she'll look weak in front of the others. Then again, letting three strangers join your gang – especially when one of them looks as powerful as Ivan – has a whole other set of problems. Tricky call, very tricky call.

'Alright, let's keep moving. Weapons first, though,' she says at last. Confiscating weapons isn't exactly reasonable, given what's out there, but Ivan doesn't even hesitate. He takes Boots's gun from him, despite the fact that it's empty, and then he walks straight up to me.

Explain, I signal again. I'm waiting for him to unveil the grand plan that excuses what just happened with no-name. Instead he reaches out with fighting speed ... *and takes my knife*.

'What the crap?' I say out loud, not caring who hears me. My knife was well hidden. Kell wouldn't have found it. Not until it was too late, anyway. Ivan's just disarmed me on purpose. He deliberately confiscated my only remaining weapon, and he did it for *her*.

Ivan's got every right to be pissed at me for lying about the school-girl monsters and the fact that I recognised them. That they were all just versions of the girl from my original nightmare. That somehow I was connected. And yet ... and yet instinct tells me there's more to it. That this isn't just some petty payback to even the score or teach me a lesson. Ivan doesn't play those games. Something else is going on here; something's very, very wrong.

Ivan picks up my gun – the one that *does* have bullets – and takes it over to Kell, together with my knife and Boots's semi-automatic. They might not be much, but they're all that we've got and he knows it. This isn't like him. This *really* isn't like him, but I'm way too confused for any kind of action. And so I watch. I watch my so-called best friend surrender our weapons to the enemy, and I watch as one of his claws nicks her hand in the process.

'Shit,' says Kell, dropping the weapons. Her hand isn't bleeding much, but it's enough for Superman to fly into action. He shoves Kell out of the way and pokes his gun at Ivan's chest. Well, his stomach really, given the height difference.

Ivan could take this guy out in a heartbeat, gun or no gun, but he does nothing. He just stands there mumbling apologies, with his head bowed down in this weird submissive gesture. The one to watch, though, is Kell. She's utterly furious, but whether at Ivan for cutting her or Superman for protecting her is anyone's guess.

'I apologise,' says Ivan, his hands raised in the universal gesture for 'don't shoot'. 'They're clumsy sometimes.'

He nods up at his long sharp claws, indicating that they're every bit as awkward as they look.

'Let me help?' continues Ivan, still hunched over in a parody of meek and mild. He doesn't wait for an answer, he just goes ahead and rips a neat strip of canvas off his satchel. Once the makeshift bandage is ready, he tentatively holds it out to Kell, like a tiny flag of surrender. Kell just stands there, staring at Ivan as if he's some kind of poorly trained beast.

'Man, I sure wouldn't want to be that clumsy if I had claws like those on me,' jokes Boots, trying to lighten the mood. 'You must be seriously careful taking a leak, right? Talk about a genuine need for military precision.' Boots acts out how he'd approach pissing with 'military precision' if he had razor-sharp claws instead of fingers.

'We need to keep moving,' Kell says at long last. She grabs the bandage and ties it roughly around her hand. Then she walks off, just expecting the rest of us to follow.

Boots keeps chatting away as we fall in behind her, which he shouldn't really be doing, even in daylight hours. Nobody calls him on it, though, because there's something almost calming about his voice. I tune the words out, and focus instead on his face, on the cheeky smile and easy manner. It's fake, of course. The boy has an instinct for easing tension, which will no doubt come in handy, but the cheery persona is completely put on. There's worry in his eyes, and so there should be.

Boots has been with us two full days. He's seen Ivan use his claws to talk to me in our private sign language, and he's seen him use them in a fight. If Boots is smart, and it's becoming increasingly clear that he is, then he knows Ivan's claws aren't clumsy. Despite his façade of relaxed banter, Boots must be wondering the same thing that I am: *Why did Ivan cut her hand on purpose?*

'Let's try in there,' says Kell, stopping at a decrepit Caltex that's jammed between a carousel and a burnt-out church. Petrol stations are normally good for supplies, but this one's clearly been ransacked already. The fact that she's putting up such a show of looking for food and weapons smacks of desperation. The kids in her gang probably haven't eaten properly in days, and I'm starting to think that the gun they took from me might be the only one that's loaded. Given what's out there, that doesn't bode well for them.

Kell enters the petrol station and Superman boy follows, but the blonde just mills around outside – she knows there's nothing to find here. Boots hovers beside her; after what happened with no-name, he's probably just keeping his distance from Ivan. I've been keeping my distance from Ivan too, but for very different reasons. Avoidance can't last forever, though.

'Train here yet?' I say as I sidle up beside him. The train is this sort-of game we have between us. When things are especially bad I ask Ivan if the train's here yet, and he gives me a different reason for the hold-up each time. A storm, a crash, no fuel – that's about as creative as he gets with his answers, but it's still an improvement. He must have answered 'there is no train' a hundred times before he finally got it. Before he realised that I was teasing him about always being so literal. After that it became a bit of a thing. The real joke is that Ivan was right the first time. There is no train – or anything else – to roll in and save us.

I wait for Ivan's answer. It usually takes him a while to think something up.

'We'll kill her, but I want to draw it out. Make it painful,' he says, after a good long pause.

Well, *that's* certainly a new one. He's shutting down my attempts to make peace, apparently. This is completely out of character for him, and that's not even the worst part. The worst part is that he's lying. I can tell by the tone of his voice. It's not just any lie, either – it's the kind of thing that, in other circumstances, *I* might have said. The promise of torture is what he thinks will sway me.

'I'll go keep an eye on her,' says Ivan, clearly wanting to avoid any further conversation. He picks up Boots's semi-automatic and heads into the Caltex. The gun still doesn't have any bullets, but after Kell confiscated our weapons he asked to carry it anyway – to 'help scare away any would-be attackers'.

Only, Ivan doesn't carry a gun, not ever. He doesn't like them for one thing, and he doesn't need them either – his claws are *extremely* effective. So why do it? Why infiltrate this gang at all? What game is he playing?

ALICE

It wasn't one of those cheesy movie transitions where everything goes all fuzzy and white, then fades gently into some parallel dimension. One moment I was standing alongside the old highway, then *bam*, I was in the Caltex on Perry Street. Only, the Caltex on Perry Street got demolished while I was away at Merryview, so I was actually standing in some place that didn't even *exist* anymore.

The only thing that *hadn't* changed was the gum tree: the lopsided one from alongside the highway. That tree looked exactly the same, and it was in the exact same spot as before … only now it was smack bang in the middle of a can't-be-true petrol station, growing up through the lino.

Just for the record, I didn't have one of those lame 'Am I dreaming?' moments. I didn't pinch myself or rub my eyes like a cartoon character to see if that would fix it. I don't know why they even put that crap in movies.

Just because you can have a dream and not realise you're dreaming, that doesn't mean it works in the reverse. When you're awake and bad things are happening, deep down you always know that it's for keeps.

I also knew right from the start that I wasn't going crazy. I'd lost my mind before, remember. Well, not 'lost' it exactly, but there were times at Merryview when things got slippery. I knew what that felt like, and it wasn't the same.

I guess the normal reaction would have been to focus on the whole 'not in Kansas anymore' predicament. I didn't. At that particular moment every bit of my scatty little brain was focused on you. One impossible thing at a time, et cetera.

You were standing right in front of me, still see-through as a ghost, having the mother of all freak-outs. You were spinning around with this 'does not compute' expression. You were really wigging out, and that threw me. Seeing you scared, I mean. I just wasn't prepared for it. I guess my mind had kind of buried the bit about you being human. I don't mean that I thought you were a robot or anything stupid. I just mean that I'd turned you into a bit of a cardboard cut-out in my mind. It was a good strategy, too, up until that moment. When I saw you freaking out it all fell apart a bit. People are never more human than when they're downright terrified. I discovered that for a fact, when you did what you did.

You must have thought touching something 'real' would help, because you bent down and dug your hands into the ground. It looked weird because from my perspective you were crouching on the lino floor of the petrol station. You stood up with two handfuls of see-through dirt; the same dirt that I'd been walking on a moment before. It didn't take a genius to figure out that we'd swapped places. That somehow you were on the side of the old highway, where I was meant to be.

You'd seen me too, I could tell by the way you never looked in my direction. I knew that game. I watched the parents play at it. They swarmed onto the playground, looking everywhere for their children. Everywhere, that is, except over near the monkey bars, where Sergeant Collins had ignored protocol and carefully laid out the bodies. Even after all the other parents and children had paired up, like a morbid game of snap, they *still* didn't look.

Avoidance only works for so long though. Just like those unlucky parents eventually had to check under the tarpaulin, you finally looked in my direction. And it just about floored me.

I knew that I was still messed up about what you did. I mean, it's not like I'd made peace or found God or achieved any other kind of Zen that implies you've somehow 'moved on' from cataclysmic disaster. What I didn't know – what I didn't fully appreciate until right at that moment – was the extent of it.

I had questions ... Actually, one question in particular. The general masses might have wanted a 'why' but I *needed* it. However much other people might have wondered whether I was a bad seed too, it was nothing compared to the amount of thought that *I'd* given the subject. Hell, I'd fantasised about getting an answer the way that normal girls with normal lives might fantasise about a first kiss or great hair. I'd been swallowing it down for three whole years, and I was about two seconds away from it all spewing out of me.

But then I had that feeling, the one you get when you suddenly realise there's someone *right* behind you. In the movies when the actors get that feeling they always turn around really slowly. I guess that must build the suspense or something, but it's total bullshit. Nobody has that kind of self-control. If you sense someone *right* behind you, you spin around. So I spun around, and instantly regretted it.

Let me just start by saying that they both had guns pointed right at me. Not like the gun you used. Not an ordinary gun that a regular, rabbit-shooting dad could *almost* be forgiven for keeping in an unlocked shed. Their guns were of the computer-game variety: huge efficient-looking numbers that could score you lots of dead bodies, fast.

I've got a real problem with guns. It's one of the many 'issues' they tried to work me through at Merryview. Dr Ben even brought a toy gun into one of my sessions, but it's hard to get serious about a plastic yellow water pistol. That part's not his fault, though. You can buy proper guns no problem, but toy guns that *look* real are totally illegal. Go figure.

The gunman on the left, well, there's no way of explaining this without it sounding like I've gone crazy, so I'll just say it. It was a monster. Not the goofy bubblegum variety that Disney's breeding, but a *proper* monster. The kind that when we were five and you thought it was funny to scare me, I imagined under the bed.

The thing basically had human proportions – two arms, two legs, one head, et cetera – only it was bigger. *Much* bigger. We're talking giant. The stuff of nightmares. Killer claws, knife teeth, slobbery mouth and wet little insect eyes. The skin is what *really* got me, though. It was all sticky and black, with white hairs poking out like granny whiskers.

That monster was hands-down the most terrifying thing I'd ever laid eyes on, but it was the sight of the *other* gunman that made me want to vomit. It was Jude. Not the pretty-boy version of Jude from the first film, or the improbably hot angsty Jude in the American re-make. It was the *real* Jude. The Jude I took sleeping pills to avoid having nightmares about. The Jude I tried to pretend I wasn't still in love with. Your Jude. The Jude you made a point of killing first.

The way people react to having a gun in their face is a very personal thing, I've discovered. Some scream, some pray, some run, some hide, and some just stand there as if they're expecting a 'just kidding' punchline.

I thought I knew what my 'gun in the face' instinct was. I thought that if fate was mean enough to do it to me a *second* time, my useless 'deer in headlights' reaction would kick in again. I was wrong.

With a real-life monster and your risen-from-the-dead boyfriend poking Uzis at me, I didn't faint. I ran. If I hadn't, everything would be different. For starters, I'd probably be dead.

LUX

The door of the petrol station is flung open and Kell runs out at top speed, closely followed by the boy in the Superman T-shirt. She crashes straight into a library stand, sending books flying everywhere, but that barely slows her down. She keeps on running like her life depends on it. *Shit.*

It doesn't matter which gang you're in, or how long you've been here, if you're going to survive, there are a few fundamentals. Right near the top of the list is if someone runs, you run too. If you stop to ask questions, you'll be dead. So you run.

Boots and the blonde clearly know the drill. Without so much as a word they run after Kell and the Superman boy, away from whatever the threat is. I run too, but in the opposite direction. Ivan hasn't emerged from the petrol station. Recent betrayals aside, he's still my best friend.

'Where? Where?' I yell the moment I'm inside, not even bothering with hand signals. The petrol station has been picked clean, but there are plenty of places for it to hide. Behind the crooked tree? Under the rubble?

'It' will no doubt be a special kind of nasty, given the timing. Monsters tend to only hunt at night, so the fact that this one's prowling around during daylight hours makes it unusual. Unusual: that's a *bad* thing.

Well, it's *usually* a bad thing. At the moment, part of me's glad that we're in for a serious fight. I could use the distraction. The problem is I can't get a fix on the damn creature, and apparently neither can Ivan. He just keeps sniffing the air, unable to catch its scent.

I look to Ivan … *Nothing's coming.* It was a trick. Kell must have started running to make us *think* that there was a monster, just to ditch us.

'Shit,' I say, and we're both on the move. *Shit, shit, shit.* I've lived through the nightmares; I know exactly what this school-girl monster is capable of. Right now she has a loaded gun, and Boots is totally defenceless. Bad doesn't even *begin* to cover it.

For all his recent weirdness, Ivan must be thinking the same thing because he's hot on her scent. I can hardly keep up as we run from bombed-out plane to office to yard, chasing her through the dream junk, trying to catch her before she does her worst. I'm not optimistic. At least two minutes have passed and I've seen versions of her gun down whole schoolyards in *half* that time.

ALICE

The front door of the Caltex didn't lead onto Perry Street like it should have. It opened straight onto a kiddie carousel, which was obviously impossible. But I didn't even hesitate. I just kept on running … straight into a library stand. Books went everywhere, but I *still* didn't stop. That's how it works when the whole 'fight or flight' instinct kicks in – survival first, all the other shit later.

I used to wonder what it felt like for the ones who tried to run that day. What it might have felt like for me if I hadn't just frozen up and then fainted. I don't wonder anymore. Running through that crazy place with Jude and the Monster and their guns at my back, I *knew*. I knew exactly what Rachel Dawson, who wasn't even meant to be at school that day, would have been thinking in her last three seconds.

I kept on running, straight past the carousel and into Mrs Wallace's front yard. The silly bat's 'I'm too old for water restrictions' lawn was as luscious as ever, but the rest of the scene was seriously messed up. You remember all those garden gnomes she got obsessed with after Ricky moved to Melbourne? Well they were all still there, only life-sized and naked.

That kinky garden led directly onto a plane that looked as though a bomb had hit it. I'd still never been on a plane, but I sure didn't stop to savour the moment. Jude and the Monster must have called for backup or something because I could hear more than two sets of feet at my heels.

Ten, eleven steps later the whole back section of the jumbo just kind of ended, as though some fairy-tale giant had chomped it off. The real problem, though, was the drop.

But there was a plank of wood. A *thin* plank of wood, like the ones that damsels are always being made to walk in pirate movies. I'm a bit thingy about heights, but I ran down that plank anyway. I mean, it's not like I had a lot of other options, given the whole 'being chased' predicament.

When I hit the ground I was in one of those office cubicle places with ergonomic chairs and too many cat mugs. Only, everything was black and white, like a lame TV flashback or someplace 'artsy'. I kept on running, straight through a door that said *Gents,* but which actually opened onto a dusty old food-court.

As far as reality goes, one screwed-up place leading straight onto another when there should be nothing but highway is a fairly major glitch. You'd have to be a goddamn *vegetable* not to clock that you're in trouble when that starts happening. Having said that, it's not as if I had time to stop and ponder it all, right at that particular moment.

Just for the record, being chased is way harder than it looks. It's fine for the person doing the chasing, all they have to do is hang in there and wait for you to trip or cramp or come up against that ubiquitous 'tall wire fence' scenario. If you're the person being *chased*, though, well, it's a totally different story. You've got to plan a whole strategy on the run. Left on that alley, down the driveway, around the pool, over the gate. It's a real skill, actually. All it takes is one wrong turn and you're cornered quicker than the bad guy in a cop flick.

I kept on running, and they kept on chasing, right up until the big red door. I shoved it open and was a few steps in before my surroundings registered. That's when I stopped absolutely dead in my tracks.

You know how Mrs Colby used to say 'a picture paints a thousand words' whenever someone whinged about her stupid art class? I always thought that was a really dumb expression. I mean, I understand the concept and all, but the fact is you can say a lot in a thousand words if you don't bullshit around too much. Well, my apologies, Mrs Colby, wherever you are. You could have written me a frikkin' *thesis* on the crazy place I'd suddenly found myself in and it still wouldn't have hammered the point home quite like what I saw next.

It was the old graveyard on Dirk Street. Well, that's what it would have been but for the headstones. They didn't poke up like granny teeth anymore – they were shiny and new and totally nameless. The half-house was all wrong too, of course. I'm not sure whether I ever told you, but I kind of had a soft spot for that crumbly old thing. Don't get me wrong, it wasn't the sentimental stuff that I went in for. Marcie and the girls might have gotten all gushy about that settler and his pretty wife. About how 'romantic' it was that he tried to build her an exact copy of the home they had back in England, even though she was blind and couldn't see it anyway. Not me, though. I liked the story because of the way she just dealt when he died. She didn't get all dramatic and leave town, or crumple in a heap, despite the fact that she apparently loved him. She just went about living her life in the half of the house that was already standing. Even before I got fully acquainted with total disaster, I knew that took some class.

Anyway, the half-house was there right alongside the graveyard, just like always ... only it wasn't. Instead of the old sandstone pile that had weathered a century half-built, it was *our* house that I was looking at. Our crappy 1970s green weatherboard, missing the whole left-hand section. I knew that if I went any closer I'd see that the edge cut straight through our bedroom and that all of our measly possessions were spilling out onto the dirt. I knew that's what I'd see because I'd dreamt it that way. The graveyard with its shiny new headstones, half our house right alongside it – the only place they had ever existed exactly like that was in one of my nightmares.

It wasn't just *any* nightmare either: it was the nightmare I had not long after you did what you did. I woke up screaming like a psycho, which is probably what sealed the deal on the whole 'off to Merryview' solution.

But even after I'd left town, that nightmare stayed with me. It was about you and me and Jude and that day. Not the day you shot up our school, but the *other* day. The day the three of us spent hanging out at the half-house until well after dark. The day that, looking back, it probably all went to shit for you, for the last time.

Well, staring at that nightmare, a fairly important point hit home: this wasn't the real world. And the girl I'd swapped with out there on the highway? *She wasn't you.* Not the real you. Not my actual sister. Does it amuse you that I'd thought she was, even for a moment? In my defence, she *had* looked the part. And when things go crazy, you don't always think straight. Not when you're busy swapping worlds and seeing monsters and running for your life. And besides, sometimes you just see what you want to see, right? But I'd come to my senses. Whoever I'd swapped with, she wasn't you. And she wasn't me either. Which begged the very good question: *Who the hell was she?*

How long did I just stand there, wondering? I guess the cheesy thing to say would be 'lifetimes'. In reality? Five seconds, tops. That's about how long it took for the others to catch up to me. My pursuers didn't waste much time; they tackled me straight to the ground and piled up on top. My head clipped one of the headstones on the way down, but that was nothing compared to the winding. Seriously, I hadn't been so squashed since Johnny Milzaric realised that stacks-on was a good ploy for a surreptitious groping.

'How many?' whispered Jude right in my ear, all breathy from running. And do you know what I thought right in that moment? I thought *he's touching me*. Not *he's alive* or *there are guns* or *this is crazy*, just *he's touching me. Jude's lying on top of me, in the flesh, for real.*

Let's get this bit out of the way, shall we? Yes, I thought about it, even after the two of you got together. I know that's probably some cardinal breach of the sister code, but I was in love with him and I couldn't help it.

Actually, that's crap. The truth is I never even *tried* to help it, especially after he was dead and I suddenly didn't owe you a goddamn thing. Jude kind of became my 'safe place' after that, to use Dr Ben's wanky terminology. When I was in bed waiting for the pills to kick in, he's where my mind went. I'm not going into the details. Let's just say that, when I found myself lying on the floor with Jude panting on top of me, it wasn't exactly the *first* time I'd imagined that particular scenario. Well, not that *exact* scenario, but you get my drift.

'How many?' Jude repeated, so close that I could feel his breath on my ear. I muttered something endlessly clever like 'Eh?', while my tummy did the butterfly thing.

And then the 'Jude lying on top of me' moment was over. The bodies that were squashing me to the ground peeled off, and Jude did too. I'd been wrong about that black-skinned monster chasing me; it was actually Jude and two other kids who'd run me down.

As for those two kids, at first I couldn't see their faces. Well, 'couldn't' is probably the wrong word. It's not as if they were wearing masks or anything. It's just that at least one of them had a gun, so I was distracted. I just kept staring at that gun instead of their faces, like boys do with boobs, even while you're talking.

Eventually I forced myself to focus. I was looking at a boy and a girl, both of them nearly my age. Other than the gun, they had that clichéd homeless look about them – greasy hair, filthy clothes, skinny past the point of being chic. And then I had one of those 'magic eye' moments.

Did you ever have a go at that book Marcie's brother was obsessed with? The idea was to stare at these blobs of colour until your eyes adjusted and the whole thing turned into a 3D dinosaur or a seahorse or whatever. Well, I was staring at those kids when my vision sort of shifted and I *really* saw them. Those two kids weren't strangers at all – underneath the grime and skinniness, I knew them.

The girl was Maggie Cooper. I know for a fact you'd remember her. Hell, *everyone* in Collector remembers Maggie. I don't know exactly why she was such a local celebrity, even after she left. I guess it was on account of her being the only girl in town with that blonde-hair, blue-eyes version of pretty.

But this wasn't quite Maggie, not really. You know how Maggie always smiled with her mouth shut because her teeth were wonky? Well, the street-kid Maggie had Perfect American Teeth. There were other Barbie type 'improvements' too – bigger bust, longer legs, smaller waist et cetera. I mean, she even had an adorable little dimple on her cheek just like the beautiful people on jeans ads. It was as though she'd been airbrushed in the flesh or something.

Alongside Maggie, wearing a pair of drastically oversized boots, was Marcus Blue. Actually, you might not remember Marcus on account of your 'hang out with the older kids' cool, but I knew him. He was the year below us at school, and he was super bright, but also smart enough to hide it. Man, that kid could make a joke out of anything, and he was always doing skits that had even the teachers chuckling.

The Marcus who'd just climbed off me was skinnier than the one I remembered, and his cheeky grin was gone altogether. Otherwise, though, he was exactly the same. Only, 'exactly the same' wasn't right anymore.

The thing is, I'd seen Marcus since getting released from Merryview. I was walking out of town one morning and there he was, cutting school just like me. I didn't recognise him at first on account of the whole muscled thing he had going. Seriously, it was as if some gym junkie had swallowed up the lanky kid who used to fake-fart at school assemblies. I guess Marcus must have done nothing but lift weights for the whole three years I'd been away, because that kind of change doesn't just happen overnight, you know, despite what the infomercials promise.

I've got no idea why Marcus decided to dedicate his life to biceps and triceps. Maybe beefing up was the boy version of an eating disorder, and instead of starving or puking his guts up he punished himself at the gym.

Whether or not you remember Marcus, I assume you remember his kid sister. I assume you took aim or chose her in some way. Then again, maybe you didn't. Maybe it was just a stray bullet that slid through her spine and you

43

never even noticed. I've wondered about it a lot over the years, but the truth is I still don't know. Maybe that's why the real-life Marcus turned into such a beef-head. Maybe every time the not-knowing threatened to crush him, he lifted something heavy.

Anyway, staring at the tweaked versions of Maggie and Marcus wasn't exactly helping, so I did what I always did in times of trouble – I looked to Jude. He was wearing his tatty old Superman T-shirt, which I knew like a treasure map. On the one hand, the paint splotch on the sleeve was exactly where it should have been. On the other hand, Jude's Superman T-shirt stopped fitting him when he was twelve, and I know for a fact that he chucked it out the year his dad skipped town.

I tried to get a proper look at Jude's face, hoping for answers, but it was no use. He was too busy staring back at the giant red door we'd just run through. In fact *all* of them were staring at that door looking nervous as hell, guns at the ready. After going to all the trouble of running me down, I was apparently irrelevant?

'Stand guard,' whispered Jude, shoving the skinny Marcus towards the door.

'But I don't have a weapon!' said Marcus, and it was true. Jude and Maggie both had guns, but Marcus didn't have a thing, not unless you counted those ridiculous boots he was wearing.

'Do it,' hissed Jude, in this no-nonsense voice that really wasn't like him.

It worked though. Marcus positioned himself just outside the doorway and shouted, 'Stay back, or else!'

LUX

'Stay back, or else!' comes a shaky threat from somewhere nearby.

Ivan adjusts our course to follow the voice. Sure enough it leads us straight to Boots.

'It's just them,' says Boots the moment he sees us, clearly relieved. He *should* be relieved. Thanks to Kell, he doesn't even have the *pretence* of a weapon. If Ivan and I had been any kind of actual threat, he'd be dead already.

And why *isn't* he dead already? Why would Kell pretend that she was being chased, but then not make her move while she had the chance? I'm about to follow Boots through the door to find out, when Ivan grabs my trench coat and whispers, 'Give me until dawn.'

He could have grabbed me anywhere, but he's gone for the pressure point. Shrewd move. I can't help wondering if it's deliberate, a reminder that, although I can't die, I still have one heck of a weakness.

'No dies,' I say, which is mean of me. I could have just told him to get stuffed, but I'm angry. 'No dies' is a reference to the time we first met, when even simple human expressions like 'no dice' were beyond him.

'I know you,' says Ivan, choosing to ignore my dig. 'You're a good person. You won't just leave Boots and the others. You'll stay with them. You'll *protect* them.'

'What's your point?' I say, because for once he's actually right. I won't leave them, but it's not because I'm a good person, quite the opposite. It's because pretty soon it will just be me in here with the monsters, presumably forever, and I'm desperate to put that moment off for as long as possible. The kids themselves have very little to do with it.

'The point,' says Ivan, looking right at me with his wet black eyes, 'is if you give me until dawn, I won't tell them the truth about you.'

Instinctively I tug the trench coat even tighter to my body, as if I'm cold. I'm not cold. I'm sweating from the run and the heat and the stress, but no matter how hot I get, the coat stays on. I've been wearing the filthy, stinking thing every single day for years. Before that I had to weather their hope, which was infinitely worse. The only thing more unbearable than everyone dying by the minute is when they expect *you* to fix it.

Ivan doesn't agree with my trench-coat philosophy, but he's always helped me keep my secret. I assumed that he understood, but now I'm not so sure. I'm starting to think that maybe I've had it all wrong, right from the very start.

ALICE

Marcus didn't come back through the door alone; he was followed by that freaky black Monster, together with a boy. The boy was about my age, maybe slightly older (seventeen? eighteen?), and he had that annoying 'edgy male model' bullshit about him. You know the type – stupidly good-looking, blonde hair cut deliberately messy, a few tough scars, eyes so blue they look phony. He even had an 'I'm so misunderstood' trench coat that was probably designer and cost hundreds. The look he gave me, though – that's what *really* got my attention.

I've had experience with hate. Hell, by that point in my life I was a goddamn aficionado, I'd had so much stinking practice. Only, copping hate from people in town was different. At least they thought they had a reason. Him, though? Some perfect-looking perfect stranger, who'd probably had some sickeningly perfect life? He didn't have a reason. He was no better than the vultures who sent mail to Dad's doorstep, even though they'd never met us. Goddamn tourists.

I suppose the boy's hate shouldn't have bothered me. I suppose I should have had thicker skin by then, or been too busy worrying about all the other madness going down. It *did* bother me, though.

'I thought they only came out at night,' said Jude, sounding panicked. 'You're sure you didn't see how many?' He was talking to me … only, how in hell was I supposed to answer a question like that?

'Nothing was coming,' said trench-coat boy, shooting daggers at me with those Windex-blue eyes. 'Ivan and I waited behind to fight if we had to, but nothing came. The truth is—'

'It was a false alarm,' said the Monster, in this super deep voice. 'There's nothing to worry about.'

Nothing to worry about, hey? Well, call me crazy, but I didn't exactly find that reassuring, considering how it was coming from a *talking monster*. Not to mention the fact that I'd recently bumped into some ghosty girl who looked exactly like us, but wasn't. Or that I seemed to be stuck in a world of nightmares, with a trench-coat boy who hated me, and a gang of kids from our town who should have been either different or dead. Oh, and let's not forget that there was clearly something 'out there' that they were all shit-scared of.

'Nobody asked either of you,' Jude snapped at trench-coat boy, which for no good reason made me feel a bit better. 'Kell, what should we do?'

I just sat there, waiting for this Kell person to answer, but nobody did. Jude actually had to repeat the question before I got it through my thick head that he was talking to me.

Looking around, it wasn't just Jude either – they were *all* staring at me, waiting for an answer. Is it normal to get distracted when you're under pressure? Well, normal or not, I do it sometimes. Or at least, I did it back then. The fact that they were all staring at me made me think of that lame 'everyone's staring at me because I forgot to wear undies' dream, which is how I came to realise that I wasn't wearing a bra.

When you've got less-than-a-handful, free-boobing obviously isn't a crisis. Truth be told, I mostly just wore bras to avoid hippy associations and high beams. Having said that, if your bra spontaneously disappears, it's the kind of thing you notice. Correction: it's the kind of thing that, when you're done running for your life, you notice.

I looked down, and my T-shirt and jeans were gone. Instead I was sporting a grotty singlet-and-camo-pants ensemble. I was wearing that other girl's clothes. After the crazy world swap, I'd apparently scored the 'tough-chick' attire. And that's when it hit me; the girl I'd swapped with? *They thought I was her.* They thought I was someone called 'Kell'. We had the same face, after all. Me wearing her clothes was all that it took to confuse us.

But it wasn't just clothes. Hanging around my neck, there it was: your convict love token. Well, talk about a 'holy shit' moment. I hadn't seen that coin up close in years – you always tucked it in, kept it private. I don't know why you liked it so much, but you did. It was your talisman, your treasure, *and you never took it off*. Out of everything in the world, that token screamed 'you'.

I looked at Maggie, who wasn't the real Maggie. And Marcus, who wasn't the real Marcus. And Jude, who wasn't the real Jude. They were all different versions of kids that I knew, or had known. *And Kell was a version of you.* That's why she looked like you and sounded like you and had your token. It explained why, when I first saw her, I'd gotten confused. Kell wasn't some random girl who just looked like us. *She was literally a version of you.* Not my actual sister, but still somehow connected.

'Kell?' said Jude, looking straight at me. 'Kell, what should we do?'

And that's about the time I realised that things were a whole lot worse than my initial estimate, because this 'Kell' person didn't exactly seem to be one of the minions.

I guess I should have seen that one coming. I mean, she was a version of you, right? And you were never exactly a wallflower. Even the older kids would shut up and listen when you were telling a joke or making a point. Probably that's just something you're born with.

Wherever it comes from, maybe you got my whole share, because nobody ever listened to me, *especially* not the cool kids. Whenever I was around them, I'd laugh too loud, or be too keen, or say 'totally' until even *I* found me annoying. Maybe that's why you let me hang out with you guys from time to time, to reinforce how cool you were by comparison.

Anyway, my point is I wasn't exactly equipped to pull off an everyone-looking-to-me-for-leadership situation. Hell, I hadn't even had a proper conversation with a kid my age in three whole years, unless you count Higginson at Merryview. He *doesn't* count, by the way. I'm not trying to be dismissive of the mentally ill or anything, it's just that having someone rant about *Star Trek* while they squeeze and un-squeeze their pecker doesn't exactly a conversation make.

'Kell, what do we do?' said Jude again.

Everyone was still watching me, waiting for some kind of guidance that I sure as shit was not okay to give them. Actually, scratch that – not *all* of them were waiting for guidance. The boy in the trench coat was staring at me, looking as if he might literally vomit. I mean, hate to the point of chucking your guts up? That was a whole new low, and I made a mental note to hold it against him.

I turned my attention back to Jude, waiting for him to realise that I wasn't Kell, and blow the whole thing wide open. The real Jude never confused the two of *us*. He wasn't even fooled that time I deliberately wore your denim skirt and blue-striped top, just to see what it would feel like to have him look at me all gushy, even for a moment.

But the Jude in front of me just kept waiting for an answer along with the others.

My first instinct was to tell the truth. To blurt it all out about the highway and the swap and the fact that I *really* wasn't who they thought I was. That I wasn't Kell *or any other* version of you.

I used to be a big fan of telling the truth, as evidenced by the 'dobber' nickname you gave me. Times change, though. I'd learnt the hard way that sometimes people are itching for an excuse, and that if in doubt you should shut the hell up.

And so I shut the hell up. I just sat there, doing my best deer-in-headlights impression. Who knows, maybe I was secretly praying for a miracle, because a miracle's exactly what I got. Not a walk-on-water class of miracle. If there is a God, which I highly doubt, it's clearly not *that* fond of me. A minor miracle, though. Well, a medium stroke of good luck, at any rate. You see, as I sat there wondering how the hell I was going to 'not talk' myself out of this one, my head started bleeding from the crash-tackle fall.

Bleeding from the head might not *sound* like good fortune, but I suddenly had the ultimate excuse: concussion. Short of losing your voice, getting concussed is about the least conspicuous way I can think of to avoid difficult questions. And trust me, when you find yourself in a crazy place surrounded by kids and monsters with guns who think you're someone you're not, *all* questions are difficult.

'She's concussed,' Jude finally deduced, using that voice he reserved for captaining the rugby team. The one reeking with alpha male that always turned me on more than a fraction.

He knelt down so that we were at eye level, looking exactly as I remembered him, only older. He still had the scar on his chin from the time Trevor Campbell clipped him during a game of British bulldog. He still had those perfectly almond eyes that inspired Melissa Jones to write that sappy 'anonymous' love poem for the school newsletter. He still had that indescribable something that you can't teach, and that pretty boys almost never have.

Jude went to hold his T-shirt up to my bleeding head, but he stopped himself. I'd seen his mum do that a thousand times, instinct curbed by violence.

'I'm just going to wipe off the blood, okay?' he said, asking permission. And that question, *that hesitation*? Well, talk about deja vu. Now, don't get me wrong – I still knew that Kell wasn't you. Not my flesh-and-blood sister. Not the *actual* girl I grew up with. She was just some 'other' version, but she still *reminded* me of you. And she clearly inspired the same reaction in this Jude. The way he'd just acted like Kell might lash out, simply for trying to help her? I'd seen that dynamic play out, too many times.

I don't know why it annoyed you that he was one of those boys with an instinct to protect. He didn't mean any harm. It was because of his dad, and what happened with his mum, probably. It was part of who he was. And yet, it clearly infuriated you. Personally, I would have killed for that kind of attention. Then again, as I used to tell the doctors and the police and pretty much anyone who'd listen, *I'm not you*.

'Thanks,' I said, giving Jude the green light to dab at the cut above my eyebrow. I knew that letting him fuss over me probably wasn't exactly in character for this Kell person, but I truly didn't give a shit. Being with Jude in that moment, him rescuing me ... it was perfect. Unfortunately, the thing you come to learn about perfect is that it has a fairly limited shelf life.

Let's just get one thing clear so you don't start thinking I've turned into a *total* sissy. Other than when I got my first period, I've only ever fainted twice. The first time saved my life, apparently. Dr Ben said you didn't shoot me because deep down you loved me, but he didn't know you like I did. Personally, I think it was the fainting that did it. With all those falling bodies and all the confusion, you probably just figured 'been there, done that'.

The next time I fainted was about twenty seconds after I saw Jude's hand. You see, as he dabbed at my head, I noticed there were scars that hadn't been there before. For some reason, that prompted me to look down at my *own* hands.

One of them was covered up with a bandage, but the one that I *could* see was laced with all kinds of unfamiliar scars and scratches. There were hundreds of them cutting into each other at strange angles, like fishnets over chunky thighs. And my biceps were all wrong too. Instead of looking as if they'd lose an arm wrestle to a five-year-old, they had muscle. *Proper* muscle.

That's when the full truth sunk in. I hadn't just swapped *clothes* with that girl who looked like you out on the highway. I was actually in her body ... and if she was anything like you, that pretty much meant I was in the skin of a monster.

But it got worse: if I was in Kell's body, then she must be in mine.

Talk about an *oh shit* implication. A version of you – messed-up, murderous you – was trapped inside my body? Not good. Seriously not good. There had only been 1,348 steps – just 1,348 measly little steps – between Kell and our sitting-duck town. There was a distinct possibility that things were about to go to shit in Collector, again. And you know what? This time they really *would* blame me. This time the whole 'she just looked like me' excuse would be dead in the water.

Right before the blood rushed from my head and everything went black, I reassessed my previous assumption. I decided that the old graveyard with its nameless headstones and our half-house wasn't my worst nightmare after all. *This* was.

LUX

Black splotches of pain are exploding in front of my eyes, and my knees have given way completely. I'm aware that Ivan's grip is the only thing holding me up, but only vaguely. Agony, that's the hell I'm in right now, but the others are sweetly oblivious. They have no idea that I only got as far as 'The truth is—' before Ivan crushed the bones in both my shoulders, just to stop me from talking.

The others. Something's happened? There's a commotion, but I can't make it out through the throbbing. All I hear is background natter. Then there's a whisper, right in close to my ear. It's Ivan. I think he just said, 'Trust me' ... or maybe '*Try me*'.

My so-called friend lets go of my arms, making sure I don't keel over. I wobble a bit, but nobody's watching. All eyes are on Kell. She's ... you've got to be kidding ... she's *fainted?*

There seems to be some kind of fuss over who'll carry her – Ivan versus Superman. Ivan has the strength, but the fact that he *wants* to? The fact that he's *volunteering* to carry one of the school-girl monsters? I can't deal with this, not in my current state. Instead I concentrate on the small stuff … like not screaming or puking or falling facedown from the pain.

With difficulty, I force myself to focus. I watch as Ivan picks Kell up in his arms. He won the prize, apparently. I figure that settles the matter, but no – Superman's getting something out of his backpack. It's not until the rope's actually looped around Ivan's neck that I realise what the compromise is. Holy. *Shit.* Ivan gets to carry Kell … *but he's being kept on a leash by way of insurance?*

An hour ago, Ivan would never have submitted to this kind of humiliation, and I would never have let him. Then again, an hour ago I didn't have two broken shoulders.

The gang is moving out, so I hang at the back, where the others can't see me. Walking is torture at first, but after a while the pain cools off slightly. I'm lucky like that. Mending might be agony, but at least it's reasonably quick. By this time tomorrow the bones should have healed, but the friendship?

I need to talk to Ivan … only, that's not exactly an option. Ivan's tall, so the rope has limited slack. That puts Superman right by his side, playing beast master. Usually that wouldn't be a problem. *Usually* I could rely on our sign language, but not now. My shoulders are currently useless. I can barely wiggle a pinkie, let alone argue it out with subtle hand-based gestures.

I try to catch his eye, but it's no use. He's deliberately avoiding me. Instead I drag my gaze across our newfound companions – Kell, Superman, the blonde with the assets. Looking at the blonde was a mistake. The moment I make eye contact she smiles like it's an open invitation.

'That's a pretty scary-looking pet you've got there,' she says, falling into step beside me. When I don't respond she gives a nod towards Ivan, just in case I'm dumb enough to have missed who she meant by *pet*. She's not actually trying to piss me off; I can tell by the smile and the fact that she's flirting. Still, under normal circumstances I'd get stuck into her anyway. I can get pretty defensive when it comes to Ivan and people's stupid assumptions. Not this time, though. This time I say nothing. I'm not in the mood to defend him, even to strangers. Instead I give a half-arsed smile that I hope conveys 'piss off' as politely as possible.

'They call me Goldie,' she says, not taking the hint.

I respond with the obligatory 'Nice to meet you, Goldie', but I make a point of looking bored. I've got rather a lot on my mind right now, and there just isn't the time for pleasantries. I need to think of something vaguely insulting to say to her that will put an end to all this. Perhaps a tactless comment about the size of her …

'Shhh,' says Superman, as though he's somehow the boss of me as well as of Ivan. I'm very tempted to *disabuse* him of that notion, but I hold my tongue. The little admonishment served its purpose; Goldie has shut up, and I'm glad of the quiet. I *really* need to think.

Ivan's still avoiding eye contact, so I use my time to size up the enemy. *Kell.* The way she's cradled in his arms with her eyes closed, she almost looks innocent. I try to focus on what a monstrous joke that is ... but her face? The pendant around her neck? My heart races and I find myself stuck in thoughts of my ugly little truth again – the one that not even *Ivan* knows about. As far as secrets go, it's not exactly a small one. The damn thing's caused me so much pain it makes two broken shoulders feel like an absolute treat.

Ivan must sense that something's up, because he finally turns around and looks at me. Whatever he sees in my face prompts him to twitch his claws signalling, *Okay?*

Okay about *what*, I wonder. The fact that my best friend just maimed me? The fact that we're inexplicably making nice with one of the school-girl monsters? The fact that this particular version of her is somehow dredging up feelings that need to stay buried? The fact that ...

And then I notice the bandage. Holy. *Shit.* I was wrong to focus on the part where Ivan cut Kell's hand on purpose. The cut has nothing to do with it. Suddenly it all makes perfect, horrible sense. I know what Ivan's up to, what he's been up to ever since he first saw Kell with my pendant around her neck.

I know exactly what he's trying to do and it's worse than I thought.

ALICE

I guess it would sound better if I told you that while I was passed out I had some meaningful moment. Something cheesy, like running in a meadow full of flowers until the sound of voices 'brought me back to consciousness'. Utter bullshit, of course. I don't know how fainting works for other people, but from my limited experience it's dead time. Like a whole chunk is missing from your life completely.

When I did finally come around, my first move was to not open my eyes. I faked it, to buy myself more time. You see, I knew that the ever-chivalrous Jude would be carrying me, and I figured I might as well enjoy the occasion while I worked out what to do next.

I thought about making a run for it, but that didn't seem like such a genius plan. For starters, there were guns. I'd seen the kids who tried to make a run for it when it was you with the gun. Some of them made it, but some of them didn't. And besides, I had no idea what was out there. I mean, life hadn't exactly been playing by the usual rules.

I'd watched enough B-grade sci-fi to guess that the trick to going home was finding Kell again. That's how it's supposed to work, right? If you touch some weird ghosty creature and end up stuck in a wacky new world, then touching them again is how you swap back. Simple. Only not so simple; I had no idea where Kell was anymore. Thanks to me running off then passing out and getting carried away, I had no idea how to find the Caltex again. And who's to say that Kell had stayed put anyway? She could have wandered off down the highway. She could have been anywhere by now. Shit, *Kell could have been anywhere.*

I started thinking about those 1,348 steps. Of Kell strolling back into town, producing a sequel. Of Dad and everyone – all the people I so desperately wished that I could help – suffering, again. Literally at my hand.

But no, I'd been down that road before, too many times. Dr Ben had spent session after session helping me understand that history wouldn't repeat itself. That I was just being paranoid. That fixating on something so morbid, so exquisitely unlikely, was simply a product of trauma. That the nightmare of what you did playing out all over again was not a rational fear.

So I did what I'd been taught to do: I shut that line of thinking down quick smart. I told myself that the town would be fine, even if I wasn't, which was all that really mattered. Even if I could never go home again.

And then I realised … I didn't actually want to go home. Maybe that sounds a bit unlikely, given the mess I was in, but I'd spent three whole years totally consumed by 'not knowing'. Years where I was desperate for answers about whether we were the same and whether everyone was right about me. I had to know if, deep down, I was a monster like you. I had to know more than anything. I'd lived it and breathed it year after year, and suddenly there I was practically in your skin; this was my one big chance to see how I'd react surrounded by life-and-death pressure and guns and I wasn't skipping out on it for anything. Certainly not for the sake of going home to my miserable world and my miserable life. I was getting my answer, no matter what.

And besides, hell came complete with the ultimate silver lining – Jude. Jude, the love of my life. Jude, who was perfect in every way. Jude, whose arms felt a lot stickier than I remembered them.

I opened my eyes just a sliver, and let out a very girlie scream.

'I knew she wouldn't like it touching her!' said Jude, as I tried to wriggle free of the Monster's grip. But the Monster didn't let go.

'Lux, make it put her down!' said Jude.

But the boy in the trench coat said nothing.

'Please put me down,' I finally managed.

The Monster gave me a long look with its beady insect eyes then lowered me to the ground.

Coward that I am, what I really wanted was to just stare at my shoes or something. I didn't. As we resumed our silent march, I forced myself to look – and I mean really look – at the place I was stuck in. And you know what? Turns out all the random junk that we were trekking through wasn't all that random after all. It was connected … to our town.

Well not all of it was connected to our town, obviously. I mean, there were TVs and cars and other generic stuff that could have been from anywhere. But most of it seemed to focus on Collector if you knew what to look for. The aqua ten-speed that Tony King's mum made him ride to school, even though it was clearly a girl's bike. The vinyl chair from Cheap Cuts that stuck to your thighs, regardless of weather. The road sign for Dirk Street that was forever having its 'r' converted.

The worst part, though, was the little differences. Just like Maggie and Marcus were a bit wrong, a lot of what we passed was a twist on the familiar. Like the way the front door to the fruit shop was only half the height it should have been. Or the way the school library had that ugly orange carpet on the walls instead of the floor. All of this might not sound like a massive deal to you, but trust me, when the world as you know it has been given the Picasso treatment, it can be majorly off-putting.

Then again, similarities can be off-putting too, as if I needed a reminder of that particular life lesson. I got a reminder, though. I got one big time. After about half an hour of silent marching, we walked through a decrepit old playground … and through the gaps between the swings, I saw it. Off in the distance, out past all of the crap and accumulated junk, there was the familiar sprawl of red dirt and gum trees. And just like always, there was Dumbo's Peak. The rock formation that, if you squinted and used a bit of creative licence, kind of resembled an elephant's face (assuming you went with the PG interpretation).

I knew right away, just from the angle of the rocks. It wasn't some mystery 'other world' that I was in – not really. I was in the exact spot where some long-dead pioneering genius had decided to build our little outback town, right in the middle of nowhere. I hadn't 'gone' anywhere – there were just two versions of the same place, and I was in the wrong one. *But they lined up exactly.* That's why the lopsided tree hadn't moved when I swapped over. And why Dumbo's Peak was precisely where it had always been. And why it was the same time of day. And why the sky was the same and the dirt was the same and why everywhere was flat and dry and hard, just like back home. They might have been filled up with different things – crazy junk versus a broken town and old highway – but the dream world and the real world? They were the same underneath. Twin landscapes. Like that time you cut your hair off because I wanted ours both to be long – different surface stuff, but still identical.

Well, thoughts of you was all it took for the fears to creep back in again. For me to start worrying about what Kell might have done – or been about to do – to the people that I knew and loved back in Collector. To the ones who were left.

I reminded myself that I was just being paranoid. That,

really, what were the chances? That everything was fine and that there wasn't a problem and all of those well-worn excuses. I mean Kell wasn't *actually* you, right? She might have been some other version but she wasn't the specific girl in question. She hadn't led your life or walked in your shoes, and didn't that count for everything? Wasn't it supposed to have been 'a combination of factors' that broke you? Nature *and* nurture, adding up all wrong? So Kell *must* be different. For starters she hadn't killed Jude, which was one up on you.

And then, right when I was busy convincing myself that all would be dandy, a little voice in my ear whispered, 'It's not safe.' Don't worry, it wasn't some lame inner monologue, or the voice of my conscience. It was Jude, urging me to keep moving.

At 'not safe' my eyes went straight to the one threat that I *was* prepared to acknowledge – the boy in the stupid trench coat. The one who was absurdly called 'Lux'. Sure enough, he was staring at me with the black-and-white hate that had become a second skin on me, thanks to what you did.

I wish I could say that I'd suddenly become the sort of person who stared straight back and held my ground and all that stand-tough palaver, but we both know that's not me. Not really. Not when it counts. The truth is, I held Lux's gaze for all of about two seconds before I looked down like a dirty coward. And you know what? Maybe the universe *does* work in mysterious ways, because the fact that I looked down is the only reason I saw it.

He must have had it tucked underneath his T-shirt before, because otherwise I would have noticed. I *definitely* would have noticed. You see, hanging around Lux's neck on a piece of grotty string was your convict love token.

I double-checked that he hadn't swiped it from me, but he hadn't. Somehow there were two copies, when even seeing *one* was strange enough.

Damn you were weird about that thing. Do you remember the day you came home with it? We were about six at the time, maybe seven. You refused to say where you'd gotten it, probably because it was stolen. Finally, when Dad really pushed for an answer, you said you'd found it under a swing, of all places.

Dad knew you were lying. He knew that you'd stolen it, just like you'd stolen the Andersons' cheese grater for no particular reason. He told you to hand it over, but you point-blank refused. And eventually he backed down, just like he always did when it came to you.

After that day, I never once saw you without it. It didn't matter that you always wore it under your top, hidden from view – I still knew it was there. At first I thought you did it just to tease me. To remind me that the really cool stuff in life was always yours and you weren't sharing. But it was probably a bit of a 'screw you' to Dad too. To remind him that when it came down to a battle of wills, you always had him beat.

I looked them up on the internet, by the way, convict love tokens. Apparently the convicts were so dirt poor they'd scratch love poems into old pennies as mementos for the people they left behind, back in England. The one you 'found' was too old to be fully legible, but I assume it once held a poem of some description. That it was faded words of love that hung around your neck the day you took Dad's gun to school instead of a lunchbox.

The thing is, convict love tokens were always made by hand. Every painstaking letter had been scratched there by some long-dead criminal. It meant that, unlike people, no two were identical. Every single one was unique, and I knew exactly what yours looked like. So how and why did Kell and Lux both have it? What was the connection?

And guess what? I was so caught up with that old penny, I completely failed to register the big-ticket item. You see, even though Lux was standing right in front of me with the coin around his neck, my mind didn't go to the one place it should have. You can tell where I'm heading with this, can't you? You know full well that, looking at Lux, I should have been thinking about your Scribble Book.

You don't know everything, though. For example, I'm prepared to bet good money that you have no idea about the *full* implication of that last picture you drew. How, even three long years and a whole goddamn world away, it was still connected to everything.

LUX

We arrive at the gang's lair eventually. It appears to be a Movie World gift shop, or rather what's left of one. The place isn't exactly in tourist-friendly condition anymore. All the cuddly toy creatures have been gutted to make beds, leaving the floor covered in piles of dirty fluff and polyester 'toon skins.

As soon as we're inside, Goldie and Superman boy – apparently called Jude – go about their 'home now' routines. Kell doesn't; she just stands there, doing nothing. She doesn't spell out the rules or tell us where to sleep. She doesn't even point out the exits.

'So, should we just make ourselves at home then?' I say, hoping to provoke a reaction. 'Take our pick and generally help ourselves? *Mi casa es su casa*?'

'Sure,' says Kell, which is *not* the right answer. Ivan and I have never been part of a gang, but we've encountered our fair share. There's a hierarchy, especially when it comes to new members. I'm not too clear on the details, but it sure as shit doesn't involve first picks or helping yourself to anything.

Goldie and Jude are clearly as surprised as I am by Kell's hospitality, but neither of them says a word. I'm guessing our inglorious leader isn't the type who's fond of being questioned.

'Well, you heard her,' says Jude, after a moment's pause. '*Mi casa es su casa.*' He empties his pockets onto the counter, and Goldie follows suit. Between them they produce two broken biscuits and a mouldy bread-roll – a measly haul by anyone's standards.

Judging by the half-starved look about them, this gang's used to going hungry. *We're* not though. Ivan's a master at sniffing out a meal and I don't eat, so food's never been a problem. In fact, right now my pockets are stuffed with enough to last Ivan and Boots two days, maybe three. It gives me an idea.

'Gosh, I'm so embarrassed to arrive empty-handed,' I say, hamming it up. 'If I'd known it was a party, I *totally* would have brought something.'

Ivan takes the bait. He strides over, reaches into my coat, and produces our supplies. *All* of them. He's sold us out, just like he did with the guns, but this time I was counting on it. I wait for Jude and Goldie to register what just happened. For them to notice that Ivan extracted at least nine different items from my pockets *in one effortless motion.* For them to realise that his claws aren't 'clumsy' and that the cut to Kell's hand was therefore no accident.

I want them to start asking questions, given that Ivan's so hell-bent on not letting *me* ask any.

The plan is clever enough ... but Jude and Goldie are not. They're so focused on the food that Ivan produced they don't even *notice* his claws. *Crap.*

'That's from all three of us,' says Ivan, 'Lux and Boots and me.' All eyes are on Kell now; she's the only one who hasn't pitched in her share.

'Well?' I say, when it's clear that no one else plans on saying anything. 'You waiting for a formal invitation?'

Kell looks confused for a moment, then she thrusts both hands into her pockets. One comes out holding a squashed cheese stick. The other comes out holding a gun. *Shit.* I try to shove Boots out of the way, but my arms won't move, the bones are still too broken. I'm about to just run straight at Kell, drawing fire ... but she's not holding the gun as if she plans on shooting it. She's holding it as if it's something to get rid of. To get rid of *quickly.* Sure enough, Kell puts the gun down on the table, right alongside the food. After that, she backs away until she reaches the wall, then she slides down it into the shadows.

I don't understand. Kell goes to the trouble of confiscating our weapons then just leaves her own gun on the table? It's some kind of message or threat, clearly, but I'll be damned if I know *what.*

I look over at Goldie and Jude, trying to gauge whether this is normal behaviour by her standards. It's no use; they're still too focused on the food to either notice or care. So I turn my attention back to Kell. It's dark, but I can still make out her face and she looks so … *vulnerable*? That's *not* okay. Half the problem is that I know it's all just an act. The other half is that it's the *right* act. It plays perfectly into my feelings and the secret and … I need to speak to Ivan. *Now.*

Ivan's busy using his 'clumsy claws' to help divide up the food, so I position myself right in his line of sight and signal, *talk*. Well, I *try* to – my thumb isn't working yet. It makes no difference; Ivan's not looking anyway. I dramatically clear my throat, but he still refuses to give me his attention. I'm *really* not in the mood for this.

I go over and stand right beside him, so that we're shoulder to elbow. I'm about to say something out loud, when Ivan preempts me with, 'I don't feel like being taken for a *walk*, but thanks for asking.'

So he *did* see my hand signal, then – he just pretended not to. That's annoying. What's even more annoying is the way he just spoke loud enough for the others to hear. The 'taken for a walk'? It was a deliberate choice of words – he's pretending that my botched attempt at 'talk' came out as 'walk', even though the signs are nothing alike. More to the point, he's pretending that even *I* view him as a pet, which is just plain insulting.

I glance back at Kell – she's hugging her knees in a way that's even more absurd than Ivan's docile routine. Well, I've had enough of all this subterfuge and bullshit. If Ivan doesn't want to talk to me, then fine, I'll just talk to someone else. Let's see how much he likes *that* as an alternative. I scan the room and decide that, yes, the vacuous blonde will do nicely.

ALICE

Okay, so I might have wanted to 'push myself for answers' and all that personal-insight stuff, but the thing you have to understand is that I really, really have a problem with guns. Being surrounded by them was bad enough, but having one in my pocket? On my actual person?

Some of my worst nightmares – the ones I had before the pills – were of me as you. Where *I* was the one with the loaded gun and the nasty perspective. I'd wake up all sweaty with guilt and it would take me days and days to shake the feeling. To get it into my head that it was just a dream and that the gun wasn't real. That I wasn't to blame for who you turned out to be or for what you did.

I looked down at my hands. Except that of course they weren't my hands, not really. The dirt under the nails wasn't there from anything that I'd done, and the scars weren't from cuts that I'd felt. The bandage wasn't covering a wound that *I'd* been given. But it was what I *couldn't* see that had me worried. As I stared down at those hands I couldn't help wondering what terrible deeds they might have done without me knowing.

You're probably thinking that my own hands weren't exactly 'clean' in the scheme of things, and lord knows that you're right. At least I knew their story, though. I knew the scrawniness from Merryview, and the sunburn from my punishment walks, and I knew why the nails were always bitten so low.

And just like that I was thinking about home again. About Kell, *who carried a gun in here.* About a playground full of schoolkids, like fish in a barrel. About it happening again; my worst nightmare playing out, all over …

I knew the drill: the deep calming breaths, the 'be rational' mantra. None of it helped. I just sat there, back against the wall, feeling utterly overwhelmed. That was the exact moment Lux decided to *really* stick the knife in.

'So, Goldie, how long have you been in here?' he said. It was an innocent enough question, but he said it in a fake-nice voice, like the one that Dr Ben used when he wanted results.

'Two months,' said Goldie. I was staring at Kell's shoes again, but I would have put money on the fact that Goldie was running her fingers through her hair or something. Some time-honoured girlie gesture that says 'I think you're hot', because you could totally hear it in her voice. The Beautiful People always pair up, eventually.

'How about you?' continued Goldie, somehow making

the question sound sexy. Looking back, I think that was probably the moment I realised that the girl in front of me was actually a stranger. I mean, she might have looked just like Maggie, but she was a whole world away from the small-town girl who favoured the 'sweet' routine when it came to boys.

'Ivan and I have been here since before it all went bad,' said Lux.

'Bullshit,' said Jude, not even trying to hide that he was eavesdropping. 'I've never heard of anyone surviving in here that long.'

'Well *we* have,' said Lux.

'Yeah right,' said Jude, but his voice was kind of limp, and not an actual challenge.

'How did it all go bad?' said the too-young version of Marcus, now calling himself Boots.

'Don't,' said the Monster, giving Lux a warning look.

'Why? Afraid I'll give them nightmares?' said Lux, and was rewarded with a few nervous laughs. The Monster wasn't laughing, though. Not even a little bit.

'It all started one night a few years back, when everyone in Collector had almost the exact same nightmare,' said Lux, ignoring the Monster. 'About a girl in a school dress. With a gun.'

And just like that he'd raised the forbidden subject. Back home, nobody ever talked about what had happened. That day three years ago – it was like this big, deadly elephant in the room. They'd say it with their eyes and their spit and their hate, but never with actual words. Hearing it out loud, I don't know whether it was a relief or a new kind of torture. Either way I'm pretty sure that I was shaking.

'It used to be that each night only one or two people in the whole town would have a proper nightmare,' said Lux. 'That meant there were only one or two *bad things* let loose in here at a time. Not so many that we couldn't handle them. But *that* night …' Lux let his voice trail off. He sure as hell had our attention, especially mine.

'With everyone having the same nightmare, it wasn't long before there were hundreds of versions of the girl in the school dress stuck in here with us. It was too many, especially since almost every one of her *had a gun.*'

It all made a sick kind of sense to me. I was in a place where the dreams and nightmares of our town piled up like junk at Old Malone's. After what you did, everyone in Collector had nightmares about you. Whatever this place used to be, after what you did it was ruined. Just like Collector was ruined in the real world. Just like everything was ruined for me, no matter where I went or where they sent me.

Kell wasn't just some generic 'other' you, then – *she was a nightmare version.* Someone in town had literally dreamt her up. She was their impression of you, post-shootings – the monster who looked like a girl, plaguing their sleep. But *whose* nightmare was she from? Someone who lost a brother that day? Or a sister or a daughter or a son or a niece or a friend? One thing was for sure: if Kell was their version of you, they would have imagined her as the very *worst* kind of monster.

'There never seemed to be any reason behind it,' said Lux, staring right at me. 'The moment she found herself in here, she just started shooting. Hundreds of versions of the same girl killing at random.'

Lux paused, letting the word 'random' hang in the air for a while. Letting the absurdity of it sink in and start to rattle, just like it had rattled the people in our town day after day, year after year.

'When everyone else was dead, they still kept shooting. Killing each other, or themselves,' said Lux, with hardly any emotion at all.

I could picture it. I could picture it exactly, without even trying. Countless versions of you in that school dress, aiming Dad's gun with psycho-steady hands. Kids running for their lives over and over again. Puddles of blood like the ones on the bitumen, but everywhere, so much that it looked fake. The sound of screams and gunshots and death just like I heard that day, but played on constant rotation. One horrific soundtrack laid over another and another, until you wished you were deaf. Bodies laid out in a line like I'd seen before, but stretching on forever. Versions of you gunning down other versions of you. *Kids escaping one, only to come face to face with another.*

Lux's voice was under tight control. He sounded calm, but not in the way Dr Ben always managed to sound calm about terrible things. It was more of a white-hot calm – like the one that kept your hands steady even as you pulled the trigger.

'Before that night, people in Collector didn't dream of guns, not really,' said Lux, warming to his subject. 'That meant we didn't have any weapons. We couldn't even fight back. By morning, more than half the people in here were dead.'

'Then what happened?' asked Boots, almost a whisper.

'It went on for months and months,' said Lux. 'Everyone in the real world kept having the same nightmare over and over until there were only a few of us left.'

I couldn't help thinking back to that time. I was whisked away to Merryview pretty quick smart, but I saw enough before I left. I saw the 'when will I wake up?' look on everyone's faces, as if they couldn't quite compute what had just gone down. As if the idea of aliens landing in our little outback town would have been easier to process than one of their own doing what you did. I guess back then I was only seeing half the story. In addition to wandering around like they were in a bad dream during the day, after dark they had nightmares too. Every moment of their lives had become about what you did, and they didn't get a break from you even when they slept.

Don't get me wrong, I knew everyone in town was messed up by what you'd done, but I thought it was only me who couldn't shut my eyes without seeing you in your school dress, holding Dad's gun. I figured that since I was the only one who got sent away to Merryview, I must have been the only one that happened to. Not so, apparently.

'Eventually, the people in Collector stopped having so many nightmares about her,' continued Lux, 'but that didn't fix things. They still had nightmares about guns and death and monsters instead of the harmless dreams they'd had before. There were always more nightmares, more monsters. We were always outnumbered ... and now the monsters are finally closing in,' said Lux, in an almost-whisper. 'From time to time people will still dream of the girl in the school dress with the gun, though. We take particular care to hunt *her* down.'

Without looking up, I knew that Lux was glaring at me. That he thought I was one of those 'versions' of you that he and his Monster had made a mission of killing. That I was one of those mindless killers who had ruined everything, everywhere, for good.

'What did she look like?' said Goldie. 'I mean, I've heard the stories, but I've never met anyone who's actually *seen* her.'

It dawned on me that the others were totally oblivious. Goldie, Boots and Jude – they had no idea that this 'Kell' person they'd mistaken me for was one of the villains. That she was one of the dreamt-up 'monsters in a school dress' that Lux had just described. Unlike everyone I met in the real world, they didn't recognise your face. Or rather, *our* face. They might have heard the stories, but they had no idea that Kell – their so-called leader – was one of them. Lux and the Monster knew, though, and Lux was clearly about to 'out' me.

'She had dark hair. Brown eyes. About *her* build,' he said slowly, pointedly. I waited for the others to make the connection. The inevitable connection that meant I would be branded a monster, again.

I knew it wouldn't matter that I wasn't technically the one to blame. That I wasn't *actually* some version of you. I knew it for a fact because it didn't make any difference back home either. No matter what I said or what I did, I knew they'd pin their rage and their blame on me. Even Jude would turn on me, like he'd never had the chance to in real life. I was about to get crucified for what you did again, but this time there was more than spit and stones to hurl at me. This time they had guns, and were accustomed to using them.

'In fact,' continued Lux, 'if you want to know *exactly* what she looked like—'

'Then that would be impossible,' said the Monster, cutting him off. 'They weren't all the same. There were differences, depending on how they dreamt her.'

'True,' said Lux. 'But—'

'Is it just me, or is it hot in here?' said the Monster, interrupting again.

Lux pulled at his stupid trench coat as if he was cold. Only, the boarded-up gift shop was like a goddamn sauna.

'Ivan's right,' said Lux, after a very long, very worrying pause. 'The school-girl monsters did all look different. They're gone now, though, at least until the next one's dreamt up. *Every last one of them,*' and he shot me a nasty little smile, just to make sure that I knew that he knew.

LUX

I smile at Kell, hoping to convey a world of hate and loathing. My little history lesson has her looking worried, which is a welcome bonus. She wasn't my target audience, though. That was Ivan, and I've clearly got his full attention now.

'Given how *hot* it is in here, maybe I should take you for some fresh air, hey, boy?' I say, staring right at him.

'Is that okay?' he says to Kell, no doubt just to piss me off.

She nods and I head straight out the front door, with Ivan at my heels. I keep walking until I hit a plastic forest, where the others can't see us. Or more to the point, *where we can't see them.*

'You remembered about the hand,' I say, without any lead-in.

Ivan doesn't flinch, but that's just the warrior in him. I know his tells. I saw the way that his shoulders just tensed.

'What do you mean?' he says, as if all is still normal between us. He's electing to play dumb, which isn't like him.

'When I told you about the dream that created me, I told you about the bandage. That she had a bandage on her left hand. *That's* why you cut Kell.' It wasn't a question.

'Cutting her hand was an accident,' he says.

'That's *bullshit*, Ivan.'

'What if it's not?' he says, suddenly excited. 'The pendant, the bandage – what if it's fate? What if the dream that created you is somehow playing out all over again? What if it's actually coming true, like some kind of prophecy? What if that's the key to how you save them?'

'But you were the one who cut her hand!' I say, desperate to talk some sense into him. 'You …' and then what Ivan *actually* just said sinks in.

'What do you mean that's the *key* to how I save them?'

Ivan doesn't answer, but he doesn't have to, the implication's clear. The idea that I would save them didn't just occur to him a few hours ago when he saw my pendant hanging around Kell's neck. Whatever's going on, it goes back further than that … Which means, so do the lies.

'How long? How long have you had it in your head that I'm some kind of late-blooming saviour?'

Again Ivan doesn't answer. And that's when I realise … *It's always been about this.* We've been hunting versions of the school-girl monster for years, just him and me. That whole time I felt like shit for deceiving him. For not telling him the whole truth about the fact that I recognised her.

That she was the girl from the dream that stranded me here in the first place. And yet, I wasn't really the one with the secret. The *real* master of mysteries was Ivan. He's been biding his time year after year, just waiting for me to step up and do the impossible.

'You've been very patient,' I say, and as if to prove my point, he says nothing. In the silence that follows, I can't help but reinterpret the last three years, which might as well be my whole life, since it's all that I remember. On second viewing, everything's different. I'm a good liar, but Ivan? He's an absolute artist. I never suspected a thing.

There's no point asking – I know exactly what put the damn saviour idea in his head. I just thought I could count on him; that although he knew my secret he wasn't fooled. Apparently not.

'We need to get back,' Ivan says at last, glancing towards the lair. The fact that he has no line of sight to the others is making him nervous, just like I knew that it would.

'Why? If it's *meant to be*, it doesn't matter what we do, right? It'll all play out regardless. Isn't that how it works?'

I lean against a fake tree as if there's no particular hurry. I'm bluffing, of course. I know the school-girl monster better than anyone, and I know exactly what she's capable of. Every moment that we waste puts Boots and the others at risk, but this is my one shot at the truth. Ivan's not exactly the talkative type. I don't trust him to be forth-coming without incentive.

'Picnic?' I say, producing a clump of boiled lollies. The sugary mess was in my back pocket, which is why Ivan didn't find it when he fleeced me for food. I hope it serves as a sticky little reminder that even *he's* capable of missing things.

I pop a lolly into my mouth, despite the foul taste – just like sleep, food doesn't gel with 'immortal'. Then I pretend to look for a comfy spot on the too-green grass, as if I really do have all day.

'Fate needs help,' says Ivan emphatically. He squints his wet black eyes and looks at me, *really looks at me* for the first time since all this started. I've seen him use this move a thousand times, just never on me. It's how he sizes up an enemy, how he scans for weakness.

Well, he can look all he likes. Ivan might be faster and stronger and better than me, but I have the advantage. If he really does believe in all this 'meant to be' nonsense then he doesn't just need her, *he also needs me*.

'Give me until dawn,' says Ivan, cutting right to the chase. 'If it hasn't played out by then, we'll kill her.'

I should tell him the whole truth and put an end to this right now. I should tell him the *real* reason why the dream that created me can never 'replay' or 'be true', not on any level. But I can't admit it, even to him, even to myself.

'All that trouble, just to throw it away come morning?' I say, laying it on thick in lieu of honesty. 'Never mind, we'll find you another completely absurd purpose. How about a prophecy about turning this place into a five-star resort? Now *that* would inspire commitment.'

'I'm not throwing it away.'

'But you just said that if it hasn't happened by dawn we'll kill her, and you *never* lie,' I say, really hoping that, for once, he'll catch the sarcasm.

'It will happen. If there's a time limit of dawn, then it will happen tonight.'

Wow, there's just so much wrong with that statement I don't even know where to begin. The idea that his little fantasy will be fulfilled tonight just because he's created a situation where it has to be is … it's *ridiculous*. One look at his face, though, and I can tell that he won't be talked around. He believes it.

'So why give yourself such a tight deadline? Why not two more days? Or ten? Surely you'd prefer a bit of wriggle room.'

'You know why.'

'Actually, I *don't*.'

'Because you're my best friend,' he says, as if that somehow answers my question. It doesn't, not by a long shot. Does he mean that he doesn't want to drag it out because he knows what being around her is doing to me? Does he mean that he knows my self-control won't last a matter of days, and that even a few more hours is pushing it?

'Promise?' says Ivan, trying for the millionth time to raise an eyebrow.

'Fine,' I say at last. The eyebrow's what sways me. It's a reminder that Ivan's not the type to quit on something, even if it's impossible. Besides, when it comes to exposing my secret to the others, I'd say that he's way past idle threats.

And so we walk back to the lair in silence. When we arrive Ivan says, 'I'll stand guard in case anything's out there.' Only he says it with his mouth instead of his hands, as if we're practically strangers. I just nod and head inside, to where the others are sleeping.

I sit with my back against the wall and force myself to wait two whole minutes before I turn my head and check. Sure enough Ivan's positioned himself with a clear line of sight to where I'm sitting. He's not watching for monsters, *he's watching me*. So much for trust, hey, Ivan? Well, he needn't worry. I made a promise and I'll keep my word. Come dawn, though, it's over. At the very first hint of morning, Kell is dead.

ALICE

After his gruesome little bedtime story, Lux took the Monster on some kind of stroll and everyone else settled in to sleep, despite it being light outside. I mean, sleep? Really? They'd just been given the how and why of their whole goddamn world coming to an end, and they didn't even get angry. They just lay down and took it, kind of like Dad did. It requires major experience with bad stuff to skip all the way to acceptance, and I couldn't help feeling sad for them. That kind of defeat normally takes a lifetime.

I knew that I wouldn't sleep during the middle of the day – especially without my pills – so I decided to fake it. I lay down and hugged my knees, just like when I was a kid and all my fears were petty and limited.

Eventually I heard the rhythmic sounds of the others sleeping, and that helped. I hadn't heard anyone sleep in years. I had my own private room at Merryview, and once

I got home it wasn't like Dad casually snoozed in front of the footy anymore. Even when he pretended to sleep, he mostly did it in private.

It was strange hearing sleep sounds again, because up until that moment I didn't even know that I'd missed them. I'd forgotten how accustomed I was to you tossing and turning in the bed next to mine. Perhaps it was nostalgia, then, that meant the sleeping noises helped calm my nerves. Then again, perhaps I'd just learned to take comfort in the sound of people breathing. It's a luxury you can't always count on.

Well, the calm deserted me the moment I heard footsteps. I tried to pretend that they weren't coming towards me, but not even *I* had that much talent for self-deception. I knew who it was. It was Lux. I'd seen him sneak back inside the hideout a few minutes before, and now he was coming to do me damage. Coming to act on the hate that had been dancing in his eyes all morning.

Some primal part of my brain yelled at me to protect myself, to run or scream or put up a fight of some kind. I didn't do any of those things. I just lay there, pretending it wasn't happening, and that none of the bad stuff was true. It's a form of denial, they tell me, like the way Mrs Battinson keeps Kylie's room as a shrine, and the way Mr Winden still talks about George in the present tense.

I kept my eyes shut, but I knew that Lux was close. I could feel his body crouch over me, well within striking distance. I tensed, not sure whether it was to brace myself for a blow or to fight back tooth and nail. I'd come to appreciate that my reactions to danger weren't exactly predictable. Perhaps my body liked to decide on a case-by-case basis whether survival was worth it – you know, keep its options open.

'Did I do something wrong?' he whispered.

It wasn't Lux crouching over me, it was Jude.

I forgot where I was; I forgot the context. I imagined that he was asking me the *real* question. The much bigger question of whether he did something wrong in relation to you. A wrong move or wrong word that somehow, in some small way, led to what you did.

I wanted to tell him no. A thousand times no, that he never did anything wrong. That what happened couldn't have been because of anything he did or didn't do. That just because he knew you better than most, he wasn't to blame. That he was only fifteen years old when it happened – just a kid, really – and you can't blame a kid for that kind of thing. You can't blame a kid for not picking up on early warning signs when none of the adults did either. And he did nothing to deserve to die.

'You've been acting really strange today,' he said. He kind of looked down as he said it, though, so that it didn't come across as a challenge. Poor Jude, even after all that had happened he was still deferring to a version of you.

And in that moment, with him and me whispering in the semi-darkness, I almost told that him I wasn't Kell. I *wanted* to tell him. I wanted to tell him everything that had happened, start to finish, so that I could crumple like a damsel and let him save me. Let him hold me in his arms and reel off all the classics, like 'It's going to be okay' and 'I won't let anything happen to you'.

But then I saw his eyes. Or rather, I didn't see them. He was still looking at the ground, waiting for an answer. And you know what I realised? I might have had Jude pegged as Handsome Prince right from the start, but he didn't actually *want* to be doing the saving. He was looking to *me* for comfort, not the other way around. And after everything that had happened, I owed him that much.

'I think I've just been a bit concussed,' I lied, again. Never has a minor head injury been given so much god-damn credit.

'So it's got nothing to do with me?'

'No, of course not,' I said, and meant it.

'Then why are you sleeping over here?' he said eventually, clearly embarrassed.

And I finally got it. Jude had been lying on the only proper mattress in the whole place. It was a double. Kell must have normally slept there with him. Clearly they were a couple, just like you and the real Jude had been, and by retreating to a corner I'd rebuffed him. Actually, I'd *publicly* rebuffed him ... and yet there he was, crouching down at my side, anything but mad. He just wanted to know if *he'd* done something wrong.

'I want to keep an eye on things tonight,' I said lamely, half pulling myself back up to a sitting position. 'You know, to make sure everything's safe?' I shot a meaningful glance at Lux, who was still sitting in shadow against the opposite wall, minus his Monster.

It was the only excuse I could think of, but it seemed to work some kind of magic. Never underestimate people's capacity for believing what they want to hear, as Dr Ben once helpfully told me. It was good advice. The moment I applied it to him and the other doctors at Merryview, I started showing 'dramatic improvement'.

'Why did you let them join the gang?' Jude whispered, not even bothering to hide the hurt.

That was a very good question. I had no idea why Kell would have let Lux and the Monster join her gang. She couldn't have been dumb enough to think they meant her anything but harm. Maybe she had a bit of a masochistic streak, which I could relate to.

'I'll tell you later,' I said, totally bluffing. Then I gestured in a way that suggested it wasn't safe to talk. Jude gave me a curt nod and lay down next to me on the floor.

Now, when I say Jude lay down next to me, I mean *right* next to me. The whole left side of my body was touching his. I stared straight ahead, trying to focus ... but it was impossible. I mean, Jude was pressed up against me, his thigh against my thigh.

So much about what you did made no sense to me, but Jude was the hardest to understand. I mean, why him? You knew the other six, I suppose. In a school of less than a hundred, you kind of had to. But you didn't really *know* them.

You knew Jude, though, and I have to believe that in some way – somewhere in your complicated madness – you loved him. Certainly he was the closest you came to love,

90

I think. I suspect you just found Dad annoying, and you tolerated me at best. Perhaps I reminded you of the worst possible version of yourself. The way I eventually became so fixated on not being like you? Maybe that's how you'd felt about me all along. Maybe that was part of the problem.

Jude loved you though; he really did. Is that why you killed him first? Did it piss you off that no matter how cruel you were to him he *still* loved you? Did that offend you in some way?

Well, as much as he loved you, I think I loved him more, even after he died. I thought I'd never have him, first because he was yours, and then because he was dead. So you can imagine what it felt like when he moved even closer, so that our legs were intertwined. So that I could feel his breath against my neck and then his hand across my midriff, under the singlet, skin on skin.

I closed my eyes, but he didn't stop. He pressed himself up against me, even closer, and I could tell that he was turned on from his quick, sharp breaths.

His hand slid across me but I just lay there like a corpse, not moving one bit. I hadn't exactly had much experience with the opposite sex, if truth be told. I know that I told you I'd made it to second base with Eric Hughes, but that was mostly bullshit. Okay, pretty much *all* bullshit.

Now, I realise that you're supposed to kiss with your eyes shut, but I wanted mine open. I wanted to experience that kiss with every single one of my senses, it had been such a long time coming. I wanted to see those big brown eyes that I'd missed for every second since you did what you did. The eyes that I sometimes felt guilty for missing more than all the others put together.

Then Jude – perfect, wonderful Jude – gave me exactly what I thought I'd always wanted. That look. The look he reserved for you and you alone. The way he'd always looked at you and *only* you. It's funny how the one thing you think you want can mess you up the most. Like those people who work their whole lives to get famous, then do nothing but whinge about it.

When Jude gave me that look it spooked me.

I expected him to see that I was rattled. To read the sudden shift in my face or the mood or whatever. I guess I expected it because deep down I'd always believed that the two of us were 'in tune' and all that mushy stuff, despite you. Well, he didn't. He leant in and kissed me anyway.

I wish I could say it was just like I always imagined it would be. That after so many years of fantasising about him kissing me just once the way he kissed you so often, so casually, it would be everything I'd dreamt of. The truth is I was distracted. I kept expecting him to realise I was an imposter. To pull back and say '*You're not her*'. But he didn't. He just kept on kissing me like I was Kell – who was a version of you – and it terrified me. The fact that Jude – any version of Jude – could mistake the two of us in such a fundamental way scared me to the bone. Before I even knew what I was doing, I'd shoved him off me.

Jude just stared at me, totally hurt. I wanted to say something – to put it right again and go back to the oblivion of kissing. Only I couldn't find the guts to say a word. I just stared at him until he got up and went back to the skuzzy double mattress without me.

I don't know what I expected. Jude had never been a 'punch the wall' kind of guy, but to just get up and walk away? It kind of gave me the impression that what had happened wasn't exactly new to him. Kell shoving him off, I mean. Which made me wonder why he even bothered. It was kind of sad to think of him continually putting himself out there if she kept treating him so badly. Maybe he was as much in love with her as the *real* Jude had been with you. Maybe that's just what love *meant* to him.

After a while I heard Jude snoring along with the rest of them. I tried to convince myself that they were fake snores to save face, but they weren't. They were real. He wasn't lying there brooding over what had just happened; he was sleeping. And somehow it made me feel more alone than ever. It was right then, when the empty feeling inside was bigger and badder than ever, that Lux went ahead and made things worse.

'I know what you are,' he whispered, just loud enough for me to hear. His voice was stripped back to the bare essentials of hate and something else, something raw.

I held my breath … and I realised that I was waiting for him to tell me, because I honestly didn't know.

All I could think was, *What? What am I?* I wished *someone* would give me an answer, instead of Dr Ben crapping on about me being 'my own person' and everyone from town only ever seeing a monster in me. And what was I now? What was I now that I was in the body of some twisted, dreamt-up version of you?

I was so desperate for any kind of answer that I was prepared to let Lux tell me. Prepared to let *anyone* tell me. But he didn't. He didn't say another word. He just sat there, letting me suffer.

In the three years after what you did I was pretty careful not to hate anybody. Hate wasn't a good sign when you were in my particular situation. Strong emotions were to be carefully avoided, et cetera. But in that moment I made an exception. For the first time since what you did I allowed myself the indulgence of truly hating someone back. And you know what? Dr Ben was right all along – hate really *is* a gateway drug. One little taste, and pretty soon you're into the hard stuff.

LUX

'I know what you are,' I whisper, once lover-boy is snoring. I wait for her to say something – anything – but she doesn't. Instead she lets my words hang in the air, taunting me. The irony is, I was lying. I don't know what she is, not really. The other school-girl monsters had all been mindless killers … but Kell? Something about her is different … or rather, the same. The same pendant. The same confusion in me …

I shut my eyes but all I see is her kissing Jude, which just dredges things up again. I thought that after the last three years I'd wiped all that trickiness clean. Apparently *not*. I need to change tactics, to get on the offensive again.

Slowly, and with reasonable pain to my shoulders, I take the pendant from around my neck. It's been ripped off in battle a few times, but I've never removed it *willingly*. At first I wore it out of guilt, a constant, daily reminder of what I'd done. What the dream that created me had *forced* me to do. Afterwards, when the school-girl monsters started spreading like a plague, it took on a more … *motivational* quality. A solid little reminder that I had more reason than most to despise her. *Have* more reason.

I'd thought to make a little game of throwing the pendant in the air and catching it, but my shoulders won't stand for that much movement. Instead I tap it on the ground with slow, steady clinks. I can tell that Kell's peeking. That she's watching me, despite the pretence of sleep. Good. Let her feel unnerved by the subtle taunting. Let her wonder what's going on and what's coming next.

'Where did you get the coin?' she eventually whispers.

'Stole it off a corpse,' I answer truthfully. 'Planning on getting myself a matching one by the same method shortly.'

I wait for her to take the bait. For her to exchange threats or put me in my place or alert the others. She doesn't. She simply nods, then hugs her knees even tighter.

And just like that I'm swamped by those feelings again. Kell needs to behave like what she is. I *need* her to act like a monster. For her to drop this disgusting charade and quit pretending. I need … I need space. I need physical distance.

I get up and storm outside, furious at myself for letting her get under my skin again. And then I do what comes naturally. I find someone else to take it out on.

'Dawn is going to be a challenge,' I announce as soon as I get to Ivan. He looks at me, his wet black eyes brimming with concern. Concern about *what*, though? The state of me, or the threat to his precious monster?

'This is difficult for you,' he says.

No shit. This is damn near *impossible* for me, on a lot of levels, but I can't tell *him* that. I don't want his sympathy, and, besides, I don't mind him seeing my anger, but those other murky emotions? They're tied into what I'm still hiding, and they need to stay private.

'You sure we can't just get this over with?' I say, as the idea takes hold. 'If you're so damn set on the dream that created me repeating itself, then let's make it happen right here, right now. All we need is Kell, a slab of stone, a gun and some stars. If you drop the docile pet routine, we can pull that together fast enough. Everything but the stars, but, hey, mere details.'

Ivan just shakes his head and says, 'I have faith in you.'

Great. Ivan has *faith* in me. My God, if I had half as much *faith* in me as Ivan does then life would be an absolute *breeze*. Everything's so black and white for him, so clear and unsullied. He doesn't even *comprehend* the tricky knife-edge that the rest of us bleed on.

'You stay out here and get some air. I'll go in and watch them,' says Ivan. Then he adds, 'I've got this, Amigo,' quoting my usual catchphrase and mimicking my wink. Only just like the raised eyebrow, Ivan's body isn't built to wink. Instead he covers one eye with his hand then gives an exaggerated blink. Something about the gesture makes him look more innocent than ever, and I feel bad for him. I might have to endure Kell until dawn, but *after* first light? Ivan's the one it'll all come crashing down for then. He's the one who's in for some big disappointment.

97

Once Ivan's inside I carefully, painfully put the pendant back around my neck. And then I start walking; there's something I need to see.

Finding it is easy, despite all the new junk from the last three years. I have a sixth sense for where the toy box is in relation to me. But I have to see it with my own eyes ... and so I lift the lid with my foot.

Bodies don't get buried here very often: the ground and the life are both too hard. They get dragged past the Edge, if anything at all. I couldn't just *dump* her, though. At the time I didn't know she was a monster, so I did my best to do right. The pillow under her head, the plastic flowers – they're all still there ... *and so is she*. Now that her bones are laid bare, the skull looks even more damaged. It's incredible to think that just one small bullet could make such an impact.

Suddenly I feel stupid for coming. I knew that Kell wasn't the *actual* girl from the nightmare that brought me here. That she couldn't be ... It's just that they look so similar – *feel* so similar – it's messing with my head. I force myself to get a grip, to be smart about this. To think through all the possible reasons for my recent confusion. In the end, there's only one explanation: Kell's playing a part, like Ivan with his ludicrous pet routine. She's doing it on purpose, just to get to me, and the only way she wins is if I let her.

It's not far off dusk by the time I make it back to the lair, and the others are already awake. Jude and Goldie are busy cleaning and packing guns without any particular fanfare, like real-world kids might clean their teeth and pack a lunchbox. Boots is trying to make his bed, which is a lost cause. He only has toy-guts and cardboard to work with.

Ivan, on the other hand, is hanging off to the side, playing the part of obedient pet to perfection. He doesn't say a word when I walk in, but his claws ask, *Shoulders*?

I give him the finger, hoping to convey both *improving* and *still pissed at you for that* with an economy of movement.

I go through the motions of getting ready to march, but what I'm *really* doing is watching Kell. She's not giving orders or making preparations, she's just sitting in the corner, hugging her knees like before. I glare at her to prove that I'm unfazed, then I turn my attention to Jude, her dutiful lapdog.

Once Jude's finished cleaning his own gun, he starts on Kell's. She doesn't even have to ask him. Pathetic. It's like he's a real-life version of Ivan's kept-pet persona. Sure enough, once it's all nice and shiny, Jude delivers the gun to Kell, like a bone.

Except Kell doesn't take it. She just stares at Jude for the longest time then says, 'Put it down there,' indicating the ground beside her.

It's a pretty rude response, given the effort he's just gone to, but that doesn't surprise me. What *surprises* me is her hands. Why are they shaking? Is the stress of this ruse finally getting to her? Is the monster beginning to crack?

Kell just sits there for a few minutes. Then, when she thinks that nobody's watching, she throws a deflated toy on top of the gun to hide it. After that, she shuffles away. When even *that's* not enough, she gets up from her corner and moves to a new one.

It makes no sense at all. A working gun's a valuable item, but it's more than that. She's the leader of a gang – in *that* context they're damn near essential.

The fact that she's unarmed is a bonus: it'll make things simpler come morning. More to the point, there's a loaded gun that's currently going begging. Ivan's 'fate' is doing me some favours, apparently, because I'll be *needing* one of those.

I wait for a fitting distraction. It doesn't take long for one to come my way. Now that Jude's finished with the guns, he produces one of the *other* most valuable commodities in here. *Water.* There's only one small drink bottle to share, and it doesn't even look full. Given how far the creek is, though, it's still a big deal.

I edge towards the hidden gun, under the pretence of getting a better look at the glorious water. I'm in position by the time Jude carefully hands the bottle to Kell – she gets first dibs, apparently. This is my moment … but then Kell takes a sip *and keeps on drinking*. She's onto her third gulp and showing no signs of stopping. There won't be anything left if she doesn't lay off.

'Hey,' I say, when she goes for a fourth. 'Other people need to drink.'

Stupid. *Stupid, stupid, stupid.* All eyes are on me now, including Kell's. If I'd just let her finish the water I'd have the gun by now.

'It's her gang, so it's her water,' says Jude.

I wait for Kell to make a point, like with no-name back at Sea World, or get shitty at Jude for speaking on her behalf. She does neither. She just hands the drink bottle back, looking … *ashamed?*

I've got to hand it to her, as far as playing a part goes, she's clearly committed. It won't last though; monsters tend to reveal themselves, eventually.

ALICE

I felt awful about the water. I couldn't fix it, though. As we both know, sometimes in life you can't just give back what's been taken. You can't change the past and quash the thirst so that others never suffered. All you can do is try and move on, so that's what I did. *I tried to move on.* I handed the drink bottle back to Jude and did my best to 'stay calm' and 'be positive' and all of that clear-thinking jargon. It was no use, though.

The truth is, I felt alone and scared and all of the usual stuff you can expect when your world goes sideways. And then, just when I thought it might all be a bit much, a la Merryview, Jude came over to check on me. He reached out and took my hand, despite the kissing debacle, and it gave me a daring idea. *What if I just did it?* What if I went ahead and whispered the 'I love you' that I'd been holding back since we were kids? The 'I love you' that I'd said with my eyes a million times, but never with actual words. What if I told him?

But I hesitated, just like always, and Jude got in first.

'I can't believe Lux *questioned* you like that.'

And there it was. Jude didn't even *care* how I'd just acted with the water, or whether I was selfish, or whether I was wrong. He loved me regardless. He loved me *no matter what*. Or rather he loved this version of *you*. And the very idea that Jude would just 'turn a blind eye' to *your* bad behaviour? I felt sick all over. I tried to swallow it down, like I'm usually so good at, but it was no use. The love words died in my mouth.

'It's fine,' I said instead, even though it wasn't. I *never* got annoyed with Jude. That just wasn't part of the deal. Jude was my perfect guy, my one and only, which meant that the problem had to be with *me*.

Well, thoughts about 'problems with me' opened it all up again. Pretty soon I was contemplating my *other* failings and that just led me to home.

My mind zeroed in on the car that had been keeping pace with me before the swap. Had I been in danger? Was Kell in danger now? What if she *wasn't* in danger? What if she'd gotten a lift back to town? *What would she have done?*

I wondered what Dad was doing right at that moment, and whether school was at lunch yet. Whether there were kids playing handball on the asphalt, too far from cover.

I forced myself to get a grip. To stop 'fixating on morbid scenarios' and letting the fear take hold. I reminded myself that Kell wasn't you – she was just some nightmare version, dreamt up by God knows who. She probably had *far* better things to do with her time than follow in your footsteps. I mean, there was a whole new world out there for her, right? A proper fresh start? A chance to literally leave the nightmares behind? Besides, she didn't have a gun and it's not like there was much *else* to work with, not stuck in *my* weak little body. I mean, I hadn't exactly been looking after myself. We're talking nasty sunburn, punishment walks, scars to the thighs, fingernails gone, pounding headaches from refusing to drink ...

And I was back full circle to thinking about the water that I'd guzzled, suddenly desperate to wee. But I had no idea where to do the business. I hadn't exactly seen any toilets hanging about and Kell didn't strike me as the type to seek advice before pissing.

'I'll be back in a minute,' I said.

I figured there would have been toilets galore in among the junk, on account of how often *I* used to dream about them. And no, I'm not alluding to some kinky waterworks fetish. It's just that, when I was little, I had this pesky habit of drinking too much water right before bed. As a result, I'd end up dreaming that I was on the toilet having a wee, only to wake up just before I wet the sheets. Okay, sometimes just *after* I'd wet the sheets, but you take my point. I dreamt of toilets, often. I must have been the only one, though, because I walked through dozens of those crazy junk scenes and yet there was no loo to be had for love nor money. I guess the next generation of kids had better reasons to wet their bed.

Anyway, I didn't want to wander too far in case I got

lost, which kind of narrowed my options. In the end the best I could find was a slightly private corner of a wardrobe that was filled with soft toys. I squatted down and aimed for a fluffy duck, since it looked absorbent. No prizes for guessing that I didn't wake up back in my bed mid-piss, with nothing worse than wet sheets to complain of.

Alright, so this bit's kind of lame, but in the interests of the whole truth I'm telling it anyway. When I was having a wee, I wanted to look. Just a peek – a tiny glance. Hell, we've all got curiosity. Everyone wants to know if they're on track in the development stakes, and it's not like I had a point of comparison anymore.

Growing up I'd always had you to look at – not in a creepy way, but you were my mirror, my benchmark. After you were gone it was just little old me, and I suddenly felt all wrong about everything. I had no idea if I was turning out how I was supposed to; whether I was a freak on the outside as well as possibly a freak on the inside.

So I was curious. So I wanted to look. *You* would have – if you were in someone else's body you would have looked for sure, no embarrassment whatsoever. But I was shy, even with nobody watching. And so I stared at my shoes instead – I looked away.

Only I couldn't help wondering … *Was this body a virgin too*? I don't know what I thought the clues might be – especially without an inspection – but I figured you must be able to tell. That there would be a difference, right? For some reason I remembered Sarah Crow saying how her mum had told her that if she ever did it with a boy she'd know for sure. As if all mothers possess these very niche psychic powers. Mrs Crow really had me going for a while. I was paranoid that in the absence of a mother, the father would take on the mystical all-knowing. Not that it was ever an issue. Not that I had boys lining up. Not that I ever wanted to do it with anyone other than Jude, who wasn't an option. It just weirded me out to think that Dad would have been able to see it on me like some flashing neon scarlet letter.

Don't worry, I'm not an idiot. I eventually worked out that Sarah's mum was bullshitting. Sarah proved that herself after shagging Johnny Pemberton on the night of our end-of-year dance and then sitting down to breakfast the next morning with her whole family completely oblivious, mum included.

Squatting down for a wee in that wardrobe I didn't think there was going to be some virgin/non-virgin aura about the body I was in. I just figured that I might be able to tell. But if there was some difference, I was as clueless to it as poor old Mrs Crow. I guess becoming a woman is the kind of change you just can totally miss – much like becoming a monster, really.

More important than all of that, though, is what it led to. You see, when I leant right forward to make sure I didn't get wee on my shoes, your convict love token clattered against my teeth. I stretched the chain to its absolute limit to get a good look. And as I stared at those worn-out words of affection, it occurred to me: who in town would have *even known* to dream of you wearing that coin, when it was the one thing you always kept hidden?

LUX

Kell's still not back and it's making me nervous. I console myself that at least she's unarmed, but I still don't like it … and apparently I'm not the only one. Jude keeps staring at the spot where she disappeared from view, as if all life stops in her absence.

'She'll be fine,' says Goldie, following Jude's gaze. 'If she worried about you half as much as you worry about her, then this gang would grind to a halt.'

'I love her,' says Jude, completely missing the point. 'When you love someone, you worry.'

'I think the lady's trying to point out a level of … *inequality* in your relationship,' I say, ignoring the fact that it's clearly a private conversation. 'I mean, does Kell feel the same way about you? I don't see her cleaning your gun or sticking up for you *or even welcoming your kisses.*'

Jude abandons his vigil, strides over to where I'm sitting and yanks me up by the lapels. My shoulders won't let me win a fistfight, but that's fine; a punch from this boy wouldn't exactly have me quaking.

'Take that back!' says Jude, holding up his fist as if he's ready to let fly.

Ivan's signalling frantically in my peripheral vision. *I'm* not worried though. Given all the pent-up emotions of the last few hours, this actually feels like progress.

'She doesn't even *love* you,' I say, going for broke. 'Anyone can see that you're just a lapdog to her.' I wait for the punch, which I clearly deserve, but it doesn't come.

Jude just says, 'Take it back,' again.

And suddenly I feel sorry for him. He's so under the thumb he can't even stand up for himself, not to mention that the poor kid's *in love with a monster.* Shouldn't I, of all people, be cutting him some slack? I try to think of something to take the sting out of what I said, but kind words aren't my forte. Perhaps—

And that's when we hear it.

Jude instantly lets go of me and turns towards the sound.

It's coming from the same direction that Kell headed off in, but it can't be her. There's no way she'd be making this much noise ... which means there's something *else* out there.

Jude and Goldie take position near the boarded-up window. Ivan adopts a fighting stance by the door. I grab Kell's hidden gun and hand it to Boots. I really hope he won't need to be armed, but somehow I doubt it. When kids dream of monsters they tend to imagine them as creatures of the night. The rare beasts who manage to fight those instincts and prowl during daylight hours? *Very* unpleasant.

Ivan signals *Stay-Here-Stay-Safe*, but I ignore him and walk outside. Whatever this thing is, it's headed straight for us. I'm trying to think of a suitable tactic given my broken shoulders, when the source of the noise emerges.

It's Kell, smashing and crashing her way through the junk as if she doesn't even care what hears her. What the … What the crap is she thinking? How can a gang-leader be so utterly reckless and somehow not dead already?

'We were worried,' says Jude, rushing straight for her.

Kell doesn't look at him. She doesn't even *acknowledge* him. Her eyes are glued on my pendant, as if we're sharing a moment.

'Kell?' says Jude again, but she *still* doesn't look.

Shit. Given my 'she doesn't love you' taunting, this lingering gaze seems suspicious. It kind of implies that I meant 'she doesn't love *you*'.

Sure enough, Jude shoots me a look with all the hallmarks of jealousy.

I try to think of some clever way of insulting Kell to put an end to this madness. Only, I'm distracted by Ivan. He's giving the air loud wet sniffs and signalling, *urine*. Ivan's nose is superb, but he must have it wrong this time – not even *she* could be that dumb.

'You didn't piss anywhere *near* here, did you?' I say to Kell, just so Ivan will drop it.

The question snaps her out of her little gaze-fest, and she says, 'I ... I don't ... I mean, no!'

But when she says it she blushes. Monsters don't blush. They don't feel *embarrassment*. I must have read it wrong; the red cheeks must mean anger, which is good. It means I'm getting under her skin.

I wait for Jude to jump in, like always. For him to have a go at me for daring to question our detestable leader. He doesn't though; the poor sap doesn't say a word.

ALICE

Okay, so I've suffered a reasonable number of humiliations in my life. Having a bath at Merryview, for example, wasn't exactly a private affair, if you know what I'm saying. Well, thanks to Lux you can add 'the pissing incident' to my list of public humiliations.

Apparently I wasn't supposed to have relieved myself nearby. Only, how the hell was *I* supposed to know that? And what exactly was I meant to do about it *after* the fact? Hit rewind? Go back in time just to wee a bit further afield? In the end I made some vague denial and prayed that Lux would just drop it.

The conversation did eventually move on, but *I* didn't. Once I was sure that I wasn't blushing anymore, and the embarrassment was safely converted into a healthy dose of anger, I stared at Lux with all the hate that I'd been swallowing down for three whole years. The hate that I'd seen on practically every person who'd looked at me ever since what you did. The hate ... *that was totally wasted.*

Lux wasn't even watching. He was busy being bumped into by Boots. At least, that's what it would have seemed like to the untrained eye. I had a *very* trained eye, though, thanks to Merryview. The others might have missed it, but I knew what an accidentally-on-purpose knock looked like. Boots did all the 'so sorry' stuff, but I wasn't fooled. I saw the gun that he dropped into Lux's pocket when he thought that no one was watching, and it sure as hell got my heart racing.

Now I know what you're thinking – I was in a place where there were guns aplenty, so why even care about one more? Well, it was the secretiveness that got me. I'd learnt the hard way that when someone behaves like they've got something to hide, it's usually a bad thing.

I had to tell someone and so, of course, I chose Jude. I sidled up beside him, and whispered, 'I need to talk to you.'

Jude didn't even look up from what he was doing. 'Yeah? Why don't you talk to Lux?' And that reaction? I'd heard it a thousand times, from him to you. *Why don't you talk to Paul? Why don't you talk to Johnny? Why don't you talk to any of the other boys you've been flirting with right in front of me?*

Lux was glaring at me now. I tried not to act spooked or otherwise let him get under my skin, but it was no use. All that hate I'd wanted to hit him with? He threw it right back at me with a fury that left mine for dead. Then, with this nasty little smile, he said, 'We should get going. It'll be dark soon, and then *morning* before we know it.'

And that's what we did. We left our so-called hideout, and started making our way through the dream junk, like underage soldiers.

'So, Goldie, have you really been here two whole months?' said Boots, after we'd been marching in silence for a while.

'I guess so,' said Goldie. 'That's how long it's been since Jude and Kell found me, and that's the first thing I remember.'

'Well, let's see what we can deduce about the dream that landed you here,' said Boots, giving her an exaggerated once-over. 'The mini-skirt, the snug top, the obvious attributes. I'd say that we can probably rule out nightmare.'

'I pulled these clothes off a corpse,' said Goldie. 'When they found me I was wearing this.' She yanked the neck of her top right down to reveal a cheery polka-dot bikini.

'Definitely rule out nightmare,' said Boots, but this time there was no smile from Goldie.

Instead she just shrugged and said, 'If we don't remember, then how can we rule out anything?'

'Some people remember,' said Jude. 'I've heard of people remembering the dream that created them – it can happen.'

'Yeah? Well lucky them. Every memory I had started fading away the moment I got here. I've got no idea who I am or who I'm meant to be.'

There was this sadness in her voice, a depth of feeling that I'd have sworn just wasn't possible in a version of our Maggie. Not in the squeaky-clean girl who worshipped diets and clothing and nails and tans, as if the look of a person was everything. I don't know why I assumed that pretty, superficial girls would only have pretty superficial feelings. I guess it was just one of the very many things that I was wrong about.

'I don't admit this to just anyone,' said Boots, in a mock-conspiratorial whisper. 'But I'm fairly sure that in the real world I'm a superhero. I mean, the oversized footwear? Clearly made for combat. And when I found myself in here, I was wearing Transformer pyjamas, which is a dead giveaway. Just because these unoriginal clowns went and christened me Boots,' he said, gesturing vaguely at Lux and the Monster, 'that doesn't mean I've given up on my *true* identity. In fact, I've been petitioning for a name change to The Invincible Pyjama Man for a while now. I think it suits me.'

Goldie smiled, and some of her heaviness lifted. Boots had known exactly what to say, just like the real-world Marcus had always known what to say.

Then, without even really meaning to, I did something that was way out of character for me. *I spoke my mind.* It wasn't much, only a meek little, 'Maybe not knowing's a *good* thing.'

And I wasn't just talking about the past.

LUX

'Maybe not knowing's a good thing,' says Kell, in this sad little voice.

Kids in here are always fantasising about 'remembering'. I thought *I* was the only one who had it backwards, who wished instead to forget. Kell's melancholy comment is way too close to the bone.

I put my hand into my trench-coat pocket for some cold, hard reassurance. Kell's gun is right there at my fingertips, ready and waiting. I owe Boots a favour or two for that. The fact that he handed the gun back without me even having to ask is impressive. The fact that he did it with total discretion? I really am starting to like the kid. As soon as all this Kell business is over I'll find him that ammunition we talked about and teach him a few moves.

Only, now that I think about it, Boots *already has* a few moves. For someone who's only been in here a matter of days, he's doing better than okay. It usually takes kids a while to adjust; to accept that this is their home now and that they have to fend for themselves, sans mummy. The boy's a natural, clearly, but it's more than that.

When we found Boots a few days ago, I figured it was just random charity that we let him come with us. Now that I think back on it, though, Ivan did *insist* on taking him. But why? What makes him so special?

I pick up my pace until I'm in lock step with Boots. Privacy's an issue, but I've got practice at discretion. I'll just nudge him until he gets the hint to slow down and let the others pass us. Once we're at the back of the group, *then* we can talk.

'This time of night used to be magic,' whispers Ivan, as I'm about to deliver my first nudge. 'There weren't many people in here before it all went bad – just me and a few kids – and every night at dusk we'd climb the rocks and wait for the show.' Ivan is ostensibly talking to Boots, but everyone's listening. Call me paranoid, but I kind of get the feeling it's on purpose. That he struck up a conversation with Boots just to stop *me* from doing the same.

'Can you picture it?' continues Ivan. 'Watching people's dreams play out, night after night. Vibrant colours and fantastical scenes. Bubbles of imagination that naturally came and went, without leaving anything behind. None of the junk and monsters of recent years – just wide-open space. Nothing but stars and outback and silent dreams in every direction – the way it was *meant* to be.'

Ivan pauses for a moment, letting the image sink in. Letting everyone picture this place as some kind of mystical realm, rather than a shit-hole.

'Kids still got stuck here, of course,' he whispers. 'From time to time a dreamer in the real world would wake up suddenly, which was all it took. It didn't happen often, though, and it didn't happen *on purpose*.'

Times sure have changed. These days gangs will end a dream without a second thought just to get their hands on guns or knives or a bloody *sandwich*. And on top of that, you've got the monsters doing the same, just to get at the kids. Everyone and everything out for themselves, not caring one scrap about the fallout. Not *us*, though. For all our many faults, Ivan and I have never been a part of this. We've never interfered with the dreams and nightmares … *until now*.

I wonder how Ivan will react when this gang inevitably wants to end a dream for some measly pittance. I wonder how *I'll* react. I guess we'll find out soon enough, because night has arrived. The stars are out and the clock is officially ticking.

ALICE

When I was at Merryview, I could see a patch of the night sky through my window. And it was rubbish. All those street lamps and Coke signs instead of the 'whole galaxies' effect that you get in the outback.

Well, as we scavenged for food and guns I got to see that nighttime in the dream place was something else again. It was the same sky as back home. I could tell by the Southern Cross shining down like always. Only, everything was darker. *Much* darker. The effect was to make the night so pitch black that you could see about a billion stars in the sky, and it made me feel smaller than an ant in the scheme of things.

After a while it started getting lighter. I couldn't pinpoint it exactly, but there was definitely a new source of illumination. It made it easier to walk, sure, but it also made me nervous. You see, it wasn't a *normal* kind of light, and – as we both know – 'not normal' is usually a *bad* thing.

I eventually caught a glimpse of something glowing through the rubble. Although, 'glowing' isn't quite the right word. Shimmering maybe? Radiating? I don't know. Choose whatever adjective you like, the point is there was light coming from it. As we got closer, 'it' turned out to be … well, there's no easy way to say this.

You know those oily rainbow bubbles you sometimes get in the washing-up water? Well it was a bubble kind of like that, only bigger. Way bigger, like the size of our whole kitchen and then some. That's not even the weirdest part. You see, inside the bubble, there was a boy. That poor kid was running his heart out. Only, no matter how hard he ran, he stayed in the exact same spot – smack bang in the middle of that freaky-big bubble. It was like he was on an invisible treadmill.

He wasn't alone, either. All kinds of random stuff was in there with him. At first it was just trees that whizzed by as he ran on the spot. Then the trees morphed into houses and suddenly he was on a slightly creepy version of Pattinson Street. Pattinson Street became the inside of that second-hand bookstore on Lyon's Road, and the boy stopped to hide in its measly little travel section.

It took me a while to recognise him: the kid, I mean. I didn't know his name, but he was younger than us. Too young to have been there on the day of the shootings, but he might have had a relative there – a brother or a sister or a cousin perhaps? He was definitely school-age now. He might have even been one of the kids at the bus stop with

Marcie who'd spat on me the week before, but I can't say for sure. I didn't see their faces.

Even if he *was* one of the bus-stop spitters, I still felt sorry for him. There was something resigned about the way he hid in the travel section of the bookstore, which morphed into the post office and then into some American-style diner. It was as if none of it was new to him, and he never really expected to stop running and hiding.

'Nothing here,' announced Goldie, as if the boy didn't even rate.

We kept moving, towards another bubble that had sprung up to our left. Sure enough there was a kid stuck inside that one too, only this time it was a girl. A girl who was goddamn terrified, on account of the giant dogs that had her surrounded.

You remember that painting Mum loved so much – the one with the figure standing on a bridge with its hands up to its face and its mouth stretched open like a black hole? Well, the girl in the bubble reminded me of that. There was no sound, but you could tell that she was screaming.

'Is she the one from last week? The one who dreamt of dogs and then of dog food?' said Goldie, sounding hopeful.

'We should wait and make sure,' said Jude. 'If she *does* dream of food we might not have long before the dream morphs again. We don't want to miss it.'

'You know damn well she's too scared to start dreaming of food anytime soon,' said Lux, with barely contained rage.

Something was going on that I didn't understand but, big surprise, I said nothing.

Whatever happened to that screaming girl and her hell-hounds I'll never know. For better or worse we left her there, and moved on to the next bubble. Then on to the next bubble, then the next. The things had started cropping up everywhere, giving more than enough light to see by. Only, it soon became clear that the others weren't really *seeing* a thing. They looked for food and weapons, sure, but as for the kids inside those bubbles and the bad stuff that was happening to them? They deliberately turned a blind eye, just like I did that night outside the half-house with you and me and Jude.

It was maybe an hour or two and a whole shitload of bubbles later that I started seeing nightmares with older kids in them, kids our age. Kids that we went to school with, who we knew. Staring at those nightmares was like peeking into the heads of all those former classmates and friends who hadn't spoken to me in three whole years. It was as if I was finally getting a glimpse of all the things that they'd left unsaid. And do you know what I saw? I saw that they were all as messed up as me. They might not have had the nasty letters piled on their doorstep or the scars on their thighs or the history at Merryview to prove it, but they were still wrecked. Underneath their school uniforms and their 'back to normal' lives, there was so much more going on than just them spitting on me. I guess for the first time I got to see beyond their hate, to what caused it.

I'm not saying they all dreamt about the day of the shooting, because they didn't. Only, if you knew what to look for, the clues were there. I guess Lux was right; they might have moved on from having nightmares about what you did, but they hadn't moved past it. It was still the ugly hurt they saw the world through.

Watching it kind of helped, in a selfish sort of way. I guess it made me feel a little bit closer to normal.

Actually, if I'm going to be totally honest, there was slightly more to it than that. You see, no matter how much I stared at the kids in those nightmares, they couldn't see me. I guess it felt good to finally be on the other side of the goldfish bowl. At Merryview I'd endured my share of one-way mirrors, and when I went home it wasn't much better. Everyone stared at me, but there was this unwritten rule that I couldn't look back. Not without starting something.

And so, for the first time in years, I finally got to take a good long look at the kids I'd known all my life, but hadn't 'seen' in three whole years, other than through sideways glances. And you know what? None of them looked like kids anymore, not really.

Anyway, that's where my head was at when we turned a corner and saw the dream with Michael in it. Michael Henson? Or Benson? He was always the quiet type. That was a bad thing for him, as it turned out.

After what you did there was this big social-work frenzy. They pretty much identified all the 'loners' in all the schools across the country and tried to work out if they were planning on turning into psychos too. As if being picked last and having practically no friends in life wasn't bad enough, now they were also suspected of being a 'killer in the making'. It was a pretty dumb reaction, especially since you weren't a loner anyway. At least, not in a way that people noticed.

Through the skin of the bubble, I watched Michael loading guns into a sports bag. I knew it was just a nightmare he was having – that it wasn't real – but I felt sick all the same. And do you know why? It wasn't the thought of him repeating what you did. He would never actually do that, I was sure of it. Michael was just some quiet kid who only wore all black because he was chubby, and was a 'loner' for the traditional reason – nobody wanted to be friends with him. What made me sick was that I knew exactly what it was like to be trapped in that kind of nightmare, feeling as if *you're* the one who's guilty.

Poor Michael. He was a decent kid. He wasn't dreaming of death and guns because he was like you: he was doing it because that's what everyone thought of him. It's the kind of thing that everyone was paranoid about.

'Can I pop it?' said Jude, hovering his hand near the bubble.

The question was directed at me, but Lux jumped in before I could say a word. 'Don't be a coward.'

I had no idea what 'popping it' entailed, but it sounded as if it would bring an end to poor Michael's nightmare, and I wanted to help him. I didn't want him to have to go through with whatever act the guns were for, and wake up with the guilt of it on his conscience.

Actually, I'm full of shit again. What I just said, well it's true enough, it's just not the *whole* truth. If I'm being really honest, the 'coward' call was probably a factor. I know that you knew about Jude's issues with that word, because I watched you push his buttons with it. Well, here's some news for you – after that night outside the half-house, I was pretty goddamn thingy about it too. And just so we're clear, by 'thingy' I mean massively defensive, totally guilt ridden and otherwise slightly unhinged. Hell, the secret I'd been keeping about that nasty little 'c' word had ruined me the most, and I sure as shit wasn't going to let Lux splash it about so freely. So I said, 'Yes,' just like that, and to this day I still regret it.

When Jude touched the edge of the bubble it popped in an instant. Michael was suddenly standing right in front of me, together with the bed and the guns and everything else that had been in his nightmare the exact moment it popped. Call me slow, but it wasn't until then that I realised – *that* was how the kids got stuck. It was how the dream place filled with useless leftover junk from dreams and nightmares. It also explained how people who were gone in the real world came to be alive again: because, in Collector, we kept dreaming of the dead.

I wondered who had dreamt of Jude. Was it his mum? Was it Melissa Jones, after penning more sappy poems in his honour? Someone else? Looking around I wondered who had dreamt up the other members of the little 'gang' I was in. Were they from dreams or nightmares? From the imagination of people I knew, or at least *used* to know? Who was still fantasising about Maggie Cooper even after all this time? Who had dreamt of Marcus as his younger, funnier self? And who had dreamt of you, as someone like Kell?

'Drop it,' said Jude, pointing his gun at Michael.

Michael looked terrified.

And that's when it hit me. By telling Jude to pop the bubble I hadn't *helped* Michael – I'd stranded him right alongside me. I might have put an end to the nightmare, but I'd dumped him in a whole *new* nightmare that he couldn't just 'wake up' from.

And what about the real-world Michael? What happened to *him* when I carelessly said 'Yes' to Jude? Did he wake up in his bed, drenched in sweat from a nightmare that had just inexplicably ended? Or did something worse happen?

'It's okay,' I said, as calmly as possible.

Michael turned … *and he recognised me*. His memories of the real world hadn't faded away – at least not yet. He looked at my face with complete recognition … and that's when his *real* terror set in. I should have seen that coming. Hell, he had every reason to be shit-your-pants scared. I wanted to say something, to do something to make it better, but I was too slow.

I'll never know what was going through Michael's head. I don't know why he put that gun in his mouth. I don't know why he pulled the trigger.

I didn't run away or faint. I stood perfectly still, staring straight ahead at where Michael's face had been just moments before. I knew that if I looked down I'd see the blood and the gore of it, and I couldn't do that. I couldn't add the mess of him to my inventory of horrors, not without losing it Merryview style. And so I just stood there, wondering … was Michael dead in the real world too? Did that bullet kill two versions of the same kid?

When my eyes finally came into focus I saw Jude. He was standing by the bed, next to where Michael's body was, if I'd had the guts to look down at it. And do you know what he was doing? He was holding Michael's sports bag, handing out the guns like some doomsday Santa.

And suddenly I wanted him *not* to be my Jude. I scanned his face for small discrepancies, evidence that he was a whole other person in the ways that count. A very different version of the boy I'd been in love with ever since I reached the age where boys weren't gross after all.

I looked away. I might have wanted to find out the dirty truth about myself, but not about *Jude*. Jude needed to stay exactly the same, both perfect and true.

'There aren't even any bullets,' said Lux through gritted teeth. He snatched one of the guns right out of Jude's hand and fired it into the air. Sure enough, nothing but *click, click, click*.

He threw the useless gun at Jude's feet, right alongside poor Michael.

'Bullets don't matter,' said Jude, trying to save face. 'They're still worth it to scare off the monsters. Besides, you don't know how things work in this gang.'

With that Jude took the biggest, most horrific gun and held it out to me. He hadn't actually met my eyes since we were back at Movie World, or spoken to me. And yet, in an insane way, the gun seemed to be some kind of peace offering. A gesture instead of flowers or chocolates? Now I like a gift just as much as the next girl, but Jude handing me a gun made me want to vomit. I shook my head. That's all I could manage.

Jude gave me his betrayed look – you know the one I mean. It was the look he got the time you made that big touchy-feely fuss about Greg Smith's six-pack, right in front of him. The look I swore to myself a billion times that, if he were mine, the world would never see again. And yet there it was.

Jude's look made me feel like you, and that scared me even more than the guns did.

I took a deep breath and said, 'What happens to the kids in the real world when you just ... *end* their nightmares?'

It was a strange thing to ask, apparently – even Lux gave me an odd look, but I didn't back down. Jude just shrugged, which meant *I don't know* or maybe *I don't care*. Either way, I felt sick all over. How could Jude be goddamn *shrugging* right now? I wanted to yell at him or shake him or kick him in the shins until he behaved like himself. Until he behaved like he was *meant* to.

And then, of course, there was the *other* problem. I tried to tell myself that the churning in my gut was *only* about Jude ignoring what he shouldn't. *But hadn't I done the exact same thing?* I mean, I'd been telling myself that Kell wouldn't cause any harm out there in the real world, but you never know for sure, do you. *Sometimes you assume someone's no genuine threat, and you get it terribly, tragically wrong.*

But no, I was jumping at shadows again. Kell wouldn't have done what you did; there were lots of other options. An infinite range of better choices she could be making instead. The town would be fine, but poor Michael?

As we walked from one new nightmare to the next, I decided that Michael – the one back home – couldn't have just *died* or anything. It's not as if real-world kids had been dropping like flies since things got bad in the dream place. They weren't connected like *that*, clearly. But what *was* the connection? Did Michael just wake up safe in his bed when Jude popped that bubble? If so, how many times a week did it happen? Did he sit through school like a zombie because he rarely slept through the night anymore? Was his sleep *always* broken because kids stuck in a world that he didn't even know existed were ending his nightmares?

If so, I doubted he was the only one. Maybe there were a lot of people in our town never really sleeping anymore.

Maybe, as much as the real world was ruining the dream place, the opposite was true too.

Maybe the destruction was mutual.

LUX

We're into the busy time of night now so screaming is standard, but I'm accustomed to that kind of noise. No, it's the constant clicking that's grating on my nerves – the soft, relentless sound of Ivan trying to get my attention without *drawing* attention.

Well, he can click all he likes, it won't do him any good. I've been ignoring him since that poor kid with the guns blew his brains out, and I plan on keeping it up until morning. Until Kell is dead and all of this mess is behind us. Then we can talk, if there's anything left to say. Then we can – Dammit, he just *will* not quit with that clicking.

'What?' I finally blurt out, loud enough for the others to hear; not that they're listening. Ivan doesn't answer. He just holds his hand out to me, palm up. This gesture isn't part of our sign language; it has a much more *practical* purpose. I'm about to tell him to get stuffed, but then I notice his expression. If I didn't know better, I'd say he almost looks *pleased*. I hesitate a moment, but curiosity gets the better of me and I take his hand so that he can lift me onto his shoulders.

From up this high I can see the various nightmares playing out around us. All those silent bubbles, surrounded by screams and chaos. Bedlam spilling out from the ones that have already been popped. Right away I know exactly which nightmare Ivan's been watching. Everything about it is totally sharp, totally focused. I can see every detail – the freckles, the sweat, the sunburn that's pinking her whole face but is worst on her nose. The jeans and T-shirt that make her look like just another girl, almost. It's so clear, so real, that I can practically feel the heat bouncing off the highway, and hear the hum of the car that's keeping pace behind her.

The car eventually stops, but I'm consumed by the girl and how she looks so much like she did in the nightmare that landed me here. She looks the same as Kell, but also somehow different. Softer, perhaps?

And then I see who's just gotten out of the car that was trailing her. It's Boots, only he's bigger and older and brimming with the kind of hate that always ends badly for someone. In this case I'd say it's the school-girl monster's unlucky day, which works for me.

Through the skin of the bubble, I watch as the muscled Boots creeps up behind her. He's just a step or two from letting his emotions fly, and it's as if I'm right there with him … But then something happens. The girl in the nightmare freaks out, as though she's suddenly gone crazy. She spins around on the spot a few times, then crouches down and grabs two handfuls of dirt for no reason. She must have seen Boots by now. She must have realised the threat, but she doesn't even *try* to protect herself. She just stares at the dirt and does nothing.

Something about that combination – her helpless, him on the brink of violence – and I'm there again. I'm back in the dream that stranded me here all those years ago. The stars above, the stone beneath, the flashes of lightning ...

No, that's *not* a good place. Instead I focus on the nightmare that's playing out before me. They're talking now, Boots and the school-girl monster. Whatever she's saying is making him crazy with rage. Even from this distance I can see the hate bubbling up in him, so it's no surprise at all when he lashes out. When he starts laying into her with kick after vicious kick.

Boots is the one who's dreaming this dream that I'm watching. Or rather, his real-world self is. I can tell by the perspective – the way the dream sometimes shifts, so that I'm seeing things through his eyes, from *his* point of view. Somewhere in Collector he's asleep right now, beating her up in his head. I can relate to that. *Only, it's not just a dream.* The events that I'm watching play out inside that bubble? They're not being imagined, they're being remembered. I can tell by the focus, the sharpness, the absence of blur. This is a true dream – the kind that comes from memory. Boots is dreaming about something that actually happened in the real world. Something *he did*.

I keep watching the dream play out. Watching as Boots delivers another kick, even though she's down. I should be enjoying this. It should be sweet release, but there's something in her eyes that I just can't shake. Something that reminds me of the girl *before* the monster, and suddenly I don't want to watch. I don't want to see the blood that's spilling from her mouth and gushing from her nose.

I *do* watch, though. I stare and stare as it all plays out. I see what Boots does *after* the beating and I see how it ends. The whole thing has the ramped-up speed of adrenaline – it doesn't take long. Once it's over, the bubble starts fading. There's nothing nearby to interfere – no kids or monsters to pop it, trapping things here, creating more junk. The dream just fades away, like it was meant to. I stare at the spot where it used to be. It's not until I hear the cry of 'Help' that I finally look away.

The 'Help' is from a kid somewhere nearby. I scan the wasteland but all I see is the red glow of nightmares in every direction. A moment later there it is again, a high-pitched 'Help' from off to my left.

This time I see where the voice is coming from: not a kid, but a monster that just *sounds* like one. It's standing on top of the Lookout, crying wolf. I have no idea why it's playing victim. Then I notice the movement *outside* the nightmare bubbles, the shadowy figures that are weaving a path through the junk, towards us. The figures that are *moving in basic formation*. The rumours were true, then. Someone – or something – really is uniting the monsters.

The 'Help' is some kind of signal … *and if I can see them, then they can see me.*

I jump down from Ivan's shoulders, swearing at myself for being so careless.

'Did you see how clear it was?' whispers Ivan the moment I hit the ground. 'It must have been about something that actually happened in the real world. We haven't seen a *true* dream about her in years. And Boots too? It means that it's finally coming together.'

'The only thing coming together is the monsters,' I say, ignoring the rest of it. 'And they know *exactly* where to find us.'

I don't wait for an answer. I have to get the others moving without starting a panic, and there simply isn't time for Ivan's nonsense.

But as I shove my way to the front of the gang, I have to wonder about the 'Boots too' comment. Ivan, it seems, has left something out in the telling.

ALICE

I knew things were bad when I heard someone cry 'Help!' ... and true to form, I did nothing. Even when I heard the 'Help!' a second time I just stood there, lost in thoughts about *other* cries for help that went ignored.

Lux snapped me out of it. Before I knew what was happening he'd barged right to the front of the group, put his finger to his lips, and given a few very simple hand movements.

Now I'm no sign-language expert, but those gestures were pretty bloody clear, even to me. They meant that (a) there was something bad in the direction we were heading, and (b) we had to backtrack. *Quietly*. Funnily enough, there were no objections. Hell, not even Jude made a peep.

We were retracing our steps almost exactly ... only, this time there was a lot more gore than I remembered. At first I thought that maybe all the blood was just part of the 'scene', you know? That some kids had been watching horror films, so they'd dreamt about blood?

Then we passed the white-on-white apartment. We'd seen that one about half an hour ago. It hadn't been a nightmare – it was just some wannabe dream about dance moves. Except that now the bubble was popped and there was a scarlet lump where the kid had been, plus lots of blood on the carpet. It wasn't a 'just unexpectedly got your period' or 'knocked the bandaid off a massive scab' puddle of blood either. We're talking 'lost a limb' quantities.

I kept walking, one foot in front of the other. I even tried counting my steps as a distraction, but it was no use.

Then we turned a corner and there it was, the prissiest bedroom you've ever seen in your whole entire life, plonked right alongside all the blood and gore. And do you know who was sitting on the frilly bed? It was Penny's daughter Lauren, still wearing her trademark tomboy overalls in the middle of all the pink and floral. I know you'd remember Lauren, because I saw you talking to her from time to time. I think maybe she was one of the few people in town that you genuinely *liked*. I had a soft spot for her too, actually. Hell it's hard *not* to like a kid who always gets picked on but never once cries about it.

Lauren looked maybe five or six, which wasn't right – she should have been older now. And as for the room she was in? In the real world, Lauren and her mum were still living in that caravan out the back of Mason's place. I'd never been inside, but unless it was some kind of Tardis there sure as shit wasn't enough room for the kid to have her very own bedroom. *Especially* not the kind of bedroom I was looking at. Picture one of those 'got every present you ever asked for even when it wasn't your birthday' bedrooms, right down to the canopy princess bed.

Maybe that was the kind of bedroom that the tough little tomboy secretly wanted. The kind that deep down she wished for, or would have liked to try on just for size. Then again, maybe she hated all that crap and the prissy pink room was her version of a nightmare. I suppose it doesn't really matter.

The important part is that Lauren was cowering on the big princess bed holding onto this very cute little puppy for dear life. Like I said, back in the real world Lauren was tough. She hadn't even cried when Frank Milano's brother broke her arm for no particular reason … but now she was packing it. I had no idea who'd popped the dream she'd been in, stranding her. But when she looked up at me with her big brown eyes, they were full of all kinds of terror.

And do you know what that bastard Lux did? He whispered, 'Keep moving.' He wanted us to leave the girl there, despite the fact that she was alone and scared and there was clearly something out there to be scared of. I couldn't believe it. I mean, what kind of monster *does* that?

What I *really* needed was good old Jude; it was exactly the kind of thing he would have put his foot down about. The problem was, the *new* Jude didn't seem to care. He just acted as if it wasn't his problem. I waited, hoping he'd change his mind and say something. Hoping he'd be the hero and save the day. He didn't. He just pretended not to notice Lauren sitting there, pleading with her big kiddie eyes to not get left behind.

'Keep moving,' whispered Lux, urging me on. The others were getting antsy, but I shook my head.

'They're tracking us,' said Lux through gritted teeth. 'Given how you insisted we leave that little kid outside Sea World, I *know* that you know they'll smell her.'

Now, I had no idea which little kid he was talking about or who 'they' were and I sure as shit had no desire to know what 'smelling her' entailed. I guess it didn't matter, though; my mind was already made up.

'I'm not leaving her,' I said. I was freaking terrified, with Lux and the Monster staring me down, but I walked over to the princess bed, gently pried the puppy out of Lauren's arms, and picked her up.

It wasn't a hug exactly, but it was the closest I'd had to one in three whole years, and I knew from that moment that I wouldn't let her go, no matter what. Not even if the so-called gang left us *both* behind, which I had to admit seemed likely. I mean, the others were all looking at me as if I'd just picked up a goddamn landmine.

Then the Monster hissed, 'Run,' and shoved me hard to get me moving.

I'll save you the suspense and tell you that in that par- ticular life-and-death situation I *did* run. I ran my sorry little heart out, around a ship, through a house, over a car, under a bridge … right up to the point where I rounded a corner and smacked straight into the back of Jude.

We'd come to a dead end, trapped by a fence that looked like it belonged in some uber sadistic war movie. I mean, the whole thing was covered in these extra spirals of razor wire as though it was being cuddled by a giant deadly slinky.

Lux and the Monster arrived last, and for a sickening moment I thought to myself, *It's a trap*. Maybe there was nothing following us after all, and Lux and the Monster had somehow rounded us up for the killing.

But then they turned around, so that their backs were to the rest of us, and I realised that it wasn't so much a trap as a last stand.

I put Lauren down beside me and stood there with the others, in front of the impossible fence. A few moments later, a man came around the corner. The first thing I noticed was his gun, all pearly and white as teeth. The *second* thing I noticed was his belt, or rather, what was hanging from its buckle. It was that cute little puppy, threaded onto the leather like a meaty charm bracelet. There was a scream, but I don't know who it came from. Maybe it was Lauren, because she'd seen the man's belt. Then again, maybe it was me, because I'd seen who was standing behind him.

Her hair was long, almost down to her waist, and somehow as shiny as ever. I knew her face. Hell, the whole *world* knows her face. She has those shit-all-over-the-rest-of-you good looks that will get you rich and famous without even trying.

There was a lot of controversy when they cast her in the Hollywood re-make, especially since she looked nothing like you. Or nothing like 'us', I guess. Some people thought they were glamorising what had happened. That a model-good-looking American with a woefully shit Aussie accent was somehow insulting. It doesn't matter. The movie made money regardless, but no surprises there – the promo poster showed a lot of cleavage and a massive gun. Boys appreciate that combination, apparently.

Anyway, that actress's interpretation of you was pretty goddamn frightening. She clearly didn't have the talent for nuance so, in her version, you were just this cold psychopathic killer with dead eyes and nothing human about you. Her performance didn't exactly win her any awards: well, not unless you count those teen awards where they have meaningful categories like 'best kiss' and 'most awesome scream'. It got watched by a lot of people, though, especially in our town.

I got to watch it too, thanks to Dr Ben and his liberal take on therapy. And you know what? Looking at the girl in front of me, the pretty green eyes were every bit as dead as I remembered them. Whoever's nightmare she was from, they'd dreamt her up exactly the same as in the movie … which was bad. As in, *very* bad.

LUX

'Ivan?' I whisper, not turning around or taking my eyes off the monsters. The one with the puppy on its belt is standing right in front of us, but others are gathering behind it.

'Razor wire,' says Ivan.

Shit.

I take a closer look at what's closing in on us. Including Puppy-belt, three of the five are beasts designed to scare. It's the *other* two that have me worried – they look like ordinary people, which is always the worst kind of monster.

Still, the fact that there are five of them works in our favour. Monsters don't play nice with others, even when it comes to their own kind. There's a good chance they'll end up fighting one another to compete for the kill, and we can try to escape while they're distracted. Only, something's not right. The way they're inching towards us … *They're doing it in unison.*

Puppy-belt might be standing in front, but it doesn't have the look of a leader – you really can always tell. I scan the other faces gathering behind it … and sure enough, there she is – monster number six.

You see a lot of very beautiful girls in here, but she's exceptional. Tall and slim with honey-blonde hair all the way to her waist. Textbook stunning, but I'm not fooled for a second. Her eyes might be the perfect shade of green, but there's zero good in them.

I take another look at her gang, doing a quick inventory of their guns and knives and claws and fangs. There's no way we'll win a fight, which would explain why they haven't attacked already. They're savouring the moment, taking time to appreciate the kill. We need to get out of here, fast, but Jude's led us down a dead end with razor wire behind us. We're trapped.

Me. Fence, Ivan says with a flick of his wrist.

I shake my head. Ivan is tough, but razor wire is tougher. It'll cut him to pieces.

Cover us, he signals back. Then, without waiting for a response, he moves to the back of the group, within reach of the fence. There's no time to argue – monsters aren't known for their patience, and they won't hold off killing us for long.

Cover us. What he wants from me has nothing to do with guns. There's only one way to cover him in this situation. Only one way I can help, and that's to *literally* cover what he's doing from view. To block the monsters' line of sight long enough for him to rip a hole in the fence and get

141

the others to safety. And of course, there's only one way to do that.

I can't help but smile to myself at the symmetry of the thing. That the one thing Ivan's wanted all along is what just might save us now. I know he can't possibly have engineered this situation, but as coincidences go, it sure is a neat one. If I believed in fate, which I don't, then right about now I'd be thinking that she has a nasty sense of humour.

I toy with the idea of *not* doing it. There's no escaping the fact that Ivan and the kids are going to die anyway, if not here then somewhere else, and soon. Perhaps I could just let it all end now. But no, I can't let them die like this, not if I can help it. As much as I want to keep my secret until the end, until there's nobody left to hope, there's no real choice anymore. And so Ivan gets his way after all.

'New around here?' I say, as I force a smile that isn't even close to being real. And then – very slowly, because of my broken shoulders – I take off the trench coat. The monsters are waiting, watching, especially the blonde.

My T-shirt's already torn at the back, so it doesn't take much to rip it off completely. Then I start undoing the belts. There are four of them in total, crisscrossed over my chest. The buckles are a problem because the leather's pulled tight, and it's hard to get a grip. I manage, though.

The last belt clanks to the ground.

But my wings stay flat against my back.

This particular set of belts has been strapping them down for eight or nine months straight. I have to pull each wing out by hand, which hurts and is strangely humiliating.

I avoid looking too closely, but I've seen it all before – the blood, the raw patches, the missing feathers. Not exactly pretty, but I prefer it to the pristine alternative.

These aren't my original wings, of course. I hacked those off years ago, but the damn things grew back like weeds, bigger and stronger than ever. I just hope they're wide enough to 'cover' what Ivan's doing from view.

He'd better hurry – the silence makes it worse. I know that silence, and all that goes with it.

It's absurd. They forget their own names in a matter of seconds when they find themselves in here, but hope sticks. The kids behind me probably think they've somehow stumbled across salvation. Hardly. My wings are every bit as mangled as my shoulders. The best I can do for them now is to bullshit and to stall.

ALICE

You know how I said before that sometimes my brain works a bit slow, especially when it really counts? Like the way I saw you take Dad's gun out of your bag, but at first it didn't register? I've given that detail a lot of thought, and I still don't know exactly what happened. I think that maybe my brain was having a 'what's wrong with this picture' moment, and things were so badly wrong that it just didn't compute. That's what I tell myself, anyway.

Well, looking at Lux in that moment was kind of the same. I mean, it's not as though I didn't see the belts cutting into his chest. I saw them all right, just like I saw Dad's gun. I watched him unbuckle them and everything. And yet it took me way longer than it should have to really *see* what the belts were for. For me to register that they were crushing something down against his back. And for my brain to accept that the something they were crushing down was wings.

I don't know what I expected to happen next – certainly not choir music and rays of white light. Nothing *did* happen, of course. There was just silence, especially from Jude and the others standing behind me. They were dead quiet, but whether it was from awe of the 'angel' or fear of the 'monsters', I had no idea.

'You have wings,' said the actress version of you, stating the obvious.

And that was the exact moment the Monster grabbed me by the arm and yanked me back behind Lux.

The first thing I noticed was that the others – Jude, Boots, Goldie and Lauren – were all standing on the far side of the fence. The second thing I noticed was the blood. It was coming from the hands of the Monster, and it was coming thick and fast. Not green gooey blood like you'd imagine would be running through his veins, but red blood, just like a person's.

'Go,' whispered the Monster, nodding me towards the hole that he'd ripped in the fence, clearly at great personal cost. And yet, for some reason my feet weren't moving.

'Go,' he said again, but I guess I must have hesitated a moment too long because he picked me up with his mangled hands and shoved me through the fence. When he put me down he whispered, 'Tell Boots the truth about who he is,' as though there was some secret understanding between us. There wasn't. I didn't have a goddamn *clue* what he meant.

As for the others, they were just waiting on the other side of the fence, staring at Lux and his crusty wings. They had that sick hope all over their faces. I knew that look. It was the same one that the parents had when they still didn't know if it was their kid under the tarpaulin.

Now, I wasn't buying into those wings – not even a little bit. I was stuck in a place where monsters with sticky black skin were considered normal. In that context, a boy with his own set of feathers didn't mean much. No, what got me was the reaction. The way the others just stood there, staring. Lux must have gone through his whole life with this totally unfair get-out-of-jail-free card, where everybody assumes you're good just because of how you look. Kind of like everyone assumed I was bad, for the exact same reason.

I know it wasn't the best time for it, but their hope in Lux made me furious. That's probably how I managed to act like a leader for the first time in … well, forever. How I managed to hiss 'Run' in a way that snapped them out of their goddamn love fest and got them moving.

I ran too, of course. Given that the gunshots started a few moments later, the running probably saved my life, again. But turning around might have changed everything too. If I'd turned around I would have gotten a good and proper look at Lux standing there, naked from the waist up, wings stretched out like a beaten-up angel. Maybe if I'd seen him in that context, I would have made the connection.

LUX

'You have wings,' she says, as though she's telling me I've got something stuck between my teeth.

'Yes, I have wings,' I say, wondering how I can drag this out just that little bit longer. I haven't turned around to check, but it sounds as though Ivan's almost got everyone through the fence and safely away. We're lucky it's dark. If it were any lighter, the monsters would see them escaping. As it stands, they're still taking their time, thinking we're trapped. Their patience won't last much longer though.

'I've been looking for you,' says the beautiful monster, which is *not* what I was expecting.

'I've been looking for you too,' I say, trying to play it cool. 'You're the one who's been organising the monsters?'

'Guilty,' she says, sounding as if guilt is the very *last* thing she feels about it.

From behind me I hear whispering, and then the unmistakable sound of feet running away.

'Can I ask why?' I say, hoping to buy them a head start. The kids should manage okay but Ivan will be badly hurt from the razor wire. He'll be moving slowly, and no doubt losing a lot of blood. The longer I can give him to get away, the better his chances.

'Self-preservation, of course,' she says, smiling, but not with her eyes. 'Word got around that a monster and a boy in a trench coat were hunting down anyone who showed up in here wearing a school dress. I felt the need to … protect my interests.'

It takes a moment for that to sink in. She looks nothing like her, but as I always say, looks are usually deceiving.

'You're one of the school-girl monsters.'

'And you're the boy in the trench coat. Which means *you*,' she says, looking behind me, 'must be the monster.'

I spin around, and sure enough there's Ivan. He should have gone with the others.

Go now, I signal to him.

He just stares at me and says nothing … then I realise: he *can't* say anything, at least not in our language of gestures. *His hands.*

For a moment I think I'm going to puke, just like a novice. Thankfully it's dark and I can only see the wetness of the blood, not the full extent of the damage. There's no escaping the *drip, drip, drip* on the concrete, though, and the fact that it's speeding up, not slowing down.

'No,' I say, without even meaning to. I've seen Ivan heal

from gunshot wounds and knife attacks and all manner of battles. Nothing like this, though. Nobody survives something like *this*, except me.

Another nightmare begins somewhere nearby, giving off an eerie red glow. It's enough extra light to see that Ivan and I are standing in a giant pool of blood, and that no one's standing behind us. The kids are gone.

If she's mad, she doesn't show it. No emotion makes it to her eyes at all. She just stands there, holding her monsters in check with an iron-clad 'Wait'.

'So,' she says to Ivan and me, once her entourage has settled. 'Who wants to die first?'

ALICE

We weren't all that far from the razor-wire fence when I had to carry Lauren again. She was just too little to keep up. Only, after the adrenaline wore off she started getting heavy. I mean, *really* heavy, but if I put her down her little legs wouldn't be fast enough, just like Casey Blue's little legs weren't fast enough.

When Lauren got too heavy, my very first instinct was to leave her behind. It's true. After making such a massive fuss about bringing her with us, that's where my cowardly self went. The fact that I kept carrying her wasn't the point. I knew that I had it in me not to, and it made me feel like a dirty fraud. It also made me wonder whether the gap between you and me was getting smaller.

But the more I felt like you, the tighter I hung on to Lauren, despite the pain in my arms. It was as if I was holding on to the distance between the two of us, and I sure as hell wasn't letting go, even a little.

One hundred steps – that's what I promised myself. I'd keep going with the girl in my arms for one hundred more steps, and then I'd give myself permission to collapse in a heap and accept whatever was coming. I was up to eighty-seven when the others slowed to a stop. We were back at the Movie World hideout, and that's not all – sitting right there at the entrance, someone was waiting.

Now, when I said everyone in town was pretty horrible to me, that wasn't entirely true. Mr Lilly was the exception. Every so often I'd pass him on the street, and when nobody was looking he'd smile. He gave out these secret little grins, just between him and me. I figured that was decent of him.

Well, there he was – Mr Lilly in the flesh, sitting right outside the hideout. I tell you, I could have just about kissed the man. Right then, seeing a friendly adult had this very 'save the day' feel about it. Like I could just sit back and let him make everything better.

I paused a moment to put Lauren down and take a breath. That's when I noticed that Mr Lilly was holding something up to his face and sniffing it. I let out a little giveaway squeak the moment I recognised the shape of a fluffy toy duck – the one that I'd recently pissed on.

The tiny noise was enough to get his attention. With lightning-quick speed he snapped his head around to face us. It wasn't Mr Lilly. At least, not any version of him that *I'd* like to meet. His eyes were too pale and they kept streaming water, like fake tears. His grin was the worst, though. It was just like the secret smile he used to give me, but now it was perverted and sinister.

Did Mr Lilly smile at me back home because he was being nice, or because he thought we were kindred spirits? Was he smiling at me because he was a good man, or because he wasn't?

I didn't have time to wonder for long, because that freaky Mr Lilly dropped the fluffy duck and ran right for us.

He got about half-way, give or take, before Goldie pegged a knife straight into his esophagus. Goldie, who looked so very much like beautiful Maggie Cooper, the girl with the perfect nails who would blow-dry her hair every single morning, even just for school. Our sweet little Maggie, whose greatest ambition in life was to be a regular on *Home and Away*. She wasn't Maggie. She was Goldie, and she'd just killed a man without flinching.

'What do we do?' said Jude after Mr Lilly hit the ground.

Goldie cut him off with 'Shhh', while she listened to hear if anything else was coming. When nothing did, they all started whispering about where we could hide, given that Movie World had somehow been compromised.

All the talk of where to hide made me think of those epic games of hide-and-seek we used to play down by the creek, back when we were kids. Damn, you were a legend at it. I mean, nobody could ever find you. One time I peeked and watched you run straight out into the bush. I have no idea how you hid out there. It seemed to me that there was nowhere to hide at all, but somehow you managed it.

'Let's go out into the bush,' I said, half to myself. 'We can hide out there until morning.'

'*Hell* no,' said Goldie 'And besides, I'm not following

you anywhere.' She shot a pointed look at Lauren, as if I'd brought along a ticking time bomb, instead of just a girl.

'She's still in charge,' said Jude in my defence, though he sounded a bit half-hearted.

'Bullshit she is!' said Goldie. 'Lux and Ivan are probably dead thanks to that stunt she pulled bringing the kid, and it could've *easily* been the rest of us too.'

'We can't decide this now,' said Boots. His voice was as calm and soothing as ever, but for once it didn't help. I felt panicky and freaked out and definitely not okay.

'I'm going,' I said. 'Come or don't come.'

As soon as the ultimatum was past my lips, I regretted it. But I took Lauren by the hand anyway and started walking.

I counted my steps – *ten, eleven, twelve*. Now if I'd been properly tough I would have just kept on walking, playing it cool. I'm not properly tough, though, as we both know only too well. So I turned around to check.

They were following all right, but they sure as shit weren't *okay* with it. I assumed that was about me, that the idea of following me anywhere was a worry. I should have realised there was more to it. I should have known from Goldie's '*Hell* no'.

Instead I kept my head down and stared at my shoes, one foot in front of the other, counting my steps.

I suppose it's ironic that of all the possible acts of avoidance, it was *shoes* that I chose as my focus. If I'd paid half as much attention to *Boots's* footwear as I did my own, then I might have recognised Dad's Blundstones – the ones that went missing right around the time that it all went wrong.

LUX

'Are you dead?' I say, unwilling to turn my head and see for myself. I'm lying facedown near the razor-wire fence. The blood is sticky and cold on my cheek, which means that the bleeding has stopped. I've been here a while, then.

I listen for an answer, any kind of noise that will tell me Ivan's still alive. I can hear the usual racket of death and dying off in the distance but nothing else.

I've been shot in the head before – it's a particular numbness, followed by a very special kind of pain. Normally I just lie still for as long as it takes for the agony to pass – hours, days sometimes. Right now I don't have that luxury. I open my eyes, trying not to move any other part of me, then gently roll my head to the side.

Bodies surround us, but they all belong to the honey blonde's monsters. We must have scored a few hits before going down, despite only having one gun and no working hands between us. That counts for something, I suppose.

I can see Ivan now. He's lying about a metre away, staring at me with vacant eyes. Judging by the blood that's oozing from his chest, he must have been shot. *Several* times, probably, but I can't remember. All I remember is the pain to the head and now this.

I turn away, staring up at the clear night sky. *So this is it, hey, Ivan?* Not exactly how I pictured it, although the feeling's dead on. The all-over sadness, smothering me like a second skin. It's precisely what I imagined. I'm about to shut my eyes and just give in to it, when I hear a murmur, something about baggage?

'Ivan?' I say, turning back to him.

Sure enough, he blinks, which isn't much, but it's a damn sight better than dead.

'The train,' he says, talking slowly, through a mouthful of blood. 'Running late because too much baggage.'

It's a joke. *Ivan's making a joke*. Talk about timing. I … I have no idea how to respond to that. Given the context, *smiling* is out of the question, so I just stare at him.

'Be here soon, though,' he says, and starts coughing.

He's not talking about our stupid mythical train anymore. He means that he'll be dead soon, and I believe him. His wounds look awful, and Ivan's not one for exaggeration. He's dying while I'm mending, and we both know it.

'Thank you,' he says.

If it was anyone else I'd think he was being facetious, but Ivan doesn't do facetious. He lies, apparently, but as far as I know he doesn't pretend.

'Thank you?'

'For taking the coat off.'

Damn you, Ivan. If ever there was a time to be selfish, it's now. Lash out, or wallow in self-pity. Do any of the normal, indulgent things that people do before dying. Focus on yourself for once, not on the fact that we managed to save some kids that we barely even know.

Well, saved them briefly. The blonde monster isn't among the corpses. She must have left us for dead. Chances are she went through the hole in the fence, after the others. It's possible that everyone in the little gang we were so briefly a part of is dead already, but there's no point in that kind of honesty now.

'You're welcome,' I say, because it's the only simple answer I can think of.

'I lied to you,' says Ivan, clearly not sold on the simple approach.

'It doesn't matter,' I say, but it's not what I'm thinking. I'm thinking, *I lied to you too, and more than you know.*

'It matters,' he says.

Then there's a silence and I think, *Maybe that's it; maybe he's dead.*

'I lied to you about the dream that created me,' Ivan says, ending the worrying pause.

'I forgive you,' I say, hoping that we can talk about something other than lies before he goes and dies on me.

'In the dream I *was* sitting on a rock, but I was talking to two boys. The older one told me that I would help him save the last survivors. We talked, and then the boys were gone. They disappeared before the dream ended, so that when the bubble *did* burst I was left in here alone.'

'The boys?' I ask, because I know he wants me to.

156

'The younger one looked like Boots. The older one had wings. I saw them under his trench coat.'

And so there it is, the truth, finally out in the open. Ivan's hopes for me go much deeper than the fact that I look like a so-called heavenly creature. His idea that I would save them goes right back to the start. When he found me three years ago it wasn't some random act of friendship. He'd probably been looking for a boy with wings all along, just to fulfil his ludicrous prophecy. Chances are he's been waiting for me to live up to his expectations ever since.

'In my dream you said that your nightmare would play out again. That when it did, I'd help you kill your monster. That killing your monster would save the last survivors. That it was the key to everything.'

Ivan, you poor delusional bastard. The dream means nothing, of course. It wasn't me on that rock with Ivan and Boots, spruiking salvation. Best-case scenario it's a coincidence, but I doubt it. Hope can twist the facts better than anything, and Ivan's far more prone to hope than most. I'd say that over the years he's done whatever it took to make things fit, just like with Kell and the bandage. That's not the point, though. The point is he believes it, that he's *always* believed it. Our whole friendship – this whole time – has been based on … wishful thinking.

'It had boats,' I say.

'What?'

'The bandage on her hand. In the dream that created me it had little boats on it. Yellow ones.'

It's a cruel move, even for me. The decent thing would be to let him have it – his hope, I mean.

In the silence that follows, I know that he understands. On the very first night we met, when I told Ivan about the dream that created me, I told him the gritty details, right down to the rag tied around her hand. What I *hadn't* mentioned – what wasn't important until now – was what that rag looked like. I remember it vividly, right down to the cheery sailboats bogged down in dried blood.

Ivan's attempts to engineer fate haven't worked. The bandage he tied around Kell's hand wasn't the same as the one in the dream that created me. It wasn't a prophecy unfolding; it was just Ivan grasping at straws. I have to feel for him. His whole plan for salvation has been undone by some lousy yellow sailboats.

And, of course, by me.

'Boats mean nothing,' he says at last.

Are you kidding me? He's actually sticking with it? That's just … That's just perfect. Even in the face of cold hard facts, he *still* believes.

The silence stretches on and on. There's absolutely nothing I can say.

'You don't believe me,' says Ivan, stating the obvious. 'That's okay. In the dream you said that might happen.'

Very convenient, I think to myself, then feel like a bastard for it. This might be madness, but it's the madness that he's lived his soon-to-be-over life by, and it's a prick of an act to mock him for it now, even if only in my head.

'In the dream you told me what to say to convince you. You told me to tell you,' says Ivan through a mouthful of blood, 'that you were in love with her.'

I try to stay focused, but it's no use. All I can think about is the dream. Of the lightning showing me her face in flashes. Of kissing her neck and lifting her top. Of her hand, wrapped in that yellow-boat bandage, gently trailing down my chest …

It's true, my dirtiest secret of all is that I *was* in love with her. In the dream that stranded me here, all I felt for her was love. Given what happened next, and what she turned out to be, that tiny detail has ruined me the most. Only, I've never told anyone that I loved her, not even Ivan. Half the time I don't even admit it to myself.

I shut my eyes to gather my thoughts in darkness. I have no idea how Ivan knew to say that. It's a coincidence or a trick, clearly, but that doesn't matter. The point is there's no time to talk him out of this. He believes it and I'm not going to change his mind, not now. Whatever has led him to guess right is irrelevant.

I open my eyes and Ivan's staring right back at me, waiting for an answer. I can't give him what he wants without sounding like a fraud, but I need to say something. I need to say the right thing, and I don't want to lie.

'You're my best friend,' I say, because it's the truest thing that springs to mind.

'Not much competition,' he says.

It's a joke – that's two now.

'Well whatever you do, don't go *pulling through* or anything. I'm …' but I don't finish the sentence or follow it up with the double nose tap that means *Reverse psychology, you idiot*.

There's really no point – Ivan's eyes are closed.

ALICE

Counting the steps you take in life can lead to some interesting trivia. For example, you might not know how many years it will take to forget the sound of Eric Hughes dying, but you can know exactly how many steps it takes to avoid his memorial on your way out of town. Or how many steps there are from the chemist to home when you're running. Or how many *more* steps it takes if a group of your once-upon-a-time friends start pegging rocks, and you have to go the long way.

Well, here's another tidbit of useless trivia: there were 312 steps between the Movie World hideout and the Edge, as they called it. Almost all of them were uneven steps, over junk that it was hard to see in the dark. But the 313th step was onto level dirt, the kind that I'd been scuffing around on practically my whole life.

I stopped and stared out into the distance, but there

was nothing but blackness and stars. Standing there like that, with everything behind me and just nothingness in front, I felt as if I was on the edge of a cliff or something, even though I knew that, except for Dumbo's Peak, the bush that surrounded our town was basically flat in every direction.

I started walking. In a way, it was like a real-life version of the game I'd been playing since Merryview – the one where I walked out of town each day, daring myself to go just that little bit further. The truth is, those walks scared the shit out of me. It was as if they tapped into my primal fear of being totally alone in the world, forever and ever. The only reason I took them at all was to push myself or punish myself, or something like it. I never actually planned on leaving. I always intended to turn back and retrace my steps, day after day. Year after year, probably.

Well, walking out past the Edge into the total blackness had me feeling the exact same fear, only more so. I started walking faster, just to prove that I could take it. That I wouldn't flake out or freak out, or worse. I slammed my foot into the dirt with each step and it hurt in a good way, like with the cuts at Merryview.

Pretty soon I was walking so fast that Lauren had to jog to keep up, but she refused to let go of my hand. I guess saving a kid's life will buy you that kind of loyalty. Well, maybe. Perhaps she just realised that holding onto *some-one's* hand in the almost-total darkness was a sensible move, even if that hand was only mine.

As we walked, there was that bush-at-night smell – you

know the one I mean. Only, there was something else too. It smelt like the furry carnage that's forever lining the highways, all sticky and bloated.

And then of course there was the crunching. Most of the time my shoes would plonk onto dirt, but every so often there was a crunch. It was dark, but I wasn't taking any chances. I kept staring straight ahead, worried that if I looked down there might be enough light to see what I was stepping on.

One hundred and seventy-two – that's how many steps I'd taken past the Edge when Jude put his hand on my arm, bringing me to a stop.

'Sleep here?' he said. I didn't see his face, but he sure as hell *sounded* worried.

I was glad of the excuse to stop, because otherwise I'm not sure if I would have known how to.

'I don't like it,' said Goldie.

'It's not far off dawn. We'll be safe now,' said Boots in an actually reassuring way that most people can't manage. He can't have known if we'd be safe or not, so I suppose he was lying. It was a well-placed lie, though, and we both know how liberating *they* can be.

We made camp beneath two gum trees, although I suppose 'made camp' is a bit misleading. It sounds all toasted marshmallows and sleeping bags, and there was none of that. All we had were the clothes we were wearing, and, for some of us, a gun. Nobody complained, though. There was no fussing or bitching. Jude passed around what was left of the water, and I made a point of going last, but otherwise, everyone simply found a spot on the ground and claimed it, kind of like a soldier or a bum.

I sat with my back against one of the tree trunks, and Lauren sat next to me. She was still holding my hand, despite it dripping with sweat. Except why was only one of my hands sweating?

I let go of her, and brought the hand up close to my face. It was too dark to see much, but there was no mistaking the metallic smell. Not sweat, then: blood. For a horrible moment I thought I must have hurt Lauren – that I'd somehow squeezed until she bled. But then I remembered the bandage – the one that was covering a cut from before my time. The blood wasn't Lauren's, it was mine. Well, it was *Kell's* really.

'It'll get infected,' said Lauren. Up this close and personal there was just enough light to see her eyes, which is all you really need with kids. The fear she had back at the princess bed was gone altogether – now she looked exactly like the tomboy I remembered from home. The girl who never cried and never wore pink, and once told me that she was going to be just like Captain Cook some day. That she was going to sail the seas and discover new lands, despite the fact that she'd never even seen the ocean.

Lauren reached into the pocket of her overalls and produced a hanky. She spat on it like a mother would have, then methodically cleaned the wound. When she was finished she tied her hanky around my hand, replacing the old bandage.

'He had *wings*,' said Goldie, barely above a whisper. There was reverence, though, no mistake about it.

'They were just wings,' I said. 'Get some sleep.' And the way I said it? Well, it was a little bit forceful. Okay, the truth is I snapped in the kind of voice that you would have used to get results. It worked too. They might have all still been thinking about those wings but they sure as shit weren't talking about them, which was good enough for me.

I scrunched down, so that I was lying with my back on the dirt and my head up against the roots of the gum tree. Lauren curled into me, making a pillow of my armpit.

In between the black outlines of branches I could see millions of stars, that billions of people thought were hiding some kind of heaven. I knew better, though. I'd seen the world at its worst, and I knew that no God worth a crap would stand for such rubbish. I knew that the people you killed hadn't 'gone to a better place': they were just *gone*, end of story. No meaning, no purpose, no secret grand plan – other than maybe yours.

LUX

'What are you doing?' says Ivan when he finally comes to. I turn away so that he can't see my relief. In the last few hours there were times when I thought that I'd lost him.

'Rumour has it I'm some kind of saviour,' I say, dumping a corpse roughly at his feet. 'So I'm getting down to business.'

'You're saving dead monsters?'

'Just you,' I say, grabbing a second body by the feet and dragging it towards the first one. There are four in total, which means that Puppy-belt and the green-eyed blonde got away. That's okay: four's enough for my current purposes.

I dump the second body in Ivan's lap, but not carefully enough. It knocks him off balance and he slumps forward.

'*Shit*,' I say, pulling him back up to a sitting position.

There's a very long pause before Ivan takes a deep breath and says, 'What's with the corpses?'

'Camouflage,' I say, putting another dead monster in place next to him, more carefully this time. 'If anyone comes, you play dead.'

'How convincingly?' says Ivan ... and did he just try to raise an eyebrow?

'*Not* to the point of actually dying,' I say, glancing at his hands.

I bandaged them up as best I could while he was unconscious but they still look awful. Just stumps, really, and he's lost a lot of blood.

I busy myself rearranging cold limbs, getting bodies in place, then I take a step back to see the total effect. Sure enough, Ivan's more or less covered. All he has to do is close his eyes to look like just one of the pile. As far as plans go it's certainly not flawless, but Ivan's badly injured and bloody heavy – moving him is not exactly an option.

Ivan watches in silence as I fumble with the buckles, trying to get a proper purchase. I've never put the belts on without his help and one of them slips from my grip.

'Need me to give you a *hand*?'

I turn around to see if that was meant to be a joke ... and yes, he's smiling. *Thank goodness he's smiling.*

After a few more failed attempts I get the belts in place, more or less, then manage to pull the trench coat on over the top. Everything's lumpy and my back looks hunched, but it'll do. For now that's the *least* of my worries.

I slowly turn around, taking stock of our surroundings.

From a tactical point of view I'd be better to sit opposite Ivan, for a clear line of sight. I choose to ignore that and sit down beside him instead.

Ivan doesn't look at me. He stares up at the sky, which is bruising with morning colours. And then, after a very long pause, he says, 'I wish I had more time.'

I honestly don't know what to say to that. The bullet wounds weren't as bad as I thought, but his hands? I've never seen another creature quite like Ivan, so I have no idea what constitutes a mortal injury for him.

'Just … just hang in there,' I say, which is the best I can manage.

'Not *me*,' Ivan scoffs. 'The deadline. It's almost dawn. I wish I had more time.'

You've got to be kidding me. Even now he's thinking about Kell and his ridiculous prophecy? I don't say a word, but the look on my face speaks volumes.

'What, I don't even get a dying wish?' says Ivan, but not in a joking way.

'No, because you're not dying,' I say, refusing to look at him in case he can tell that I'm not sure. 'Saviour, remember? This is me in action.'

Maybe it's the blood loss, but something about him looks greyer. Less full of life.

'I was dreamt up by a woman who'd been blind her whole life,' says Ivan. 'She had no idea what good and bad were *meant* to look like, so she pictured me like this. She didn't see me as a monster.' There's a flatness to his voice that sounds all wrong. 'She was different. *Special*.

Everything in the dream that created me seemed so *clear*. And the part about you? About the dream repeating itself and me helping you kill your monster? About that being the key to saving everyone? I've waited for it to come true ever since,' he says, still not looking at me. 'I've been waiting and believing for more than a hundred years.'

A hundred years? A whole *century*? It seems impossible. I knew that he'd been in here for a while before he found me, but nothing *close* to that long. I should say something, but the tone of his voice has thrown me. Even when the chips are down – which is most of the time – *Ivan's* not down.

'I'm sorry,' he says at last. 'I'm sorry for everything. When I saw the coin around Kell's neck I was so sure. I *believed* it would all play out and that I'd help you kill your monster and ... I just thought ... I can't explain it. I was wrong.'

Actually, the one who was wrong was *me*. All this time I thought that hope was the worst kind of burden, but I was mistaken. It turns out the *absence* of hope is far worse. Looking at Ivan now, hearing the defeat in him ... suddenly I'll be damned if I just let him fail. If this stupid dream-repeating-itself business means so much to him, then he's going to bloody well have it.

'Fate needs help,' I say, quoting his mantra of yesterday. 'And I'm all about *lending a hand* to those in need of one. Or two.'

Ivan doesn't even smile; he just takes a deep breath and closes his eyes.

'I'll do it tonight,' I say, talking faster. 'I'll kill her under the stars on a slab of stone, just like in the dream that created me. I'll *force* it to play out again.' There won't be lightning or sailboats on the bandage and I sure as shit won't *love* her. More to the point, it won't lead to anyone being saved … but hey, mere details.

Ivan still doesn't respond. He just sits there with his eyes closed and his face turned towards the so-called heavens.

It goes on for so long that I think maybe I've left it too late, that either he's given up on hope for good or that he's dead already.

But then out of nowhere he whispers, 'Now? Wouldn't it make more sense for you to bring her here now?' He has some of the old spark back. 'We could tie her up and wait until nightfall. I think it would give me … motivation.'

He doesn't say motivation *to not die,* but he doesn't have to, it's implied. I'm about to object, but actually, it's not a bad plan. It makes more sense to retrieve Kell now, in the relative safety of morning, than to wait until nightfall. It means I won't have to leave Ivan alone after dark, for one thing.

In the end I nod and say, 'I've got this, Amigo,' which has always been one of Ivan's particular favourites. I pull the gun from my pocket. Ivan might despise these things, but I don't care, he's taking it anyway. Leaving him alone in his current state is bad enough, but there's no way I'm leaving him here *completely* defenceless.

'No arguments,' I say as I hold the gun out to him. But then I stop short. *Ivan has no way of pulling the trigger.*

169

The silence stretches on and on with Ivan looking right at me. I don't know where to go from here so I basically stand still, caught in the moment. Eventually I clear my throat and give a gruff 'Remember, *play dead*' as I awkwardly pocket the gun again.

Ivan responds with a 'Woof', in homage to his stupid pet routine.

I should keep the mood light. I should say 'There's a good boy', or make some other joke, but I can't. I feel sick to the stomach, so instead I just turn to leave.

'Tonight?' says Ivan, wanting one last reassurance. I take a deep breath and say, 'I swear on the heavens above,' but he doesn't get that I'm being ironic, given the wings and all. So I add, 'Yes, tonight.'

'Swear on my life?' says Ivan, which just makes it worse.

'*What* life?' I say. 'You're as sad and pathetic as I am. Other than hunting monsters, we have no life.'

I meant for my words to lighten the mood, but now that they're out I can't bring myself to smile. Instead I add, 'Yes, I swear,' while my hands urge, *Living. Keep living*.

Ivan nods, but I'm not sure whether it's in response to the promise or the plea.

ALICE

At dawn I got my first proper look at where we were, and it will haunt me forever.

We weren't sitting out in the empty bush that surrounded our town, not really. There was the red dirt and spinifex grass and the shimmery heat, just like always. But what we were *really* sitting in was a graveyard. Or rather, a dumping ground for bodies. There were bodies as far as the eye could see. They weren't buried. Unlike the dead of our town, there were no little white crosses or marble headstones or memorials marking where they lay. Just bodies, dumped like nothing but flesh.

It was probably a good thing I hadn't eaten a scrap. If I had, I'm pretty sure I would have puked it up when I remembered the crunching underfoot the night before. Then of course there was the smell I'd noticed. No wonder Goldie and the others had wanted to avoid going past the Edge.

For a while I just sat, staring. The makeshift graveyard was so horribly wrong, but what made it even worse was that it also seemed … right. As if in a weird way our town surrounded by all those dead bodies was more honest.

In our town – the *real* version – they buried the seven kids you killed. They put them under the ground, out of sight, so all that was left were the shiny memorials. So that no one could see how everything was still sinking into the holes they'd left behind.

The sight of all the dead bodies dumped out there on the dirt reminded me of an exercise Dr Ben made me do one time. He gave me a big piece of butcher's paper and asked me to draw what I was feeling 'on the inside', as if I was a goddamn child or something. Well, if Collector had a giant piece of butcher's paper, and could draw how it 'felt on the inside', then I think the dumping ground of bodies that I was looking at would have been a bloody good start.

After a while, I realised I was crying, which is something I hadn't done in practically forever. In precisely the number of days that had passed since what you did, plus three. Given what a sook I used to be, you'll probably find that hard to believe, but it's true.

I don't know why I couldn't cry after what happened, but it wasn't one of those 'meaningful' things. I guess I just didn't really feel in the mood, no matter how bad it got. Maybe it's because things get past a point where tears can help, you know? That's not to say I didn't try, though.

I tried very hard to cry after the shooting, for two reasons. Partly because in those dark days I was desperate to prove that we weren't the same. The fact that you never cried and suddenly I couldn't? Well, it seemed like a bad omen. Like, discovering a 666 birthmark kind of a bad omen.

The other reason I tried to cry is a pretty cynical one, if you must know. Before Merryview, the newspapers were mad for taking my picture and writing awful things about me 'showing no emotion'. The fact that you'd killed people in cold blood and I looked like I wasn't even all that fazed by it was a really top story for them. By 'no emotion' they meant that I wasn't blubbering all over the place. Apparently that's the only kind of grief that translates well to the general masses. So I tried to cry.

I thought about everything. I thought about what Lisa Jenkins would have felt as she gripped her stomach and tried to stop the bleeding but must have known it was hopeless. And George Winden when he realised there was nowhere to run. And Casey the moment the bullet burrowed into her tiny, not even fully grown spine. And Rachel's parents when they arrived and couldn't find her and knew – just somehow *knew* – that their whole reason for living was about to get buried.

I thought about Peter when he heard the shots and realised that his little brother would be out in the courtyard, playing handball. And Mrs Battinson, who was half deaf and didn't hear the sirens and so she ended up watching a re-run of *Wheel of Fortune* while her only grandkid bled to death just down the road.

I even thought about Dad and what that moment must

have been like when Sergeant Collins finally tracked him down in Henson's back paddock.

None of it worked, of course. I'd cried about thousands of utterly stupid things over the course of my life, from being picked last, to breaking my arm, to the fact that you got the boy, but when it really mattered I was dry as a bone.

Dr Ben said I was probably in shock. And then of course they put me on the pills, and crying through that fog would have been damn near a miracle.

But sitting there, staring at the wreck of our town that wasn't even really our town anyway, the tears just kept on rolling. They were proper tears too, the type that come with snot and puffy eyes and gaspy little hiccups. The sort of tears that you can't stop, even if you want to. And just like that, with snot and tears streaming down my face like I was a lonely kid again, I knew what had to happen.

I'd like to say that Kell is what made my mind up. That I'd finally admitted the truth – that she *might* be a threat. I mean, so what if she was only a *version* of you, as opposed to the real thing? So what if a few kids in the nightmare world seemed to trust her? We all trusted you, didn't we? And as for Dr Ben's 'you're just being paranoid' mantra, well, he clearly hadn't factored in a world swap. I'd like to say that because of her I had to go home, so that I could save the town, unlike last time.

It's a plausible explanation I suppose, but the truth? No, the truth is it was the crying that did it. *That's* what made my mind up. You see, I hadn't felt a huge amount of emotion in three whole years, and crying scared the shit out of me. What if I lost control? What if, without the dulling numbness, I really *was* like you? What if all the guns and death and monsters nudged me in the wrong direction?

As I sat there crying, I realised ... *I didn't actually want to know.* I didn't want to know whether, push come to shove, we were more alike than not. I didn't want to find out exactly what kind of person I was capable of being. I'd been looking for an answer to a question that, deep down, I didn't want to know at all.

There, *that's* the dirty truth of it. It wasn't fear about what *Kell* might be capable of that tipped me over: it was fear about what *I* might be capable of. *That's* what made me decide I had to swap back, no matter what. I had to get out of the nightmare place and back to my pills before it was all too late. Before I discovered my true colours ... and maybe even did something awful.

But I didn't have a clue how to get back to the real world. I mean, there was no instruction manual and it's not as though I could just casually ask around. And so, in the complete absence of any other options, I had to hope that finding Kell would somehow provide the answer. The thing is, she could have been anywhere. Back at town, *not* back at town. She could have hitchhiked to Sydney for all I knew. I had no idea where she was, so I latched on to the classic *check the last place you saw them.* Isn't that what Mum used to say? *If you ever get lost, just stay where you are and wait.* So that was my plan. I'd go back to the Caltex and just pray that Kell was there. Pray that, despite all the other options that seemed *way* more likely, she was just sitting there patiently waiting, like I needed her to be.

The more I thought about it, the more it really took hold. I became convinced that if I could just get back to the Caltex it would all be okay. That I'd find Kell and swap back and return to my pills and their safety.

Maybe that sounds plain crazy to you, but here's the thing – I was desperate. Desperation can make you latch on to all kinds of stupid ideas, wouldn't you say? If you're *desperate* enough, you can talk yourself into just about anything. Hell, some people even end up taking a gun to school.

At any rate, the moment I locked onto the Caltex solution, a kind of calm came over me. I had a plan …

But that plan didn't involve Jude or Lauren or the others, and I suddenly felt sick about just leaving them while they slept, like you once did to me.

I told myself they'd be better off with the devil they knew, as opposed to yours truly. I mean, at least Kell seemed to be *competent*. She'd kept them sort-of safe and sort-of fed, hadn't she? That was far more than *I* could manage. And yes, *of course* I still hated the idea of leaving them with a version of you … but just because I'd been secretly worried about what Kell might get up to in the real world that didn't *necessarily* mean she'd be a threat back where she came from, right? No, being rid of me was clearly their best option.

I thought about waking them up to say goodbye, but the same thing stopped me as what probably stopped you.

I didn't want to be talked out of it. And so I did what you did; I took the more cowardly option.

Goldie and Lauren were first. I mentally bid them both farewell, then I turned my attention to Boots. Back at the fence Ivan had asked me to tell Boots 'the truth about who he is'. Instead I just watched him sleep for a while, thinking how peaceful he looked as compared to the real-world Marcus.

And then, when I couldn't avoid it any longer, I went over to Jude. It seemed impossible to believe that I could walk away from Jude. That I had it in me to leave him behind of my own free will, let alone do it without a goodbye.

I toyed with the idea of quietly waking him up while the others slept so that we could finally have that epic farewell we missed out on the first time. So that he could hold me like I wanted to be held and kiss me like I wanted to be kissed and tell me what I wanted to hear, just like I'd always imagined. The problem was, with Jude asleep like that? He wasn't fawning over me or pissing me off or making me love him less. He was perfect, and really, who dares mess with perfection?

LUX

Crap, I say with a flick of my thumb, which is a ridiculous instinct. There's no point using hand signals without Ivan. Still, a well-placed expletive seems necessary, given the werewolf-style monster that's lurking nearby. Kell's to blame for that.

She's been stomping her way through the dream junk again, not even *trying* to be quiet. That initially worked in my favour. I was half-way back to the Movie World lair when I heard her, which saved me some time. Only, I'm clearly not the *only* one who's tracked her.

I could let Kell know that I'm here, but there's no fun in that. I decide to stay hidden instead and see how she handles wolfie. She must know that it's tracking her. She must know that *something* is tracking her, given all the noise she's been making. Besides, the occasional wafts of burnt-flesh smell that it's omitting aren't exactly *subtle*. Pretending to be oblivious must be a ruse of some description, but it's a dangerous game that she's playing.

The beast closes in for the kill. It lets out a growl then lunges right at her … *and she does nothing*. She's a gang-leader, a school-girl monster, and she doesn't even *try* to fight back? I'm so surprised that it takes me a moment to respond, to draw my gun and kill the creature, like *she* should have.

The beast collapses dead on top of her, and she screams. She actually screams, despite what could be out there. Shit, you'd think she'd never seen a werewolf before.

Once she's scrambled free she just stands there, staring at me. It's the wings. It's always the bloody wings that have them staring. I might have managed to get the trench coat back on – more or less – but she knows that they're there.

It's not until Kell puts her hands in the air that I realise I still have my gun drawn, and I'm pointing it right at her. I should lower my weapon, I suppose. Well, 'no dies'. I keep it aimed at her head as I ask the question that's been on my mind since I tracked her down and saw that she was alone.

'Did you kill the others?'

'What?'

'Boots and the others, did you kill them?'

'No!' she says, and has the gall to sound indignant. 'I left at dawn, while they were still sleeping.'

She doesn't *appear* to be lying, which is some small mercy. The others should be safe enough at the Movie World lair during daylight hours. As soon as the stars are out and I've killed Kell, I'll go back for them, assuming Ivan's well enough to travel.

And then I see it.

Kell's hands are still above her head, in the gesture for 'don't shoot'. The canvas bandage that Ivan tied around her hand is gone. There's a new one in its place. It has boats on it. *Yellow ones.*

I'm breathing hard, trying to get a handle. Is it a joke? A trick? And then, just as I'm feeling right on edge, she makes it worse. She closes her eyes and takes a deep steadying breath … and all at once she looks vulnerable. Like a girl instead of a monster, and it reminds me of the dream that created me. It reminds me of that dream even more than the bloody bandage. I feel like the fundamentals are slipping – like the lines are getting blurry …

'You're a monster,' I say, mostly for my own reassurance. To remind myself that, when I pull the trigger tonight, it won't be a *girl* that I'm killing.

Kell just stares at me, and there's something in her eyes. It's anger, the kind I haven't seen in her since she condemned that no-name kid back outside Sea World.

'Maybe,' she says, looking right at me. 'But I'm not *your* monster. I'm not Kell, alright? I saw some ghost who looked like me and we touched and we swapped and … I'm from the real world, okay? I have to find the Caltex so that I can touch her again and swap back.'

'Right,' I say, after a lengthy pause. 'And I'm from the land of the unicorns. Tell me, do I *come across* as stupid?'

'It's the truth,' says Kell, but the words are not what

180

gets me. It's the look. The fervent, absolute, totally-sure-of-it conviction that I've only ever seen before in Ivan. Holy. Shit. *She's not lying.* Kell actually believes she's from the real world, which is the last thing I need right now. The question, I suppose, is how best to handle it.

Crazy can be fun to mess with, and part of me would rather enjoy the sport. Then again, crazy's also unpredictable. If I taunt her, what are the chances she won't say something or do something to provoke me? Something that results in me killing her too soon, thus breaking my promise. No, all things considered, it's probably best to just play along – to indulge Kell's delusions until I've got her back to Ivan.

'Okay,' I say.

'Okay what?'

'Okay, I'll take you back to the Caltex.'

'I can find it myself.'

'Really? If you left the others at dawn then shouldn't you be there already? Get a bit *lost,* did we?'

'I don't need your help,' she says, which is an absolute joke. *Me* helping *her*? Never happen.

'Oh, but I *insist,*' I say instead. I pocket the gun with exaggerated slowness, to emphasise that the one who's making the decisions right now is me.

Kell just stares, then says, 'Why would you help me?'

'I'm not helping you, I'm *getting rid* of you,' I say, which is precisely the truth.

Kell looks a bit alarmed by my little double entendre, though, so I temper it with, 'Isn't that what you *said* would happen? That when you get to the Caltex, you'll swap back to the real world?'

'Yes,' says Kell, after a moment's hesitation. 'Yes, that's *exactly* what will happen. All I have to do is get to the Caltex, then I can swap back.'

It's hard to say whether she's trying to convince me or to convince herself. Either way, I'm sold on the fact that she's crazy.

ALICE

Lux promised to take me to the Caltex.

He didn't; he took me back to the fence instead. As soon as we rounded the corner I knew exactly why I was there. Goldie had said that getting attacked by the monsters was my fault, and now Lux wanted payback. He wanted me to see what I'd done: the blood, the death, the carnage. It hadn't escaped my notice that the Monster – Ivan – was gone, presumably dead.

I waited for Lux to start with the yelling, which is normally what comes first. He didn't. Instead he bee-lined for a pile of dead monsters, and started hunting through it. After that he looked around, getting more and more desperate.

It wasn't until he actually whispered 'Ivan?' that I finally understood. Ivan wasn't dead, then, just missing ... and it was making Lux *very* worried. Underneath all that nothing-can-touch-me cool there was definite panic.

Part of me just wanted to shut my eyes. I mean, I was on a very important mission of non-discovery, right? But Ivan had risked his life to save us, and that kind of trumped my instinct for avoidance.

So I helped. I looked under beds and behind swings and in fallen-down scenes of perfect-life bliss. And then, after all that, I found myself over by the fence again. The place where, for the second time in my life, I'd expected to die amid kids and at least one monster.

I stared up at the hole in the razor wire, then down at the blood beneath it. I wondered how it must feel to be brave in a crisis. To have put yourself to the test and not let yourself down.

'Come over here to gloat?' said Lux, suddenly right behind me. He made a point of looking at the blood at my feet, as if he expected me to spit in it or something. The old me probably would have gotten her hackles up about that, what with Lux just *assuming* I'd behave like a monster and all. Well, I didn't.

Instead I carefully rested my hand on the fence. Lauren's little yellow sailboats up against all those sharp edges. I touched the gaping hole, still covered in Ivan's blood. Ivan, who I'd thought was a monster. Ivan, who'd *actually* done that one incredible thing – *risked his life to save a bunch of kids.*

'People always think that they'll act like a hero under pressure, but they don't,' I said, thinking about the schoolyard and that night outside the half-house. 'Most of us are cowards when it counts.'

'You're talking about Ivan?' said Lux, eyeing me suspiciously. 'Most people don't count Ivan as *people.*'

'Most people are idiots,' I said, with a level of conviction that really wasn't like me.

It must have struck Lux as odd too, because he stared at me with this look that I couldn't quite read. Then he said, 'Agreed.' And you know what? For a weird moment it was as if we had a connection. A thread of understanding … and then, like seven unsuspecting schoolkids, it was gone.

Lux cleared his throat and gave our surroundings another once-over. He *seemed* purposeful enough, but I wasn't fooled for a second. I recognised the lost vibe about him. It was the look of a person who doesn't have a next move. I'd felt that way myself, many times, which is how I knew about the goal technique. When you're totally lost, you've got to find yourself a goal. Something to latch on to, even if it's silly or far-fetched … like me with the Caltex.

Did Lux *ever* plan on taking me there? I mean, he'd clearly come back to the fence for Ivan, but *after* that? I suddenly found myself focusing on a few practical realities. Like the fact that Lux hated me. And we were alone. And he had a gun.

Do you suppose I behaved true to form and ran away or fainted? No, not that time. Instead I sucked it up and asked Lux the million-dollar question. The question that I probably should have asked of myself, and sooner, but which I put to him instead. I looked him in the eyes and, with a forcefulness that would have done you proud, I said, 'Why am I here?'

LUX

'Why am I here?' says Kell in this no-nonsense voice that's utterly fake. She's scared, clearly, and that look in her eyes? I don't get it. What happened to the ruthless girl who made us abandon no-name?

'Why did you *really* bring me back to the fence?' she says again, when I still haven't answered. I should be enjoying this moment. I should be dragging it out and scaring her more and telling her, *Yes, very bad things are in your future*. But for some reason, I find myself looking away and muttering a pathetic, 'Wrong turn.'

Kell must know that I'm lying but she doesn't call me on it. She just stares for a moment, then says, 'And now?'

I have no idea. I still have a promise to keep, that much is clear, but nightfall's most of a day away. I can't just wait it out *here*. I have to find Ivan ... Only, *I have no idea where to look*.

Did he take himself off somewhere to die? Was it always his plan to make me promise then simply disappear? I'm itching to call out for him again, but I force myself not to. If he left of his own accord, he won't answer. If he *didn't* leave of his own accord, he won't *be able* to answer. Either way I'm still going to find him ... but what to do with Kell while I look? I suppose I *could* just tie her up here then leave, but what if someone – or something – else finds her? *Shit.* I don't have a next move or a new plan, so I do what worked for me the last time. *I lie.*

'*Now,*' I say, with as much kindness as I can fake, 'I take you back to the Caltex.'

The look on Kell's face tells me that she doesn't buy it – not this time.

'I'm keen to get rid of you, remember?' I say, trying a different approach. 'As far as I'm concerned, the sooner the better.' Yes, that's a smarter tactic. Kell seems *far* more willing to swallow the idea that I'd rather see her gone. She drops her gaze and stares down at her shoes.

'You'll really do it?' she says after a moment or two. 'You'll really take me back to the Caltex?'

In my head, I should be mocking her for being such a fool, but I'm not. Her voice is the problem, the way it's crying out for reassurance, just like Ivan when he made me promise and then promise again.

'We head north,' I say abruptly. North was a random choice. I don't actually have a destination in mind. I figure I'll just keep us moving while I look for Ivan. Under normal circumstances I wouldn't have a hope of pulling that off, but

Kell's sense of direction seems to be woeful. I don't know how long she'll believe we're still on our way to the Caltex, but I'll cross that bridge later.

'Let's go,' I say, not meeting her gaze.

Progress is slow and the day is hot; it's not long before I'm sweating. Sweat I'm used to; it's the *blood* that I don't like. I'm covered in it, both Ivan's and mine. The stickiness is awful, but the smell is worse. Combined with those occasional wafts of burnt flesh that somehow haven't left us, there's stench to the point of distraction.

As we walk Kell occasionally glances at me. Her expression almost resembles sympathy, except of course that it's fake. I wonder what's *really* going through her head at the sight of me like this. The hunchback effect from the coat, the dried blood, the head wound, the flies that have started to circle – I must look downright horrific. Good. Let her be scared and revolted. Let her … Kell has stopped in her tracks, and that almost always means danger.

'What?' I whisper, reaching for my gun. 'What?' I ask again when she still hasn't answered.

Kell doesn't say a word, she just points to a tiny gap between a skate ramp and a rollercoaster. I'm expecting something horrific … but no.

She has surprised me, again.

ALICE

Is it possible to do a thing and not even really know why? A random act of kindness perhaps? Or in your case, the extreme opposite? The truth is, I'm still not sure why I showed Lux the little beach that I'd spotted. He clearly didn't deserve any sympathy from me ... and yet? Well, I'd been covered in blood myself, once upon an awful time. *Not* a good feeling.

The beach itself wasn't much, not by Australian standards. In fact, the whole scene was more like a giant cheap postcard, brought weirdly to life. We're talking cheery plastic umbrellas and lounge chairs plonked straight onto sand that wasn't quite real. Opposite all that was a brick wall covered in a painted-on sunset. Hardly impressive.

No, it's what *separated* those things that mattered. You see, wedged between the fake sand and the 2D horizon, there was water. *Actual* water that smelt like salt and was all that you'd need to get clean.

Lux didn't waste a moment. He led us straight onto the sand ... And then he realised his problem – *the gun*. He couldn't get it wet, but he clearly didn't want to leave it unattended near me either. Dilemma. In the end he put it on the nearest sun lounge then warned, 'I'm quick. If you make for the gun I'll get to it first.'

'I'm *not* going to make for the gun,' I said. Only I was so adamant, so *emphatic* that I kind of sounded phony. At any rate, Lux was suspicious.

'Even if you get to the gun, it'll do you no good because *I* can't die,' he said, implying that dying was a very real option for me. Perhaps I should have been impressed or simply not believed him. Instead I said the first thing that popped into my head at the thought of living forever. I blurted out, 'Jeez, that must be *awful*.'

Lux just stared and stared with this cryptic expression that kind of got under my skin. I figured he was probably just annoyed that I wasn't wowed by his whole 'immortal' claim.

I moved away from the gun, proving that I *really* didn't want it, and headed to the far end of the tiny beach. I took off my shoes and waded straight in fully clothed.

I floated on my back, shutting my eyes to the clear blue sky and painted sunset. My body felt light and sounds were muffled. I wished I could stay like that forever. Not quite hearing or seeing the nightmare world, let alone the real one. Not quite feeling the weight of things.

In that floaty state I dared to wonder what was next for me. What would happen once I got back to town, and returned to my old way of living? I'd gone home to find answers. But now that I was committed to *not* knowing, maybe it made sense to just leave. To retreat back into Merryview and the pills and my memories of Jude. Leave Collector and its troubles far behind me. This might sound a bit tragic, but I kind of *liked* that empty fantasy. The idea of living out my days in foggy penance held a gentle, righteous appeal.

But the fantasy was ruined by Lux wading into the water, distracting me. He waited until he was out nice and deep before taking off the trench coat. It was as if he didn't want me to see him, to watch him, you know? And then, in no time at all, it was over. Lux was back on the sand, wearing his coat and a scowl, just like always. Time to go, apparently.

I headed for the shore and was almost out of the water when the whole bra thing became an issue again. As in, *how I wasn't wearing one*. The singlet I had on was sticking to my skin in a way that left nothing – *and I mean nothing* – to the imagination.

I guess some of the panic must have shown on my face because Lux jumped to his feet and ran over. 'What is it? What's wrong?' he said, scanning the water as if he expected aquatic horrors.

I didn't have time to respond before Lux had waded in, boots and all, grabbed me by the arm and pulled me behind him. That was the first time he'd touched me. His hand, my arm ... I couldn't help it. In a cruel twist of betrayal, my heart sped up, despite how I *really* wished it wouldn't.

And do you know what I thought, right in that moment? What crazy idea was running through my head as my pulse behaved like an absolute traitor? I wondered *how had he known?* How had Lux read the change in my face – the subtle nuance that said something was wrong – when not even Jude had managed that much when he kissed me?

LUX

'What did you see?' I say, trying to get a fix on the threat. Kell doesn't answer, so I glance back at her. I don't understand, then I see the way she's hugging herself, trying to hide her chest. I spin around, putting my back to her. Turning around is *not* about being a gentleman. It's about hiding my face. Hard to be sure, but I think I might actually be blushing. *That's* a definite first.

I should just tell Kell to get over herself, that it's a hot day and that her singlet will dry soon enough. The problem is the image that's stuck in my head.

I take my coat off and hand it back to her, waiting until I'm sure she has it on before turning around. *And then I look*. Nope, the coat's not helping. I find myself focusing on *other* things – her lips, the freckles, those eyes …

Kell's staring right back at me, and I brace myself for 'the reaction'. Sure enough, her eyes travel to the wings.

'You probably need a bandaid or antiseptic or something,' she says, looking them up and down. 'That bit right there looks kind of infected.'

What the … ? She's treating the wings as a regular part of me, rather than something special? Nobody's ever done that. Nobody's ever seen past the hype to the flesh and the blood and the bone.

'The skin's all come off over there,' she says.

I could tell her that it will heal, and quickly, but I don't. The silence stretches on until she must think that I'm confused, that I require further explanation. She reaches past my shoulder and points, finger on feather … *touching me*.

I'm perfectly still, focusing everything on the tiny place where our bodies are connected, the teasingly small spot where her finger is on me, not moving away.

I've never … I mean I've never let anyone … I close my eyes and take a deep breath to calm myself down. It doesn't work. In my mind her finger trails down the length of my wing, meandering around my neck, my chest, my arms. A feathery touch as I stand perfectly still, letting her slowly explore …

Next I'm hooking my finger into the loop of her waistband, pulling her into me by the hips. I'm staring down at her, drawing out the moment before we kiss. Feeling her breath against my lips, so close but not quite touching. Letting her hear the want in me with every breath, but not making a move. Waiting, even though it's killing me. Waiting for her to stand on her tippie-toes and reach up and—

194

'Lux?' says Kell, snapping me back to reality. She's still standing right in front of me, looking confused. I should be embarrassed. I should be wondering if she has any idea where my thoughts went just now. Instead I focus on her eyes; they're brimming with ... with what? Something. *Something* when I'm used to seeing *nothing*, just the cold, flat gaze of a killer.

I'm staring at her and she's staring at me and neither of us is moving ... *and then Kell remembers the hand*. She realises she's still touching me, finger on wing, and pulls away in an instant.

I don't say anything or do anything. I try to look blank, as if nothing just happened. As if I didn't *almost* lose myself and *almost* kiss her and *almost* do all manner of things that should be completely off-limits.

'It's actually not that bad,' says Kell after a long pause. 'The sore, I mean. Jude got a much worse infection when he picked off a scab in the third grade. He didn't even cry when they popped it with a needle. He's always been really great like that.'

I'm thinking that what would be 'really great' is if she stopped talking about Jude right now. Stopped talking completely, in fact. I stare at her, wondering what I've *actually* promised Ivan.

Another dip in that water would be a good idea, since it's as close as I'll get to a cold shower. Instead I give a rude 'Are you quite done?'

I'm ostensibly talking about the unprompted Jude tribute, but I also direct a pointed look towards my wing, at the spot where she touched it. Sure enough Kell blushes, as if *she's* the one who crossed the line just now.

'We should go,' I say.

Moving's a good thing; the aimless walking helps to get me sorted. To remind me of what Kell is and what's at stake and what I've promised. After that, I turn my mind to 'what next'.

There's been no sign of Ivan. I thought I'd have found him by now and we can't just wander around all day. Even Kell would twig to that eventually. No, I need a new plan … but what? How do I occupy Kell until nightfall?

It occurs to me that maybe going back to the Caltex isn't such a bad idea after all. Without an injured Ivan to factor in, there's nothing to tie me to any particular place. I can kill her wherever I like, so why *not* at the Caltex? Getting there will fill in some time, and taking Kell where she wants to go will keep her compliant. I can simply play along until the stars come out, then turn on her.

And so, after however long of *pretending* to take us back to the Caltex, I head towards it for real. Well *mostly* towards it. I have one small detour to make along the way. *The Lookout.*

When we arrive at the Lookout, the first thing I do is check for monsters – a necessary evil these days. This place *used* to be a favourite point of navigation, mainly because it's one of a kind and practically indestructible. Not anymore – now the monsters have more or less claimed it. Every night at least a few of them climb to its roof for a bird's-eye view. As a result, gangs rarely come near here anymore. They use other landmarks to get their bearings. I'm not here because I'm lost, though. I'm here because the monsters are right: the view from the top is superb.

'Wait here,' I say to Kell. The walls of the Lookout are straight up and down, but there's junk piled up against all four sides, creating easy footholds. It doesn't take me long to climb to the roof, just like old times. As soon as I'm up top I look out across the junk, searching for movement. Ivan's way taller than average. If he's standing, then maybe I'll see him. If he's *not* standing, then maybe he'll see me. It's a long shot, but that's what I'm down to.

I don't own a watch so I wait for what I think is about five minutes ... Then ten minutes ... Then a bit more. It's no use.

I jump down from the Lookout, but land with a wobble that ends with me flat on my arse. The stupid wings are to blame, as always. Reflex made them want to open, but the belts interfered. It made me lose my balance and stumble, again.

I hide my embarrassment with a gruff 'Let's go', but Kell doesn't move. She just stands there, staring as if she hasn't even noticed my botched landing.

'What, you've never seen the Lookout before?' I ask, when she still shows no signs of moving.

'It's not a lookout,' says Kell. 'It's a *panic room*. After what happened, Mrs Bell was so scared she had it trucked in all the way from Melbourne. It cost the poor lady her whole life savings and it didn't even fit. It was so big and the house was so small they had to put it in the backyard. They ripped out the play equipment and put *this* there instead.'

I stare at Kell, and frankly I don't know *what* to think anymore. The emotion in her voice, the sadness, it seems so true. And yet her stories about the real world *have* to be lies, so how does she make them sound honest? And more to the point, why am I suddenly having trouble telling the difference?

'When I first moved back to town, Mrs Bell saw me walking along the footpath,' continues Kell, almost to herself. 'She dropped the garden hose and ran straight for the panic room. She *literally* panicked just at the sight of me.'

Watching Kell right now I decide that if she *is* a monster, then she's one that's been squarely defeated. There's no fight left in her. She's just tired and spent. And then, right when I'm thinking how tragic she looks, something changes.

Kell slips out of my too-big coat and heads straight for the Lookout. Scooters, chairs, boxes – whatever's resting against its sides – she lifts or drags away. I could help, I suppose, but I've got no idea what she's doing. The way she targets particular spots and then moves on? There's a method that I can't quite follow.

She eventually finds what she's looking for – *a door.* I never even knew it was there, hidden behind the junk. I always assumed the Lookout was solid. Kell pulls at the door, but it won't budge. She pulls at it again, but still nothing.

'It's locked,' she announces after the third try. Sure enough, alongside the door there's a little keypad blinking red. It wants some special combination of numbers that nobody knows, or will ever know.

Kell laughs. 'There's one safe place in this whole world and it's *locked*.'

I just stare at her.

'What? You don't think that's funny?'

'No,' I say. 'It's not funny at all.'

'You're wrong,' she says, tears mixing in with the laughter. 'You see, for a second there, I thought I'd actually done it. I thought I'd found a way of keeping everyone in here safe, even after I'd gone, so that I'd never have to feel guilty. That *I* of all people could believe that, even for a moment? It's goddamn *hilarious*.'

ALICE

After my little meltdown at the panic room, Lux kept his word. He took me back to the Caltex. I felt just like Dorothy finding herself back on the farm. I'd done it, right? I'd found the Caltex, which meant that I could swap back and reacquaint myself with those tiny little pills and their glorious oblivion. The whole moment had this very 'end of the road' feel about it, and right away I started calling out, 'Hello? Hello?' as if I expected a ghostly version of Kell to pop out from behind the drinks fridge and give me a wave or something.

She didn't, of course. Not that *that* stopped me. I looked inside dusty freezers and under empty shelves and behind that lopsided gum tree. I looked everywhere.

When I realised Kell wasn't there, it made me look even harder. I checked places I'd already checked and spaces that were clearly too small. Mrs Dawson did the same thing when she was looking for Rachel among all the not-dead kids back behind the police tape. She just wouldn't admit that her baby wasn't among them, playing some ill-timed game of hide-and-seek.

Eventually I stopped looking, just like Rachel's mum eventually stopped looking. I had no Plan B. Nothing. I had absolutely no idea what to do next, because getting to the Caltex was it. That was the whole extent of my far-fetched solution.

'We'll wait here until the stars come out,' said Lux after I'd been standing still for way too long. And guess what? That was exactly what I needed to hear. Waiting until nightfall? Goddamn perfect. Suddenly I had myself a brand new plan, and I decided it was a good one. I decided that it was *exactly* the ticket. I mean, Kell would simply arrive shortly, right? She'd definitely show up before the sun went down and the nightmares started all over again. I'd be home in no time, back to a place where I didn't have to ask all those sticky questions about who or what I was, now that I finally knew once and for all that I didn't want the answer.

I suppose you must think that all sounds a bit ridiculous. You know, to *still* be so sure that Kell would just show up against all odds? Well, like I said, never underestimate the desperate. If you need something bad enough, sometimes that can be enough to convince you. Trust me, I should know. On so very many counts, I should *definitely* know.

Lux sat in silence, absently peeling up the lino. I tried to sit in silence too, but it didn't last.

'How long do Jude and the others have?'

As soon as I'd asked the question out loud, I knew that the guilt of it had been on my mind all along. Ever since I snuck off while they were sleeping. Earlier even?

Lux was in no hurry to answer. He just stared at me for way too long, and then said, 'What, you're not going to ask me if I can save them?'

Did I think he was going to save them? Was he kidding? *Hell no* I didn't think he was going to save them. Not in the literal sense, and sure as shit not in the fluffy white heaven sense either. I mean, really? What kind of stupid-arse question *was* that?

'I'm not an idiot,' I said. 'Wings don't mean a *thing* to me.'

In the silence that followed, I figured maybe Lux had some kind of messiah complex and I'd pissed him right off by calling him on it. Maybe I should have tried the flattery angle and implied that he really *was* kind of God-like. That had been Dr Ben's particular favourite.

But Lux didn't reach for the gun, or cut me down, or insist that he was 'special'. He just stared at me, again. Stared at me the way Dr Ben used to, right at the very start. The way that made me feel like I was a messy Rubik's cube that could do with all manner of twisting.

'The monsters are getting worse. There's more and more of them every night from new nightmares, and the ones that are already in here are starting to work together,' said Lux at long last. 'Best guess? Two days, maybe three.'

Two days, maybe three. When I'd left Jude and the others that morning, I suppose I knew that I wasn't leaving them behind to 'better things'. And yet? And yet at the same time I suppose that I'd also tried to not really think about it. I mean, there was nothing I could do, right? Nothing I could help with, nothing I was *equipped* to help with. I just wasn't the girl you wanted in a crisis, anyone from town could tell you that.

I looked around at the ransacked Caltex, so exactly like the one where we used to buy slushies. Except for the massive gum tree through its middle. That tree had grown however it liked, wonky as hell, not yielding one bit. The floor, the roof, the walls – everything had just kind of … bent around it, you know? Nothing got too close, a bit like with you.

Well, I thought about you, then I thought about our town, and what was beyond it. About Dr Ben's cheesy advice about there being 'a whole world out there'. At the time he was just trying to stop Collector being the centre of my morbid little universe, but you know what? Sitting on the floor of that Caltex it occurred to me that, for once in his life, Dr Ben might have given me some advice that was actually helpful.

'Is there anything else out there?' I said, hardly believing it had taken me so long to ask. I mean, if *I* was going to finally leave Collector once I swapped back, why shouldn't Jude and the others just 'leave' too?

Lux looked at me as if I was a Class A fool. Then, in a voice that was off-the-charts facetious, he said, 'What, you think Collector's the only place where people have dreams and nightmares?'

And so there you had it. The dream place wasn't just some mirror of our demented little town. It was way, way bigger than that. Hell, apparently it was stockpiling the dreams and nightmares of the whole *planet*. Can you even imagine? The unchecked psyche of the entire human race?

I wondered … did starving kids dream of food, so that at least in the dream place they got fed? Did poor kids dream of all the stuff they'd ever wanted? Did kids in war-zones dream of peace or just more guns? Were there pockets of the real world where things were good, and dreams were good? Sleepy little towns, perhaps, where a person like you had *actually* never existed, as opposed to just 'not existed' for the purpose of some crack-pot conspiracy website.

I mean, in the real world, there were towns spotted all through the outback, right? Towns that hadn't gone to shit like Collector. Towns that hadn't been ruined, by you. Towns where the dream place might still be okay … where it might not be filled by monsters brought about by your monstrosity. Nice towns with nice people, where bad things hadn't happened. Or at least, hadn't happened yet.

'Why not just leave then? Just leave this place and go somewhere new?' I said. As if Dr Ben hadn't asked me that exact same question, over and over, and as if I hadn't been asking myself the same question lately.

'So, everyone just walks off into the outback?' said Lux with the kind of sarcasm that would have done you proud. He had a point, of course. Any other continent on Earth and you could probably just wander off. Not here, though. Not in Australia. In Australia you grow up knowing that the outback is *not* your friend. It'll kill you a dozen ways before sundown if you're not bloody careful. There was the sun and the thirst and the spiders and the snakes and that was just the *obvious* stuff.

Maybe my brilliant idea wasn't such a brilliant idea after all. There might be towns beyond Collector, but they were so few and far between that if you missed your mark by even a fraction you'd wander the outback until you were done for.

Even if Lux was telling the truth about being immortal, Jude and the others really would die out there if they tried to leave. Not quickly, at the hand of some monster: slowly, of exposure and thirst. Slowly, as it turns out, is a *bad* thing. I've watched people die, right up close and personal. I've watched them get blinked out in an instant, and I've watched them gurgle through a bullet wound to the gut. You don't want a slow death. Those few extra seconds or minutes or days? *Really* not worth it.

So Jude and Lux and the others were trapped in the nightmare version of our town, just like I'd been trapped in the real one. The only difference was I *could* have left. I could have left a hundred times in a thousand different ways for a million good reasons ... but then again, I also couldn't.

LUX

It's been hours since Kell's naïve 'stroll into the outback' suggestion, and she hasn't said another word. I've been productive with my time, though, peeling back lino, exposing a patch of concrete. Focusing on little practicalities like whether I should bind her hands when the time comes and how I might convince her to say the words that she said in the dream, just to make it authentic.

It's no use. The closer it gets to nightfall, the worse I feel. I should be relieved to have this over with, pleased to just get it done, so that I can try to find Ivan, then go back for Boots and the others. Instead I'm feeling ... *unsure*.

I remind myself that, aside from being a monster, Kell's clearly delusional. Shit, the girl thinks she's from the *real* world. *That's* what I have to focus on.

'So we're waiting for your ghost, are we?' I say,

206

hoping to tease out a bit more of the crazy and put my conscience to rest.

'Not *my* ghost,' says Kell, instantly defensive.

'Right. You just *look* the same.'

For some reason that offends her even more, and she jumps in with, 'No, not *exactly* the same. My hair's shorter. It was in a ponytail. I was wearing jeans and a T-shirt. I'm ... I'm just *not the same*, okay?'

'What colour T-shirt?' I say, with a sudden feeling of dread.

'You think I'm lying?' says Kell. Then she gives this sigh, like she can't even be bothered, and says, 'Green. The T-shirt was green. Satisfied?'

Holy. *Shit.* The true dream that Ivan showed me. The one with the girl on the highway, who reached out to touch something and then started acting all strange? The one where a muscled-up Boots had gotten out of his car and beaten the shit out of her? *The girl had been wearing a green T-shirt.*

Kell didn't see the dream; she can't possibly have known that detail.

The swap that Kell described, her weird behaviour since the Caltex, the things she somehow knows about Collector ... *it all fits.*

'You were telling the truth. You really *are* from the real world.'

Kell just stares at me, and in that moment I realise that Ivan was right. It *is* all coming together. For the first time since all this started, *I actually believe him.*

'What's your name?'

'Alice,' she says, which is perfect. So very nearly 'a lie'.

'You're not just some *version* of the school-girl monster, *are* you, Alice?' I say, as it all sinks in. 'You're the *actual* girl. You're the one who ruined things in the real world three years ago. You're the *original* monster.'

And just like that my complicated love-hate feelings have all become *very* simple.

ALICE

And there it was, again – a whole world away, and I was *still* being blamed for what you did. I was about to launch into my self-serving little spiel about how it 'wasn't me' and it 'wasn't my fault' and all those excuses. But you know what? For the first time in years, I couldn't bring myself to do it. I simply didn't have the heart for all of the carefully worded, apologetic crap that had gotten me through thus far. Instead I did something right out of character for me, post-shootings. *I got mad.*

'You don't get to tell me I'm a monster, just because of how I look. I'll cop it from others, but *not* from you. Not from someone who looks like ... like *that*,' I said, gesturing loosely at his perfect face and heavenly wings and the whole ridiculous lot of it.

And do you know what Lux did? He gave me this tight

little smile and said, 'So how you look's irrelevant, provided you don't look like *me*.'

I stared at the belts strapped around Lux's chest. One of them had started to slip off his shoulder, but another was pulled so tight it must have been torture. Way tighter than it needed to be just to get the coat back on.

I knew that tactic. It's what got me through at Merry-view, when I cut my thighs for reasons of personal punishment. It's what I did to bring the pain to the surface, so that it couldn't eat me up from the inside. All at once, I found myself thinking about that stupid box of Ebony Dreams. Of the way I once tried to dye my hair black with a cheap mix-and-shake home job to disguise how I looked.

Lux finally made sense to me. I finally understood what his life must have been like, with those wings. Looking like you in our town was a goddamn death sentence, but looking like a saviour in a hellhole for the dying? Talk about torture.

I'd spent so long being cast as the devil it didn't even *occur* to me that the alternative might be just as revolting. That to spend your life having people always thinking the worst of you was bad, but having them always thinking the best? Was that the kind of pressure you were under? Always the 'pretty' one, despite us being identical? The 'fun' one? The one with 'promise'? Did all those expectations finally get too much? In some crazy way, did you covet the boring version of 'us' that was my miserable lot? Were you jealous of the fact that I slipped right under the radar with no expectations at all?

Lux didn't say anything, but he didn't have to. His jaw was clenched and his face suddenly wasn't perfect anymore – he was all just ugly, rotten pain. The kind of pain that I'd seen in you that night outside the half-house, and in the mirror pretty much ever since.

I figured that I owed Lux an apology of sorts, but I was no good at 'I'm sorry' anymore. I'll bet you didn't see that one coming, given the fact that my whole pathetic *life* used to be an apology. Well, that all changed. 'Sorry' got taken right off the menu. You see, there just aren't the words to convey enough regret over your identical twin killing seven kids in cold blood. And you know what? If you can't apologise for that, then saying sorry for anything else is worse than pointless.

Instead of 'I'm sorry' or 'I had you wrong', I decided to go with something actually helpful. At least, helpful from my somewhat screwy perspective.

I got up and walked the few steps over to Lux. I knelt down on the patch of concrete where he'd peeled up the lino. I reached out and took the end of one of the belts ... and I pulled as goddamn hard as I could.

When Lux groaned, I pulled even harder. Maybe that sounds like the most twisted gesture of apology you've ever heard and, hell, maybe it was. But wrong or not, there you have it. Instead of saying 'I understand' or 'I'm sorry' or 'It will be okay' or 'Life is unfair' or 'I had you wrong', I yanked at the belt until I knew for a fact that it must have hurt like a bastard.

If I could get those belts tight enough, he'd be able to fit his trench coat back on properly and hide his true self, like I wanted to. Forget 'confronting your problems' – a disguise is as good as any medicine. Hell, if I could have donned a coat and cloaked my secrets, I would have. If I could have found some easy out other than the pills, I would have been right there.

Lux didn't say a word; he just guided my hands to where I should grip. And as I pulled those belts, I tried not to think about the highway walks or the Merryview cuts or the lies that I told myself about them. I refused to think about what it 'meant', or what it meant I was *really* like, deep down. I refused to have those thoughts or to question myself or any of that trickiness. And yet … and yet as we both know, when you swallow something down, there's always a leak. Something always leaks out somewhere, now doesn't it?

The funny thing is I didn't even realise I was crying. That these big blubbery tears were running down my grotty face, and that the harder I pulled those belts, the closer I came to bawling my sorry little heart out.

'You've got snot running into your mouth,' whispered Lux. 'It's fairly disgusting.'

That made me laugh, and you know what? That was perfect. Given the choice between a sappy moment and a laugh about snot, I'll take the latter – every single time.

He was right, of course. I would have just wiped it on my sleeve, but I didn't have a sleeve. All I had was Kell's singlet, and I couldn't lift *that* up without flashing. So I untied Lauren's hanky from around my hand.

'Don't,' Lux said, all serious. He roughly wiped my nose with his coat, then started re-tying the makeshift bandage.

The moment Lux's hand touched mine, my turncoat little heart sped right up with all kinds of feelings that had no business being there. Shades of want that hadn't been around when Jude kissed me, or, if I'm really honest, through all my years of wishing that he would.

I didn't *say* anything or *do* anything. I just knelt there while Lux re-tied the bandage, staring at his hands and my hands and at those little yellow boats. When he was done he didn't look *at* me; he looked *above* me. We were kneeling beneath a hole in the roof where the gum tree pushed through, and he just stared straight up at the darkening sky.

When Lux lowered his gaze there was nothing beatific about it. Quite the opposite, actually. He had that tough, mind-made-up look about him. The kind of no-nonsense, man-of-action vibe that's always in fashion.

Our faces were only inches apart. I could see the way he was clenching his jaw and biting his lip and how all of his muscles were tense. I reached out and put my hand on his arm and said, 'Are you okay?'

Well, talk about a wrong move. Lux literally flinched at my touch, and then recoiled. I mean, I knew that he'd hated me right from the start but I guess I thought we'd kind of moved past that slightly. Apparently not. I got to my feet but there was nowhere to go, so I went over to the old lolly counter. There was nothing there – just dusty boxes where the treats used to be – but it gave me something to lean on.

After a moment I heard footsteps. Lux was walking towards me, and I knew what *that* meant. He was coming to tease and to taunt, which was nothing new. But in my head I was thinking, *Not now; please not now.* I was too raw, too close to tears, too close to a lot of things.

Lux didn't stop until he was standing *right* behind me, almost but not quite touching. I didn't turn around. I waited with both hands on the countertop, bracing myself.

Instead of delivering a jibe or threat, Lux reached one arm around either side of me … *and put his hands on mine.* He had me pinned inside a tiny jail between his body and the counter. Only, he did it so gently, so *carefully*, that it almost felt like an embrace.

I still didn't turn around. I stared straight ahead at our blurry reflection in the glass. At his muscled arms, bare against my skin. At the way he was so much taller than me and bigger than me that I suddenly looked small. *Felt* small.

Lux took another step closer, so that his feet were straddling mine. So that our whole bodies were touching, his front running the length of my back. I couldn't see his face but I could hear his breathing; it was heavy and deep and hot against my neck.

He leant in some more, nudging me up against the counter, his belts pressing hard into my back.

I let out a sharp intake of breath. I couldn't help it.

Lux tensed and pulled back. 'Did I hurt you?' he said, turning me around to face him.

I didn't trust myself to speak, not with his lips near my

214

neck and his arms still sort-of wrapped around me. I shook my head.

Lux took a deep breath, and as he exhaled he whispered, 'I don't *want* to hurt you.'

Only, the way that he said it? It was full to the brim with oh-so-familiar pain. I knew I had to say something; that it was definitely a 'speak up' moment. But here's the thing about moments. The world can change in them and people can die in them and just one is all it takes to make a mistake that will last you a lifetime. Try to hold on to one, though, and it'll slide right through your fingers *literally* quick as a flash.

The lightning only lasted a second, followed by a loud crack of thunder. That was more than enough to spook me though.

In the Hollywood re-make of what you did, it rained right after the shootings. This unnatural storm rolled in and drenched all those kids lying dead on the asphalt, then rendered your school dress conveniently transparent. That rain was supposed to be poetic, as if even the heavens were crying. As if, in our dusty outback town, what you did changed everything – even the weather.

Of course, it didn't *really* play out like that, now did it? There was no rain, just thunder and lightning, and it didn't happen after the shootings – it happened three nights before. It happened that night outside the half-house, with you and me and Jude. If the so-called heavens *were* angry it was then, and probably at me.

Well, whatever negative associations I had with

lightning, Lux clearly had me beat. The moment it struck he took two or three steps back … and his expression? The way he stared at me as if the world was going to shit for him, again?

It didn't last long. By the second flash Lux's 'nothing can touch me' mask was back in place, badder and meaner than ever. Whatever messy emotions I'd glimpsed in him were gone … and so was the boy who'd maybe sort-of held me. He'd been replaced by something blank and in control. Only, that icy expression? It melted my heart way more than Jude's sunny, carefree smile ever did.

'Looks like a storm,' I said, in a voice that was way too chipper. I mean, of all the pointless things to say, right? Funnily enough, Lux didn't respond … and so guess what I did? I kept on talking.

'We don't get them much in Collector,' I said, trying not to notice the way he'd started leaning back, increasing the distance between us. 'I hope Jude and the others are okay. They'd know not to sit under a tree in a lightning storm, wouldn't they?'

Lux looked me right in the eyes and said, 'I thought you left the others back at the lair.'

'We made camp out past the Edge. The Movie World place wasn't safe,' I said, glossing over the pissed-on duck and the part I'd played in the 'not safe' status.

It was still just light enough to see by, but I wish it hadn't been. I wish I'd missed the look on Lux's face altogether. The look that I'd only seen once before in my whole life, on Dad, when they brought him to you.

'During the day, that's where they sleep,' said Lux, with a drained-of-blood look, just like it was with Dad in that moment. Just like it had been for Dad ever since.

'What?' I said, but I was already dreading the answer.

'The monsters.'

And without even meaning to, I said those three little words that I'd whispered to myself like a mantra so many times at Merryview when no one was around to hear. The three little words that I guarded as the worst possible secret that not even the doctors knew about. I said, 'I didn't know.'

It was the second time in my life that the fate of innocent kids had rested in my hands … but, as we both know, it was the first time that those three little words were completely true.

LUX

'I didn't know,' she says, as if ignorance changes things. As if it somehow makes up for the fact that she left Boots and the others out past the *Edge*, of all places.

I try to put it out of my mind – they're probably dead already, and I've got other problems. What happened just now, the way the feelings took over? The way I somehow forgot she's a monster and got lost in the moment? I can't trust myself. If the lightning hadn't snapped me out of it I would have kissed her ... *and meant it*. I need ... I have to get this over with.

The stars are out. I've peeled up enough lino to expose a reasonable patch of concrete, which is close enough to stone. There's even *lightning*, for Christ's sake. This is my moment. It's time for her to die, as planned and as promised.

'We have to go back for them,' says Alice. She heads for the door, so I grab her arm to stop her from leaving.

'Please,' she says, begging me with her eyes, just like Ivan did back at the fence. 'We *have* to go back for them.'

It sounds like concern, but I don't buy it. Not from her. Not from the real-world school-girl monster – the *actual* cause of everything. I've seen too many kids gunned down for no reason at all to believe that she cares one scrap about a few more. I won't let her phony compassion suck me in again. Not like when she asked if I was okay *and I almost fell for it*. No, this is clearly some ploy to save her own skin, and she can forget it.

'Please,' she says again. 'It can't be my fault that they die.'

I try to think of another way, but it's no use. Boots and the others might be dead already, but then again they might not be. If I go ahead and kill her now there's almost no chance I'll find them in time, and then their deaths won't just be her fault, they'll also be mine.

'Take me to where you left them,' I say eventually, letting go of her arm. Another hour, tops, that's the extent of her leeway. Once the others are safe – *or accounted for* – it shouldn't be too hard to find another patch of stone under the stars and get things over with.

It doesn't take me long to get us back to the Edge, but after that Alice is in the lead. It's a disaster. She only knows the outback by daylight, apparently, and it's dark now. But for the flashes of lightning, it would be pointless.

'I think this is it,' she finally whispers, as we approach a cluster of gum trees. I'm so focused on looking for signs of life that I almost don't notice the corpse at my feet.

'It's one of the ones from last night,' I say, squinting down at the monster's belt, still heavy with dead puppy. 'A scout for the blonde, probably.'

There's another flash of lightning. It only lasts a few seconds, but that's more than enough to see the blood and who it belongs to. In the next flash, I don't look down at Boots – or rather what's left of him. Instead I look at Alice. At the monster who's responsible, again. I expect to see gloating, but I don't. There's no triumph there.

'Take your coat off,' she says.

I'm about to say no, but then I clock her expression. Not like Ivan with his hope or those other girls and their adoring gazes. She stares as if she understands *exactly* what she's asking.

'Actually, no,' says Alice, before I have a chance to say or do anything. 'I changed my mind. *Don't* cover him up.' She squats down and makes a deliberate point of looking at Boots, guts and gore and all. At first I think it's some kind of monster blood-lust thing, but her demeanour's all wrong. The shaking hands, the pale face – anyone would think this is torture for her, as opposed to the opposite. It's only a moment before she squeezes her eyes shut, blocking out the image altogether. Her tears still fall, though.

'Your real name was Marcus,' she whispers. 'You were skinny and funny and smart and kind.'

I wait for her to go on, but she doesn't. Just like back at the lair, when I really need her to talk, she says nothing.

Explain, I signal with a flick of my hand, before I catch myself. 'Explain,' I say again, this time out loud.

'It was something the ... Something your *friend* asked me to do. When we were back at the fence, he asked me to tell Boots the truth about who he is, and that's the only truth I could think of.'

Ivan, at it again. Well, whatever grand plan he had it's clearly over. Boots won't be involved in any 'saving' now, that's for damn sure.

'Marcus,' I say, turning the name over in my mouth, deciding if I like the fit. 'We just called him Boots because he had some.' I try to imagine him as a Marcus – as a boy with a real name and a real life, but I just can't do it. For some reason, I can't quite picture him as ... and then it hits me.

The problem is that I've *seen* the real-world Boots. I saw him in the true dream. I saw him as a muscled-up bully, who beat the shit out of Alice alongside an old highway. That boy was a long way from skinny and funny and kind. So why the discrepancy? The people in *true* dreams aren't made-up, distorted versions – they're themselves, which means Alice got it wrong. Something doesn't add up. Something's not right here.

I'm about to ask more questions, when a bullet's fired in our general direction. Instinct kicks in and I tackle Alice to the ground.

'Hold your fire – it's them,' Goldie calls from nearby.

Climbing off Alice, I'm almost bowled over by the little girl from last night, the one with the puppy. She runs straight past me and throws herself into Alice's arms, as if the monster is somehow a saviour. Alice hugs her back and says, 'I'm so glad you're okay,' just like she really means it.

'It attacked just after sundown,' says the girl, talking fast. 'The others are behind that tree over there. We didn't move because Jude's been shot.'

Alice starts to run for the tree but I grab her by the arm, holding her back again. 'The real-world Boots – is he how you described him?' I say, staring her down. 'Is he really skinny and funny and kind?'

Alice looks at me as if there are a million things she could say, instead of just a simple 'yes' or 'no'. In the end she settles for, 'He used to be, now let go of my arm.'

'And now?' I say, still pushing for an answer.

'My sister killed his sister. We weren't exactly *close* after that,' she says, straining against my grip.

'Your sister?'

'Twin sister. *Identical.* Comprende?'

And I do. I do *comprende* – I finally understand perfectly.

'You're not a monster,' I say, as it all sinks in. 'You're just a girl. You're just an *innocent girl.*'

Alice looks me right in the eyes and simply says, 'Hardly.'

ALICE

After the shootings, Jude's mum wouldn't let me near him. She wouldn't even let me visit him down at the morgue so that I could have my last-goodbye moment. I can understand that, I guess.

Well, at the foot of that gum tree there was no one telling me not to, so I did things my way. I got the others to stand right back, giving us privacy. I lay Jude's head in my lap. I put pressure on his shoulder with one hand, half to stop the bleeding, half to cover up the sight of all the blood. I must have fantasised about that scene a million times – of his dying moments being tender, and with me. I suppose I should have fantasised about healthier things, but lying in that bed at Merryview, it was so often where my mind went. I imagined an alternative ending where we'd both been shot instead of just him, and we lay together dying like Shakespeare would have wanted.

I'd thought a lot about dying words in the lead-up to that moment. About what I would have said to Jude if I'd had the chance. But right then? Well, my mind went blank. So instead, I told him the truth. Well, as close as I could come at the truth when Jude didn't even know who I *really* was and it was clearly too late to tell him. Instead, I told him who *he* was. Or rather, who he'd been in the real world.

He listened as I told him everything I could remember about the boy that I'd loved my whole life, who was dead now because of you. And because of me. And because of himself, if I'm being *really* honest.

I told him how Jude was captain of the rugby team, and how all the girls in town had a crush on him. How he could eat nine meat pies in one sitting. How he hated Fanta because it's what his dad used to bring him as a make-up present. How his Superman T-shirt was from his aunt, and it had always been his favourite. How he ate the nougat off a Mars bar first and saved the caramel for last. How the middle finger on his left hand was wonky because he'd broken it when he was seven. And as I listed every little detail, I realised … it was all this terrible cliché. It was all the pointless stuff, like when I told Lux that I was different to Kell because of a green T-shirt and a goddamn *ponytail*. It was just the on-paper rubbish that anyone can know, without even trying.

Staring down at Jude's face, I realised that I'd never even known him. I don't mean the boy in my lap, I mean the other Jude – *our* Jude. The real-world dead and buried boy. I'd worshipped him practically my whole life, but the truth was I didn't know a single thing about him. Nothing beyond skin deep. In my head he was just this construction of 'perfect' that I'd always relied on. The outline of a person I wanted to see, kind of like you were. And then after what happened outside the half-house … Well, after that I *had* to see him as perfect. I had to keep on believing it, day after day, because if I admitted his one big mistake, then I'd have to admit mine too.

And so there, I've finally said it – Jude was flawed. I know that now. But then again, I wasn't perfect either, and neither were you. People *are* flawed. That's life. Most of us manage to cope without taking a gun to school. Besides, so what if Jude *was* cowardly? Just how brave are you supposed to be when you're only fifteen years old? Just how much of a 'man' can you expect in a small-town kid anyway?

I kept on talking. It was the only decent thing to do. The boy lying in my lap was in pain and he seemed to like the stories, so I kept them coming.

I told him about how Jude's real name was actually Harry. How he'd serenaded you with that Beatles song when we were in grade 2 and he was in grade 3 and the name had stuck because everyone in the whole stinking town thought it was so darn adorable.

And that was the moment I finally twigged about his name. Jude was still called Jude in here, but how was that possible? Didn't most of them forget everything, including their names? Isn't that why Marcus was Boots and Maggie was Goldie and a version of you was called Kell?

'How is your name still Jude?' I asked him.

Jude opened his eyes and squeezed my hand. 'It's okay.

I know you forgot, but I didn't. I remembered for both of us.'

If I'd been quicker, perhaps I could have changed the subject. Said something to take the conversation in a safer direction, or prattled nonsense so that he couldn't get a word in. But I hesitated just a moment too long, and Jude started recounting the dream that had created Kell and him. Short of telling the poor boy to please shut up, I had to hear it.

When Jude finished the story there was a smile on his face. I tried to smile back, but I doubt I managed much. You see, there was this doomsday feeling creeping all over me.

I didn't remember having a dream about Jude and me on a stupid romantic boat ride, not specifically. It's the kind of dream I *would* have had, though. The sappy words and the dewy-eyed looks and the bit where I fell into the water and he did the saving? It had all the pathetic hallmarks of me. I'd even dreamt of myself wearing your convict love token, because, really, didn't I always secretly covet what was yours?

So I *did* still have dreams after the Merryview Solution. I just didn't remember them. The pills didn't fix anything. They didn't *stop* the nightmares, they only hid them from me. All those years of presumed oblivion were nothing but frauds.

I stared down at the version of Jude in front of me and finally understood that his blind adoration was *my* fault. *I* was the one who made him nothing more than a lapdog for Kell. I was the one who'd thought that love was all about clichéd devotion. My fantasies of Jude – that's all they were ever about. Of someone adoring me, no questions asked, like Jude adored you. A black-and-white love. *I* was the one who made him the kind of boy who would decide to wait for me past the Edge, even though it was a bloody *stupid* move. Even though he should have gone somewhere safer, and damn well taken the others with him.

And if I'd dreamt the dream that created Jude and Kell, then Kell wasn't a version of *you*. No, the scary gangleader who carried a gun and treated her boyfriend like shit was a version of me.

There couldn't be much doubt about how similar we were *now*, could there? Turns out I was *definitely* capable of being like you given the right circumstances, or the wrong ones. Hell, not even *I* had been able to tell the difference between a version of you and a version of myself. Whatever line there used to be in my head, I'd officially lost it.

And it wasn't just a *version* of me that was capable of bad things: the *real* me was as well. On top of my other unforgivable failings, I'd meant to abandon the others. I'd meant to swap back to the real world, back to my comfy bed and the cushy pills. I'd known that they'd die in a few days at best, but I'd crept away regardless. So no – I didn't buy that *you* killing kids and *me* killing kids was different. Dead is dead is dead.

I finally knew the truth: *they'd been right about me.* Identical meant exactly what it sounded like – no loopholes, no exceptions. And I knew what had to come next.

First, though, I allowed myself one last indulgence – something that was years overdue, and which I honestly thought was beyond me. It was a kiss. I leant down and I kissed Jude on the forehead, *like a friend*.

LUX

I wish this damn lightning would stop. Every flash shows me Alice stroking Jude's hair, whispering sweet nothings. I'd rather stay in the dark about that, frankly.

The two of them are locked in a moment under that bloody gum tree. I can't hear what they're saying, but it's probably love-related. Some epic declaration. Sure enough, Alice tops it all off with a gentle kiss to Jude's forehead. I've been around a bit with the opposite sex, back when I thought that might help. I know what a kiss that means nothing looks like. And *that* kiss? Not nothing.

Alice waves the tomboy over. Not me, not Goldie – just the kid from last night. I still can't hear a thing, and I don't like it.

After their little chat Alice gets to her feet, mumbling something about doing a perimeter check. Clearly a lie. First of all, there is no perimeter. We're out past the Edge, which *literally* means no boundaries, no borders. Also, this is *Alice* who's talking, not Kell. From what I've seen, she probably doesn't even know what a perimeter check *is*. Honestly, the girl won't even carry a gun.

'I'll go with you,' I say, unwilling to let her just wander around here alone. Alice responds with a 'No' that's far too quick off the tongue. So *that's* how it is now. Sure enough Alice is avoiding my gaze with a skill that's right up there with Ivan. Well, bad luck. She can dodge me all she likes come morning, but now is *not* the time for a casual stroll in the moonlight.

I'm about to tell her as much, then I see her expression.

'Please, just let me go,' says Alice, and I realise I've grabbed her arm again. Letting her go is the *last* thing I want, but I know what it's like to need space. To need a moment to drag yourself up from rock-bottom. Besides, after what I just witnessed between her and Jude, I doubt she'll listen to *me* anyway.

'Five minutes?' I whisper, once I've opted to cave. Alice just nods and says, 'Ample' … then she turns and walks away. It's too dark for me to get a good view of her leaving, but perhaps I *never* had a 'good' view of her. One thing's sure becoming clear, though. She might have been treated like one and she might have even *felt* like one but the girl is no monster … and so I'm sorry, Ivan, wherever you are. The plan doesn't work when it's Alice.

I turn my attention back to the gang and see that I wasn't the only one watching Alice go. Not Jude, like I would have expected. *The kid*. She's peering out into the darkness, looking downright miserable. I'm not great at cheering kids up, but Goldie's busy with Jude so we're short on other options.

'What's your name?'

The kid just shrugs and says, 'Dunno.'

'Really? I always figured that Dunno was more of a boy's name,' I say, trying to lighten the mood. 'But with those overalls you can probably pull it off.' She just looks at me like I'm a complete tosser. Still, I have to call her something and 'no-name' has lost its appeal.

'Dunno …' I start to say, but I've got nothing – this isn't my thing. Boots was good with tension and Ivan is – *or was* – good with kids. I'm crap with both, apparently.

'Dunno, you've arrived at a rather bad time,' I say, opting not to sugar coat it. 'There's a lot in the way of *dying* going on.'

'Yeah, I picked up on that,' she says. 'Is that where *you* come in?'

The wings. God, wouldn't Ivan just love this. Backs up against the wall, me the last great white hope …

'Sorry, kid – I can't save anyone.'

Dunno just shakes her head at me and says, 'I was kidding, you idiot.' Only, I can see from her face that's not *entirely* true. No, wherever Ivan is, I'm glad that he's not here to witness this moment. I really doubt it's all that he imagined.

I squint into the darkness, looking for movement. Alice should be back by now. You rarely see monsters past the Edge during hunting time, but still. If she wanted a moment alone, I should have insisted she walk in the other direction, away from the Edge where there's less chance …

And just like that it hits me. Suddenly I'm thinking of Alice and her naïve plan to just walk out into the outback. As a long-term solution it would never work, but for right now? As a last-ditch effort to buy them a bit more time? There's no food out there, of course, but they can do without food for a day or two. All they really need is water.

'We head for the creek,' I say to Goldie. 'The monsters don't venture far from the Edge, even to sleep, so it might be our best chance.'

Goldie looks over at Jude, but she doesn't come back with lame protests like 'we shouldn't move him'. She simply says, 'If that's what it takes,' in a way that's so tough – so determined – I get the impression she'll carry him the whole way herself if she has to.

'How many guns?'

'Two with ammo,' says Goldie, indicating Dunno and herself. Dunno just shakes her head and says, 'Not me. Kell took mine when she called me over.'

It's a moment like back at the fence, when I realised that Ivan was missing.

'Kell took your gun?'

Dunno doesn't answer right away – she's seen my expression and it's freaking her out. 'Am I in trouble?'

I should tell her *no*, that she's not in trouble. Instead I turn to Goldie and say, 'Don't stop until dawn.'

ALICE

You know, I used to think that you were fearless. I don't mean that I thought you were brave. I actually believed that you were missing the fear gene completely. That all of the cowardly instincts had been ripped right out of you in some prenatal joke, then left in me to fester. So that you were strong and wild, and I was, well, the opposite of that.

There were a million examples to support my theory, but the crevice at Dumbo's Peak is as good as any. How I was too scared to jump it even once, while you went back and forth, time after time.

After what you did they called you the worst kind of coward, and it's hard to argue with that. Still, I doubt that's the *full* picture. Thinking about it now, maybe 'fearless' was on the money. What if I really *did* get all of the fear and cowardly instincts? What if, when you jumped from one side of that crevice to the other you felt ... nothing? What if *that* was part of the problem?

Maybe it's no coincidence then that, after leaving Jude, I stumbled my way towards Dumbo's Peak and climbed it. That I sat on the same patch of rock where I used to watch you jump. The spot where I always felt to the pit of my soul like the lesser twin. The coward.

Well, guess what? I still wasn't fearless. My hands were shaking like an addict as I pulled the gun from my pocket. As I turned it around so that I could stare into all the potential nothingness of that tiny black hole.

Is that what it felt like for you when you put the gun into your mouth? When you turned it on yourself after killing the others? When you brought the death toll up to eight, not that your death ever counted? When you pulled the trigger *that time* were you still not scared? Was it as dull as jumping the goddamn crevice?

Sitting on that patch of rock from our childhood, gun in hand, something felt inevitable about that moment. As if the whole universe had been pushing me towards it, year after year. Like when the doctors and everyone kept watching me 'for signs', they were just seeding the thought all along. That maybe I *should* have done it right at the start, the moment you made my life unbearable. Earlier, even. The moment I made my mistake out there at the half-house?

All the punishment walks and the cuts to my thighs, and going back to Collector – deep down, I thought that maybe I deserved it. Maybe I *deserved* to die. I'd been too chickenshit to do it myself, but I'd been tempting death in a thousand ways ever since the schoolyard. And life had finally come to the party. I mean, there I was at the edge of the crevice, gun in hand. All I had to do was pull the trigger or jump.

There was no other way out. I mean, *of course* Kell wouldn't just magically 'show up' at the Caltex so we could swap back. Maybe deep down I'd *always* known it. Girls like me don't get miracle escapes. We're not princesses who wake up and realise it was all just a terrible dream.

And you know what else? My hands weren't shaking. I was calm, like you were calm. I could hold a gun to a head without my nerves going to shit. I had that in me too, and God knows what else.

And then, whisper soft, I heard, 'It hurts, you know.'

Lux was standing behind me, short of breath from running. 'The last thing you'll feel will be excruciating pain.'

Last feeling … What was your last feeling before you pulled the trigger? Were you pleased or horrified? Did you *feel* like a monster? Was pain the last thing you felt in life? And, if so, how long had it been going on for?

Lux sat down next to me. He didn't try to talk to me or save me or analyse me or blame me or absolve me or any of that crap. He just sat there, staring out at the night sky. It was dark and we were in the outback, so the stars went on forever.

They say that the universe is infinite, and that there are a billion worlds out there just like ours, only slightly different. I suppose that means there are worlds where you made better choices, or had been a better person, or were different in some tiny but crucial way. Worlds where the same could be said of me and of Jude and of everyone, I guess.

I thought about that as I sat on the rock with Lux, staring at the stars. I thought that maybe there were whole worlds where we'd been happy. Where you and I were the best of friends and everything was peaches. Where I hadn't copped out. *Where I was brave.*

And then I did something brave in *my own* little universe: I put down the gun.

Shall we pretend that 'choosing life' was a magical fix for me? That I was suddenly all about healthy thoughts and Pollyana smiles? No, I suppose you of all people know that it doesn't work like that. That changing who you are can't happen in a moment, and sometimes can't happen at all. The truth is I wasn't 'transformed'. I might have finally realised that I didn't want to die, but I still had the rest of it to deal with. I still had the guilt of finally knowing what I was capable of. Of feeling like we were more alike than not. So do you know what I did? I reached over and grabbed Lux by the lapel of that ridiculous trench coat. And I kissed him.

He tried to pull away, but I wouldn't let go. I kissed him hard on the mouth, with all the loathing and fear that I needed to get out of me. He resisted and resisted … but then suddenly he didn't. Suddenly he was kissing me right back.

Every second of that kiss I hated myself more. It made me feel just like the monster that I knew I had inside me. Just like the cruel, self-destructive force that the world had seen in you. I mean, Jude was shot and the others were defenceless and yet there I was kissing Lux? That's not the mark of a gentle heart, now is it?

Only, there's a very fine line between love and hate, fear and passion. Dr Ben told me that. Maybe for you those feelings were always connected just a little too closely. Maybe we're alike in that, because somewhere in that kiss I got caught up in the moment. Somehow, as I kissed Lux as hard and as rough as I could, all that hate and fear got turned into actual passion. Somehow I was pulling off his coat and unbuckling his belts and existing nowhere else but in that moment.

I used to practise on my pillow, just so you know. In the absence of any actual experience with boys, I'd worked out exactly how a proper kiss would go. How I'd start, where I'd put my hands, what to do with my tongue et cetera.

It wasn't like that. It wasn't the kind of kiss that you got in rehearsals.

When Lux slid my singlet off, there was no embarrassment. There was none of the stupid shyness that always did me in. None of the self-doubt and second guessing. It was as if my body finally knew what to do. I might not have known how to 'just be me' in the way that Dr Ben kept spruiking, but right then? Right then something took over, and for the first time in my whole life I felt like a natural.

And the way he kissed me back? The way he slid his hands across my skin? The way I could hear every single breath he took, even while he was kissing me? *Especially* while he was kissing me? The way he let out these tiny little moans like he'd been waiting for my lips his whole entire life? Maybe you know the feeling I'm getting at, but then again maybe you don't. Maybe you never felt it, even with Jude, and if so then I'm sorry. I'm not sharing mine with you, though. I'm not giving you any more details of that kiss because it existed outside of you, in a rare moment when you weren't in my head, and I'm keeping it that way. I'm keeping you separate.

But moments don't last. I opened my eyes and glimpsed Lux above me. His too-perfect face that was usually so controlled, but currently wasn't. His chest, finally free of the belts and the pain that they caused him. Your convict love token hanging around his neck. His wings, spread wide above us, blocking out patches of stars …

And that's when it happened, the long overdue jolt of recognition. The thing my brain had been refusing to let me accept right from the start. You see, I finally knew where I'd seen that image before. It was the very last drawing in your infamous Scribble Book.

In my defence, that picture was dark. And I don't just mean in terms of its content. There was a lot in the way of black and shadows, so that making out the boy's face was damn near impossible. I suppose that's why people assumed it was Jude in the picture. And why Dr Ben used to wonder out loud whether it was some other man from our town who was maybe molesting you or something. Does it amuse you that everyone thought that the 'who' of it was important? That we all focused on the boy and his shadowed face, rather than what was behind him? Well, if

I hadn't known that picture off by heart, not even *I* would have noticed. I wouldn't have twigged that, in the picture you drew, there were two patches of the night sky that had no stars. And that those two patches were in the shape of wings.

The 'boy' in the picture wasn't a boy at all. It was the angel from outside the half-house. The stone statue that you climbed all over three nights before the killings. The one you pretended to pash in a silly game to make Jude jealous. The one you were still draped around when Jude and I made our supersized mistake.

You and your Scribble Book. God, you must have thought we were so dumb with all our theories and interpretations. The way that book stumped everyone, even me. Well, the jig is up. Thanks to that fateful kiss with Lux, I know that it was your chronicle of nightmares. That all those sketches you made were of the things that plagued your sleep. Was sketching them some kind of therapy? A form of release, like Dr Ben always wanted from me, so that he'd have tangible output?

I thought about how thick that book was. How almost every page was filled with nasty pictures that we all assumed were of what you wanted, instead of what you'd seen. How those nightmares must have been constant for you. In the lead-up to that day, when was the last time you slept through the night? When was the last time you slept in any kind of peace at all? And which came first? Were the nightmares because you were so messed up or did you get so messed up by all those nightmares?

I'll never know about the other pictures in that book of yours – the truth of them died with you. The *last* picture, though? I knew the truth about *that*. The last nightmare you ever had wasn't some nonsensical thing. It was based on something that actually happened that night outside the half-house with you and me and Jude. The night when, looking back, Jude wasn't the *only* coward.

Me lying under the stars with Lux half-naked above me – it was exactly like your last picture. The only difference was that in the picture the angel had a gun to your head. Without even thinking about it, I whispered to myself the words that you'd written below that fateful sketch. Those two little words that had baffled Sergeant Collins and Dad and me and everyone else who cared to ponder. The words that seemed like the final clue in a riddle we so badly needed to solve, but couldn't.

I whispered, 'It's time.'

The moment the words were out of my mouth, Lux stared at me, hard. He pinned me down with one arm. He hesitated five, maybe six seconds. Then he reached over … and he picked up the gun.

'Ivan was right,' he said, in this can't-quite-believe-it voice. 'It all played out anyway, exactly like in the dream. The sailboat bandage around your hand. The pendant. The stars and the lightning and the stone. Even the words you said … Every single detail – *it's all the same.*'

'In the dream I did it. I pulled the trigger,' said Lux, looking me right in the eyes.

Lux pulled the trigger and shot you dead. Did you wake

up back in your bed the moment it happened? Did you sit bolt upright, covered in sweat, just like in the movies? You can't have known the *full* implications of that. How, a world away, the bubble would have burst, leaving Lux stranded. Leaving him stuck in a nightmare place with a gun and your corpse. *But what about you?* What did *you* do after dreaming that an angel had killed you? Was I sound asleep in the next bed when you pulled that Scribble Book from its secret hiding place? When you sketched your last nightmare – *the one where you died.*

They say that if you die in a dream, it's a very bad omen. They say that if that happens, you're going to die for real. And of course that's exactly what *did* happen. You died three days later, and took seven other kids – not to mention a whole town – down with you.

'Ask me why I never believed it,' said Lux. 'Ask me why I was *so sure* that the dream could never play out. That it could never, ever be true.'

I just lay there, wondering how three years and two worlds and seven – *eight* – dead kids could have all built up to this. I'd looked so hard for clues about your life in that last picture, when the truth is I'd had it backwards. I'd been staring at my own death all along.

'Well, maybe Ivan was only *part* right,' whispered Lux. 'Maybe the best I can do is to just save one.'

And then he did the thing that you either couldn't do or wouldn't do – *he put down the gun.*

LUX

I put the gun down and wrap my arms tight around Alice, squeezing her into me. Holding her like I did in the dream that created me, when all I felt was love. *Love, love, love ...* right before my puppet hands made me pull the trigger.

Perhaps I've made a colossal mistake. Perhaps Ivan was right, and killing her really *is* the key to everything. Perhaps that should matter, but it doesn't. What I care about most is the living, breathing girl ... *that I'm currently squashing.*

'What, you're opting for suffocation instead?' says Alice, wriggling to get some air. I release my grip a smidgen and she settles into my embrace a lot more comfortably. Her head's resting on my recently broken shoulder, but it doesn't hurt anymore. I've been quietly mending, basically since I met her.

'So,' says Alice after a few minutes of stillness. 'Are you going to tell me why you did that?' I don't know whether she means why I put the gun to her head or why I put it back down again. In the end I decide to answer the latter, since that's the part that counts. There are various things I could say, but in the end I settle for a simple 'I wanted to do things differently'. Alice leans up from her nook against my shoulder and looks me right in the eyes. She stares at me for the longest time then says, 'Well that's a damn fine reason.'

ALICE

'Well that's a damn fine reason' is what I said, but it's not what I was thinking. I was thinking about the gun. *That Lux put down the gun.*

No matter how hard life had pushed him in one direction, no matter how inevitable things must have seemed, he still chose for himself. *He* decided what kind of person he'd be. It wasn't some pre-determined, inevitable thing. He wasn't all good because of a stupid set of wings and he wasn't all bad because of the mistakes he'd made. Just like you weren't all bad. There, I said it. Hard as that is to admit, you did have good in you. You had your moments. You weren't some evil twin or spawn of Satan; you were just a girl. A sister. A friend. You did a monstrous, unforgivable thing, but you were still all of those things to me. I'd danced around that fact for years and years, but that's the truth of it. That's the painful, terrifying truth. After what you did the world had to see you as a monster. There had to be black and white because, otherwise, that nasty grey was in anyone. In *everyone*, really.

I'd been so obsessed with the 'good or bad' question that I'd missed the whole point. There wasn't some innate force lurking inside me calling the shots. *I* was calling the shots. *I* was making the choices, like Lux did when he put down the gun. You don't 'discover' what kind of person you are, you *decide* it.

I don't know exactly when the plan started forming. I'm tempted to say that it happened right there on the rock, when I had my revelations. That it 'arrived in a flash', like the lightning. I doubt it, though. I think sometimes an idea takes hold before you even know it. Sometimes it's bubbling away under the surface for a while, don't you think?

But the shocking part isn't the plan or when it came together: it's that I kept it a secret. I swallowed it down and held it back and didn't tell a soul the truth, not even Lux. Hypocritical, right? I had my reasons but, really, isn't that what they all say?

LUX

'We should go,' I say eventually. Alice doesn't respond. She just stares out into the distance. It's not until I repeat myself that she finally says, 'I'm not coming with you. I'm going back into the nightmares to look for Kell. I can't just leave her in the real world.'

Not what I was expecting. I try to shut it down fast with a dismissive 'Bad idea. Worst ever'.

Alice doesn't answer. She doesn't plead her case or try to convince me. She just stares at me in that calm way that I copped so often from Ivan … *when his mind was already made up.*

'Kell wasn't there, remember?' I say, still hoping to salvage this. Hoping to shoot it down and head for the creek, as planned.

'I'll look other places then. I have to try,' says Alice, and there it is again, the expression that tells me she won't be budging.

Crap. I try to think of other options, other ways of changing her mind, and quickly … but I can't. There's only one thing for it, then: brutal honesty.

'I saw a true dream with you in it,' I say, before I can change my mind. 'You were walking along a highway, being trailed by a car. You were wearing jeans and a green T-shirt.'

'That's what happened,' says Alice, clearly confused. 'Just before I ended up in here, that's what happened in the real world.'

'The boy in the car was Boots, only older. He *hurt* you,' I say, forcing myself to look at her as I say it. 'Or I suppose he hurt *Kell*, really, then he tied her up in some building shaped like a bird. The point is, he took her away. You'll never find her.'

Silence.

Alice eventually gives a slow nod, with this humourless laugh like back at the Lookout. Then she mutters something about irony. I don't know what she means, so I say, 'What?'

'I count my steps,' she says after a lengthy pause. 'I know exactly how many steps it is from the Giant Emu to the place where we swapped.' The confusion must be clear on my face, because she explains: 'If I can get back to the Caltex as a reference point, I think I *can* find her.'

What? She still plans on finding Kell, even after what I've just told her?

'You know the part where I said that I could just save one life?' I say. 'Just so we're clear, *I meant yours*. Kell got the short stick with the swapsies, remember? She's tied up, beaten up … She might even be *dead* for all we know.'

246

Alice just nods. She takes a deep breath and she says, 'I can't keep running away. Kell is a version of me. If I run away from her, I'm running away from myself.'

It's a noble enough sentiment, but that makes me even more determined to change her mind.

'So, you're just going to skip out on Jude and the others? Leave them here to die?' I say, with calculated cruelty.

'You have to trust me,' she whispers, resting her forehead against mine. 'I used to know Marcus. Even if he's beaten me up and tied me up, I'll get through to him. And even if I can't, I still have to try.'

She wants to go home. *Of course* she wants to go home.

I'm not ready to look at her yet, so I stare at our hands instead. She bites her nails – Alice, not Kell. They're almost half gone since yesterday.

So much fuss over whether to take her life or spare her life when that wasn't even the hard part. The *hard* part is letting her go.

'I'll help you,' I say eventually. 'I'll help you find Kell and swap back.'

Alice just gives me a sad little smile and says, 'You can't. You have to look after the others.'

She's right of course, and I know it. I should be catching up with Jude and Goldie and Dunno and keeping them safe, at least for now. I should be looking for Ivan. I can't, though. I won't let Alice venture out there alone. The girl's got many talents, but survival skills are not among them.

'They'll be fine until morning,' I say, which is a terrible lie. Really, I have no idea if they'll be safe and I hate that

I'm taking the risk. Alice doesn't have to know that, though. Only one of us need shoulder that particular guilt, and it might as well be me.

'Put this back on,' I say, throwing Alice's singlet at her chest. 'If I'm going to get us back to the Caltex in one piece, I'll need to concentrate.'

ALICE

Getting back to the Caltex wasn't easy. It was the bad time of night, which meant nightmares and monsters and chaos and all kinds of gore. I'd have been dead in five minutes if it hadn't been for Lux, keeping me safe. I won't tell you what I saw that night – let's just take all that horror as read. The important part is we made it. After however many hours, we were back at the Caltex, again.

I figured the hard part was over. I mean, I'd literally passed the Giant Emu every single day on my punishment walks, counting each step as a distraction. I knew exactly how many steps there were from it to the spot where I'd swapped. So I just had to retrace my steps, right? Since the dream world and the real world lined up exactly, that's all there was to it.

Only here's the thing: in the real world those steps were across a flat highway with nothing whatsoever in my path.

The nightmare place was a *very* different story. There were about a billion pieces of junk to climb over or around, and keeping in a straight line was next to impossible. In the end I did my best. I took the designated number of steps in what I hoped was the right direction then called out, 'Kell?'

I called out once and only once. Lux's hand clamped over my mouth quick smart. He whispered, 'Quietly,' right in my ear, so close I could feel his breath on me ... and yes, my heart did that butterfly thing all over. Impulse told me to stop what I was doing and just kiss him, but I didn't. Turns out you don't *have* to act on impulse, sister. Instead I 'quietly' blustered around the dream junk, searching for Kell, hour after hour.

I wasn't kidding myself anymore. I knew that finding her was a massive long shot. That even if I *did* stumble upon the right spot, she might have escaped or been moved or simply dropped dead. I wasn't giving up, though. I'd seen what can happen when a person just gives up, and I was choosing the *other* option.

Maybe the universe decided to reward me for that smidgen of backbone by doling out some decent luck for a change. Then again, maybe not. Whatever the reason, I turned a corner and there she was. *Kell.* The girl I'd assumed was a version of you, but was always my vision of me.

She was lying inside a crusty drycleaner's, all see-through as a ghost, just like last time. Only, she wasn't *actually* in a drycleaner's. In the real world she was tied up in the Giant Emu, right where Marcus had left her.

The bruises were the first thing I noticed. They were

on every bit of skin that I could see, but her face was the worst. Even in the semi-darkness there was no mistaking the reds and blues and yellows. The blood caked around her nose and mouth from a gash that stretched down to her chin. The way her left eye had swelled almost shut, like a parody of winking.

This is going to sound hypocritical, but seeing her like that – seeing *myself* like that – really rattled me. It's one thing to push the boundary, to push and push and tell yourself you'll go where it takes you. It's another thing to stand outside yourself and witness the result. I hadn't tied Kell up or delivered the bloody cut or the black eye or the bruises … but in a way, I had. I'd deliberately walked out on that highway, knowing what might come of it. *Daring* something to come of it, really. Suddenly that didn't seem like such a shit-hot plan anymore. Having gotten all nice and personal with violence and death – well, I guess the whole self-punishment thing seemed a little bit … gratuitous.

'Do you see her?' said Lux, no doubt wondering why I was giving an empty drycleaner's so much special attention.

'Yes,' I said. Kell didn't respond to the sound of my voice. She just lay there. I couldn't tell if she was dead or just unconscious. The cut looked bad, but then there was the dehydration to think of. My little 'no drinking' policy out there on the highway could well have done her in.

Perhaps you're thinking that I'd already seen myself dead, thanks to you. That when you killed yourself right in front of me I got a first-hand glimpse of what I'd look like with the life snuffed out. Well, you'd be wrong about that. I guess the thing they don't tell you about suicide is that it's a messy business. Those movies that make it all look like some Romeo and Juliet act of teenage torment are a hundred per cent full of shit. Give Juliet a firearm and see how 'pretty' it seems. Give the mushy twit her dad's gun and see how 'attractive' anyone finds it. So no, I never got to look into your lifeless eyes – eyes that were identical to my eyes – and have some existential moment. I got to see you literally blow your brains out. I got to see bits of you on my goddamn shoe.

Suddenly I was blurting out all the 'I'm sorrys' that I'd been holding back on for so long. I'd been clinging to our differences for years, and that whole time I couldn't admit to anything. I couldn't admit to a single fault or even a *sliver* of blame without the slippery slope taking me over. I guess once I decided that I had the capacity for good *and* bad, 'I'm sorry' was all I *could* say.

And boy, I said it alright. I gave Kell all the apologies that I should have given Jude, and Dad, and Dr Ben for my poor and cowardly choices. All the 'I'm sorrys' that I couldn't say without being complicit. All the 'I'm sorrys' that needed to be said on your behalf, but couldn't be said in your absence. I poured them all out, every little thing I'd done wrong. And I built my way up to the big one. The thing that I was *really* sorry for. The important, unforgivable mistake I'd made that night outside the half-house.

It must sound stupid, me saying sorry to a version of myself, but that's what happened. After so much silence and denial, the person who got my apologies was *me*.

And that's when I noticed the movement. It was subtle, but when I watched carefully I could see that her hands were moving back and forth. Kell wasn't dead or unconscious; she was straining against her restraints.

'You're awake,' I said.

Kell opened her eyes and looked right at me. And do you know what she said? She said, 'I want to go home.' The version of me that I'd dreamt up just wanted to 'go home' in a way that I'd long forgotten how to.

I turned back to Lux. He was leaning against the side of a washing machine, hands in his pockets, waiting. Looking at him right then, all scruffy and torn, a big part of me wanted to choose the more selfish option. To just stay with Lux, consequences be damned.

Lux had his head down. He didn't even look up when I was standing right in front of him. He just clenched his jaw and whispered, 'Hello, Kell.'

He thought I'd swapped without even a goodbye. So I kissed him.

That kiss wasn't the same as the last one. There was no anger or punishment tied up in it. It wasn't one of those delicate-flower things either, though, just so we're clear. I kissed Lux with the force of how I actually felt, without all the bullshit and drama. I pulled him into me and I kissed him properly, no reserves. He hesitated for a moment, and then he knew it was me in a way that Jude hadn't when our lips were touching. He knew it was me and he kissed me right back. It was *me* that he wanted, not Kell, not you, not some better version – the *real* me, good and bad, damage and all.

LUX

Alice eventually ends the kiss. Instinct tells me to pull her into me, squeeze her tight and keep her close forever. Instead I take a step back, and look at her one last time.

She might have the same face as Kell, but she's not the same girl. This is my Alice, the one who blurted out all those apologies just now. The one who's clearly been as messed up as me these past few years, but who somehow hung in there. The one who's fragile and tough and funny and who seems to feel sorry for almost everyone, except herself.

Now would be the time for a memorable moment, I suppose. Heartfelt words about love and a happy life, even though it won't be with me? Well, I've never been good with that kind of sentiment. Instead I flick a piece of hair out of her eyes with an arc of my hand that says, *Living. Keep living.*

She doesn't ruin the moment with 'goodbye' or 'I'll miss you' or one more hurried kiss. Instead she wipes her tears and snot off onto the sleeve of my trench coat. And then she smiles. And then she goes.

I watch Alice reach out and touch nothing at all. I know that she must have swapped back, away from me. I wait for something to mark the moment – a look or a feel or a spark or a flash or a sound. There's nothing. Apparently a girl can change into a monster, just like that, with no outward signs at all.

It's Kell I'm watching now. Kell who pats her body down, checking it's real. Kell whose hand goes straight for her pocket.

'Crap,' she mutters to herself, upon discovering that her gun's missing. She's not deterred, though. After a lengthy pause she says to herself, 'We'll have to see about that,' clearly in reference to finding another gun. Could she be any more unlike Alice?

Kell turns to leave, and that's when she finally sees me. There are no niceties. She simply says, 'You.'

'Guilty,' I say, quoting the blonde from back at the fence. It seems appropriate.

ALICE

Thirst then pain. That's what I felt when I touched Kell and swapped back, into my own skin. It was dark inside the Giant Emu. I couldn't see Marcus but Kell was right there, all ghostly in the shadows.

'Kell,' I croaked through my bruised, dry throat.

Lux couldn't hear me or see me – not from a world away – but *she* could.

'Kell,' I said again, louder. She turned to face me ... and I didn't waste a moment. I blurted out my plan as quickly as I could, hoping she'd understand. Hoping she'd be willing to take a chance and play her part.

When I was finished, Kell just stared at me, then said, 'We'll have to see about that.'

And the way she said it? It gave nothing away. I had absolutely no idea if I'd convinced her to help or convinced her I was crazy. All I knew for sure was that, as Kell walked away, she didn't glance back – not once.

After she was gone, I tested the rope that bound me. If I couldn't get free my plan would fail, no matter what Kell decided to do in the dream world.

I pulled and pulled, despite the pain and exhaustion. I put everything I had into that rope, determined to be strong enough. Determined to tap into some super-human strength, because I damn well wouldn't wimp out this time. Not like three years ago, when that's exactly what Jude and I did.

Deep down I'd always suspected that what went down that night had played a part in it. And now I knew for sure.

All at once, tied up in that Giant Emu, I had that lost cause feeling. I'm sure you know the one I mean. I kept working on the rope, but I knew it was hopeless. Kind of like how Mr Darwin kept doing CPR on you even though you were clearly, unequivocally, gruesomely dead. He was hated for that, by the way. Hated just for *trying* to save you.

Well, just like Mr Darwin must have known there was no pulse, I knew there was no point, but I didn't give up. *You* gave up, though, didn't you? You gave up that night outside the half-house, after you finally mustered the guts to confess your worst ... *and instead of getting help, we chose to ignore you.*

I yanked the ropes as hard as I could ... and that's when I saw him. He was standing in the doorway, watching.

'Finished talking to yourself?' said Marcus, when it was clear that I'd seen him.

He must have been standing by the door the whole time and overheard my conversation with Kell. Or rather, *one half* of the conversation. From his perspective, I would have been talking to no one. From his perspective, I would have sounded stark raving insane.

And that's about the time I noticed the crowbar in his hand – the one that he was clutching way too tight, given that I was tied up and basically helpless. It occurred to me that maybe he'd been working his way up to something *more* than a mere beating.

I stared at Marcus and, in that split second before speaking, I thought about all the plausible lies that I could give to convince him to untie me. But the truth has a certain ring about it. Even if we deny it, like Jude and I did that night, deep in our hearts we somehow always know.

'I've been stuck in a nightmare world that mirrors this place,' I said, taking the punt of my life. 'There are survivors there. I think I know a way to save them. I think I have a plan.'

In the silence that followed, I thought to myself, *I've done it*. Somehow, despite all odds, Marcus actually believes me.

'Casey was only *nine*,' Marcus said through gritted teeth. He wasn't talking to me – not really. He was talking to you. According to Dr Ben that's a fairly natural reaction, given that you're dead and I look so entirely the part. Given that we have the exact same DNA and we were sisters and we shared the same bedroom our whole lives and therefore

258

I *must* have known why you did it. I *must* have had some insight, right?

I could have flat out said 'I'm not her' or 'I don't know why she did it'. But instead I answered the *unspoken* question. I admitted to him the one thing I hadn't admitted to anyone, that blaming me was dead on the money.

'It was three nights before the shootings,' I whispered. 'She tried to get us to help her leave town, but we thought she was kidding. She even joked about taking a gun to school, but we pretended it was a goddamn *game*.'

So Marcus Blue got the truth when even the relentless Dr Ben couldn't session it out of me. Unlike what the papers said, you *did* ask for help. You asked the two people in the whole world who were supposed to love you the most ... and we ignored you.

LUX

We're heading through a classroom dreamscape when Kell stops mid-step, listening intently. *Crap.* I'd hoped to keep her oblivious, but she's apparently too smart for that. Sure enough she points to the south, letting me know that we're being followed. I shake my head to suggest that she's mistaken – an outright lie – and keep on walking. Not my most responsible moment. Ignoring what's coming is a dangerous game, but I'm in no mood to fight yet. I need to think.

The problem is Kell, and whether or not to trust her. I could tell her where the others are headed, so that she can find them while I look for Ivan. Or I could ditch her. But I don't know which one. Is she violent and cruel, like all of the other school-girl monsters? Is she genuinely different? Alice said that Kell was a version of her, but I don't see it. I don't buy it. I met the 'real' Kell, back at Sea World – she confiscated our weapons and made us abandon no-name.

Not exactly Alice-like behaviour. But Goldie and Jude seemed to trust her, so should I trust her too? Given my history, it's not an easy call.

Kell pokes my arm then points to the south again, warning me that the threat's still coming. I can't keep pretending she's wrong, given the noises. Whatever's approaching isn't far off … and that's when I smell it. Burnt flesh again, the same as before. *Shit*. This thing's been tracking me for hours, I've just been too self-absorbed to notice. More to the point, this particular monster hasn't acted on impulse; it's been patient, biding its time. *Not* a good sign.

There's another noise, closer this time … and Kell shoves me out of the way. She puts herself in front, shielding me from whatever's coming. She doesn't have a gun. She doesn't know that I can't die. She doesn't actually *know* me at all, but she's still trying to save my life?

This is my moment. She's distracted – it would be easy to just leave her here. Turn a blind eye to the fact that she has no gun, no way of defending herself against whatever's about to attack. It would make things simpler. I'd never have to worry about whether she is or isn't a threat to the others. Whether she is or isn't something bad, deep down.

But I can't, because of Alice. She might be a world away, but she's in me now. All those murky ideas about what makes a monster must have rubbed off, because I can't just go back to simple black and white. And so I do the unthinkable. I step out from behind Kell, ready to draw the fire. Ready to protect – and to trust – a school-girl monster.

I give Kell a flick of my hand that says *On my mark*, purely out of habit. I'm about to translate, when a deep chocolatey voice says, 'Well *this* feels familiar' … and with that, Ivan steps out from the shadows.

I want to hug him and hit him in equal measure, but there's no time for either. Instead I shove him behind me, together with Kell, while I try to get a fix on what's coming.

'Nothing's coming,' says Ivan, giving me deja vu.

I turn back around, and sure enough the flesh smell is from Ivan – he's cauterised his wounds … and it looks downright awful. His once-glorious claws have been reduced to blackened stumps, but at least they're not still bleeding.

'Took you long enough to notice me,' says Ivan. 'Been a bit distracted?'

The way he emphasises 'distracted' makes me wonder exactly how *much* he has seen? How long has he been tracking me?

Since when? I say with a flick of my wrist.

'Soon as you left me back at the fence. You're getting sloppy.'

He's been tracking me *since the fence*? All that worry about where he was and whether he was dead … *and he was with me the whole time?* The only thing I can think of to say is, 'Why?'

Ivan looks pointedly from me to Kell then says, 'Just making sure you chose to do the right thing.'

My promise. I promised Ivan that I'd kill her, tonight. The stars are still out. Kell's standing on a footpath, which is close enough to stone. I have a gun and she's defenceless. Christ, she even has the right bandage on her hand. Ivan must think that it's fate – that *this* is the moment.

Ivan. He's my only friend and I gave him my word and he believes it's the key to everything and he's hurt and he's waited so long …

I don't say a word. Instead I flick my wrist in the gesture that I've used on him a thousand times. The one that always applied whenever he wanted me to take off my coat or indulge in some other whim of hope or kindness. The one that simply means *No*.

Ivan looks from me to Kell then launches into a detailed response. Only, he's using our sign language and, without his claws, I can't make out a word of it. When he's finished I shake my head and say out loud, 'I don't understand.'

'No kidding,' says Ivan with an irrepressible grin. And then he leans in very close and whispers, 'The dream that created me? When the boy in the trench coat said that I'd help him kill his monster – that killing his monster was the key to everything? He was very specific about *which* monster.'

'Yeah, I got that part,' I say, glancing at Kell.

'Not her,' says Ivan with a scoff. '*There. In there.*' He's jabbing his stump at my chest, my heart.

'You were told to help kill a monster … *in me?*'

'Back then they called them demons, and maybe the word was defeat, but yes. Exactly.' Ivan stares at me wide-eyed, as if he doesn't understand the difference. That it's just another one of his naïve mistakes of language.

'You weren't told to help me kill my monster,' I say, putting it together. 'You were told to help me defeat my demons. You believed that *me defeating my demons* was the key to saving everyone.'

'Isn't that the same thing?' says Ivan, all innocence. But this time I see it – the intellect behind his wide-eyed expression.

Holy. *Shit.* All that stuff about the dream repeating itself? It was never about me killing the girl, just like last time. *It was about the exact opposite of that.* It was about me confronting my nightmare. Dealing with the things that lurked on the inside, under the skin. *Defeating my demons by making the other choice.*

'You were bluffing,' I say, as it all sinks in. 'You were gambling that when the time came I wouldn't pull the trigger.'

'You're my best friend,' says Ivan, but this time I understand exactly what he means by that. He means, *I know you better than anyone* … and maybe even, *I had faith.*

'But if you didn't want me to kill Kell, then why go to such lengths to convince me it needed to happen? That history was destined to repeat itself. *That I had no choice in the matter.'*

Ivan doesn't try to explain. Instead he raises what's left of his hand and taps his nose twice – one of my more specialist signs.

I just stare, dumbfounded, so Ivan leans in and whispers the translation. It's not necessary. I know perfectly well what two taps means. I *created* that sign, specifically for Ivan.

Tap, tap: *reverse psychology, you idiot.*

ALICE

Marcus didn't even flinch at my deepest darkest secret. He just launched straight into telling me his own.

'You remember Tony?' he said. 'That bald guy from the mines that my mum used to date?'

No, actually, I didn't remember Tony. Marcus's mum had dated a lot of men over the years. I didn't want to get sidetracked, though, so I just nodded.

'Well, the two of us used to get into fights, so when he was in town I'd tell Mum I was staying at a friend's house.'

'But you didn't?'

'Sometimes I'd sleep down by the creek, but it got really cold. I moved around a bit, trying to find a good spot. One night I was camping out underneath the water tower – that's where she found me.'

'Who found you?' I said, but he just gave me this look and that was enough. He didn't have to say your name for me to know that he meant you.

'She took me to the old half-house and showed me this hidden room and how to put the boards over the door to keep people from finding it,' said Marcus, watching my face.

'What was she doing at the water tower?' I asked.

Marcus shrugged. 'She used to walk,' he said, looking anywhere but at me. 'She'd sneak out at night and walk all around town. After she showed me the room at the half-house she met me there some nights.'

I couldn't breathe. The idea of you slipping out of our bedroom time and time again while I snored away, completely oblivious? I mean, I knew you must have snuck out to get Dad's gun, but I'd assumed that was a one-time-only deal.

'What did you do at the half-house?'

'Not much. Nothing, really. Sometimes we'd talk about movies, that kind of thing. She'd try and get me to stay up all night with her, but I always fell asleep eventually.'

I thought back to that time and had to wonder – were you staying awake to avoid the nightmares? When you took that gun to school, how long *had* it been since you'd slept?

'How often did she meet you at the half-house?' I said.

'Few times a week … for a few months.'

A few months? A few goddamn *months*?

'And the last time you saw her?' I said. It was the right question to ask. I could tell by the way his jaw clenched and the flush to his cheeks went patchy.

'Three nights before it happened. We'd arranged to meet up. Only, when I got near the half-house I heard voices.'

He didn't have to expand on that. Those voices were ours. Yours and mine and Jude's. So Marcus had been part of that night too, I just never knew it.

'I was mad at first,' he said. 'I thought she'd arranged to be there with Jude on purpose. So I'd have to see it. I hid behind one of the old gravestones. She must have been keeping an eye out, because she noticed me right away. For a minute I thought she might say something to you and Jude but she didn't. She just winked at me then got really … flirty. She climbed the angel statue and started pretending to kiss it to get you and Jude distracted. While you watched her, I snuck into the half-house.'

Well, chalk that up as another 'holy shit' moment. I'd spent years secretly interpreting that last night. Years deciding what the flirting meant. Why you did it and what it said about your character. Mining it for clues and meaning, but all that time I'd had it wrong. You were just putting on a show to sneak Marcus into the half-house.

Okay, maybe there was a *bit* more to it. Maybe it was some kind of ego trip too – flirting in front of both boys, me totally oblivious. Maybe it made you feel in control and powerful at a time when, clearly, you were neither. But as for all my long-stretch theories? Utter nonsense. It was all just a bloody distraction.

'I went into the hidden room and waited. There was a storm that night – thunder and lightning, and damn I was cold. The floor was stone and there was a hole in the roof. I thought I'd never get to sleep, but I must have because the next thing I knew she was shaking me awake. She had stuff with her. *That* stuff,' said Marcus, indicating a sleeping bag and a backpack near where I was tied up.

It wasn't your backpack: it was mine. Blue instead of red. I'd looked for it after Merryview, but I couldn't find it anywhere. All I could find was yours, and I wanted nothing to do with anything of *yours*. I guess you must have grabbed the wrong one that night, either because it was dark or because you were rushing. I recognised the sleeping bag too. It was Dad's, though I doubt he even noticed it was gone.

'Tell me what happened,' I said, then I added, 'Please.' In my head I was screaming *Please, please, PLEASE*, but saying it once was enough to get him going.

'She wanted to leave,' said Marcus, chewing hard on his bottom lip. 'She said she'd had a dream, and knew it was time. She said the dream was a "sign from the heavens". And then she laughed and laughed like she'd just said something hilarious.'

The dream with Lux: the dream where you'd told a so-called heavenly creature 'It's time' – and the angel had obliged by blowing your head off.

'And you said no …' I whispered, as the hugeness of it sunk in. Marcus slowly shook his head.

'I said *yes*. I wanted to leave with her. Even though I should have stayed to look out for Casey, I *would have left with her*.'

So Marcus had been in love with you, just like Jude had been in love with you. Did you know that? Did you love him back? Was he the Romeo in your tragedy, or was he just something to play with? Was killing his darling Casey not so random after all?

'Why didn't you leave then?' I said.

'There was lightning, like there is tonight. I told her we should wait until it passed.'

'And then what happened?' I said, because it was the only thing I *could* say.

'We waited,' he said, 'but the storm just kept on building ... then eventually it was morning. It was too late to run away. She told me to meet her back at the half-house after dark, and we'd go then. I went back the next night, but she never showed. The next day at school she said we'd leave *that* night for sure, so as soon as it got dark I snuck back to the half-house. I was the first to arrive so I got all of our stuff out from the secret room and stacked it by the door, so we'd be ready to leave as soon as she got there. I divided everything into two piles for each of us to carry. It was all there, everything except the gun.'

Marcus knew you had the gun. He knew you had the goddamn gun.

'She said we'd need a gun to shoot rabbits for dinner, and to protect ourselves from dingoes,' he said, almost in a whisper. 'She'd nicked it from your dad's shed. I thought she must have just taken it home in the meantime, in case he noticed it was missing. Or that she'd decided we wouldn't take it with us after all. I didn't think anything *bad* would happen.'

Now that Marcus had gotten it all out he was staring at me, waiting for me to say something. I knew what he wanted – he wanted me to absolve him, like I'd wanted absolution myself for three whole miserable years. Wanted it from Dr Ben and from Dad and from the kids who spat on me. Wanted it from myself, if I'm really honest. Wanted it so bad that I'd have taken it from anyone.

'If I'd said we should leave despite the lightning, Casey wouldn't be dead,' said Marcus, when the silence dragged on. He said it as a statement, but it wasn't a statement, not really. In his heart, it was a question. It was *his* Big Question. The one he'd no doubt been swallowing down for just as long as I'd been choking on mine.

I knew I had to give him an answer. The right thing was to just come out and say, 'It wasn't your fault'. It would have been true, too. *Of course* it wasn't his fault. I *knew* it wasn't his fault … and yet? And yet right at that moment all I could think was that, yes – he should have bloody well left despite the lightning. That everything might have been different if you'd both just gone.

Marcus was watching me, waiting. I was being unfair and I knew it, but I didn't have 'fair' in me right then, so I changed the subject. I said, 'Can I see?'

If Marcus was expecting a different reaction he didn't show it. He just kicked the backpack within my reach, but I couldn't undo the zip with my hands tied. I figured that was on purpose, a deliberate taunt. It wasn't. When Marcus realised I couldn't open the backpack he knelt down and untied me, no threats, no dramas.

Once my hands were free I carefully laid out the contents like they were artefacts … which in a way, I guess they were.

You'd packed Dad's missing boots, the ones he always said were 'bloody lifesavers out bush', even though they wouldn't have come close to fitting. You had all the essentials too: maps, a compass, the chemical that turns creek water clear. You even had printouts on how to survive – what plants to eat and how to find water.

You had money as well, just under $150, all in small notes and change. I don't know how you came by that kind of cash since you didn't have a job. It wasn't anywhere near enough to start a new life, but you were young – you wouldn't have known that. To you, $150 probably seemed like a fortune. *For you, that kind of money would have taken time to save.*

'It's all there. I didn't take anything,' said Marcus, but I hardly heard him.

You see, I'd just seen the photo. It wasn't the one that used to hang above the mantle. I had no idea where or when it was taken. There was nothing written on the back. No *Miranda*, no date, no *Mum*. Just a tatty old photo of her on a swing, with a hanky in her hair – one with yellow boats on it. And around her neck, a chain was tucked under the T-shirt. I couldn't see what was hidden against her skin; maybe there was nothing there at all.

As far as I can tell, that photo was one of only two 'indulgences' you packed. The *other* took a little longer to find. It was deep inside the backpack's hidden pocket, sketched onto the paper that I'd come to know so well. Only, there were no pages ripped out of your infamous Scribble Book. The drawing I was looking at was from *another* book, then.

I have no idea how many nightmares you had, or how many Scribble Books you filled, cover to cover. All I know is it was a single sheet of paper in the backpack. That you only chose to take one drawing with you into your new life, back when 'life' was still what you were planning. A drawing of the two of us standing side by side and smiling. A drawing with the half-house in the background, only this time fully built. But the page was folded right down the middle, so you couldn't quite tell if it was meant to be two girls and a whole house, or just one girl and half a house, reflected. Whether it was meant to be both of us, or just one of us, and if the latter, then who?

I stared at the drawing that was maybe of us and maybe wasn't and one very important point hit home. You'd gone to Marcus with your running-away bag *after* we all left the half-house. You were planning on leaving town even *after* Jude and I ignored you, and *after* that fateful nightmare with Lux and the gun.

That meant it really wasn't *just* my fault. Me saying nothing hadn't necessarily been the straw that broke you. It probably played a part, but it wasn't a lay-down misère from that point on. The last person who could have changed your mind *wasn't me*. That didn't make me any less guilty or any less to blame, but it did mean I wasn't *alone* in the guilt of it. No, right there in the thick of it with me was none other than Marcus. Poor Marcus Blue, who had once been so funny and smart and kind. Who had once known you and maybe even loved you. Who had once had a sister called Casey.

Were there others connected to you in ways that counted? Was there a reason that, three years on, Lauren dreamt of herself as a little kid with our mum's hanky? Did you give it to her in some moment of sharing, and had it been haunting her ever since? Was Dad part of the guilty-conscience club too? Is *that* why he couldn't even look at me? Did Jude tell his mum about your 'confession' after all, and did she dismiss it? Is *that* why she hated me so badly? Was it because if she knew that I was complicit, *then so was she?* Were there others who hid their guilt behind spit and hate and blame because they just couldn't face it? Did you maybe try to reach out to a lot of people and *none* of us listened? Could it have been any number of townsfolk with me inside that giant bird, confessing?

I don't suppose it matters. Just knowing that I wasn't the *only* person who could have made a difference … well, it helped me do the one thing for Marcus that nobody had been able to do for me. *I forgave him.* I said, 'It wasn't your fault,' and I meant it.

Marcus just stared at me, his eyes brimming with all kinds of emotion. Relief? Rage? He still had the crowbar. Maybe I'd said the exact wrong thing and pushed him over the edge.

The silence stretched on and on but I resisted the impulse to fill it with prattle. Instead I started packing up your things, item by item, finally putting the past away. I got as far as Dad's Blundstones before I stopped. And just like that, Ivan's 'tell Boots the truth about who he is' finally made sense.

'I met a kid,' I said. 'He looked just like you, only younger. In the dream that created him he was wearing Transformer pyjamas and these exact boots.'

Marcus stared at me for the longest time; then he said, 'I had that dream. I never told anyone.'

I waited for him to ask more questions or demand more proof but when he finally spoke it was simply, 'You need a doctor'. Then he carried me to his piece of shit car, and drove me home.

On the way he explained about the bruises. How he'd just wanted to talk out there on the highway, but then I'd acted all crazy. How I'd said that I didn't even know who Casey was. That I didn't even *care* who Casey was. *Then I'd said, 'Where's my gun?'*

He'd figured I must be a monster, exactly like you.

It was still dark when we got back to town. Marcus wanted to take me straight to Dr Appleby's but I shook my head, so he took me home.

Dad was useless. He just stared at the blood like it was all some bad dream, and did nothing. It was Marcus who dug out the first-aid kit and made me sip water. Who bullied Appleby into making a house call. Who waited by my side until I was all patched up … and then left, to go and turn himself in.

(six months later)

LUX

'Enough?' says Ivan, with his mouth instead of his hands.

'Measly,' I say, pretending to inspect the food that he's scavenged. 'Fortunately, I've done a much better job,' which is clearly not true.

Ivan waves his stumps around with great gusto. When he's finished, he punctuates the whole thing with a dramatic 'And *that's* what I think about *that!*'

Without his claws, there's no way I can possibly tell what he just said to me, which is the whole point. This has become Ivan's favourite joke.

'You've developed quite the potty mouth,' I say with a fake scowl, as if I've understood perfectly. 'You're wrong about the T-shirt, though – it *does* make you look fat.'

It's enough to spur Ivan into a whole new pretend tirade, which he's clearly enjoying. I humour him by taking great offence as I lead us home.

It's dusk by the time we make it back to the perimeter fence. I unlock the gate and Ivan hisses as we pass through, just like he always does. It's not actually the *same* razor wire that took his claws, but he likes to pretend there's still a vendetta.

'Want me to beat it up for you?' I say, giving the offending wire a threatening glare.

Ivan just raises one eyebrow – a new skill that he's ever so proud of.

When we're safely inside with the gate locked behind us, we head straight for the Lookout. Ivan and I used to refer to it as 'the bastard', on account of the way it was an *absolute bastard* to move to this particular spot, despite the help of a dreamt-up trailer. Kell's been on a bit of a warpath about that kind of negative talk, though. She says it's bad for morale and neither of us are game to challenge her on it. Besides, Kell's probably right: she usually is when it comes to that stuff.

When we get to the Lookout, Kell's already there, waiting.

'Everyone's inside?' I say, and Kell nods. I punch in the key code and open the Lookout's reinforced door. It's a growing cast in here come nightfall, but that's how we do things now. When the monsters are out, the survivors stay in. We haven't lost anyone since Boots, and numbers are slowly growing.

Ivan pushes past me and crouches down next to Polly, our newest recruit. I found her out in the nightmares just before dawn this morning. The poor kid was a mess, but she's taken a real shine to Ivan, just like they all do.

Jude and Goldie are handing out pillows and organising the rations. They're still in the honeymoon phase, and it's a wonder they get anything done. I've never met two people more prone to long, loving gazes, but Ivan made me promise I'd quit with the teasing.

'And the big hand points to …?' says Kell, reminding me to check the time. Ivan found me a working wristwatch a few weeks back, but I'm still learning how to read it. I've been counting the minutes out loud, which attracts a lot of ribbing, but I'm okay with that. Getting teased for being hopeless is a damn sight better than being revered for … well, the opposite.

I give Kell a nod to let her know that it's time, and she comes and stands beside me. Kell and I divide up the honours when it comes to running this place, but the 'goodnight' is always from us both, together. Kell says that, given how we fight half the time, the unity's important. I think that we both just secretly like doing it.

'Sleep tight, kiddos,' I say, hamming up the role of father figure.

'Sweet dreams,' says Kell, pun intended.

It's not exactly an original routine, but she's right – the kids love it, especially the little ones. I guess it makes them feel all tucked-in and looked after. And it turns out kids need *that* as much as food and water.

I shut the door, making doubly sure it's locked. Kell and I are alone out here now, just the two of us. She walks away, not saying a word.

I check the perimeter, but that's just an excuse. Bells and

pots and other noisy items are tied all along the fence, so if anything tries to attack we'll know it.

What I'm *really* doing is stalling. I force myself to walk slowly, because it's not a big enclosure. Other than the Lookout and the Rocket, not much else fits: a clothesline, a few toys in the dirt, an annex made from bedsheets. I don't know what the future holds for the kids who call this place home – I've grilled Ivan a few times for hints, but he always plays dumb. He says he never knew what would happen once he'd helped me defeat my demons – that the 'saving the last survivors' part was vague. I'm not sure whether I believe him, but I *do* trust him, and that's probably enough.

I catch my reflection in one of the pots that's tied to the fence. I don't wear the trench coat or the belts anymore. Too damn uncomfortable. Besides, the wings aren't such a big deal these days – the kids don't need *me* for hope, now they've gotten their own back. Ivan's like a pig in shit about that.

Staring at my reflection, I see there's still blood on my face from where I got knifed last night. I spit polish it off, and just like that, I'm good as new. Same as always. I might change in the ways that count, but I'll always *look* exactly like I did when she knew me.

I finish walking the perimeter and find myself standing outside the Rocket, again. We call it the Rocket because it used to be in some Mission-to-Mars dreamscape. There were closer things – *lighter* things – that we could have dragged to this spot instead, but Ivan insisted on the Rocket.

He liked the irony – of choosing something that was dreamt up *as a way to reach other worlds*. Bit of a cruel joke if you ask me, since I *can't* reach her world. That was probably the point. Now that his hundred-year mission to 'save the last survivors' is officially underway, Ivan's taking on side projects. Getting me to lighten up is his absolute favourite.

I stare at the Rocket, knowing that Alice is in there. Sort of. The rusty old spaceship lines up with her bedroom, so technically she's a world away *and* she's right through that door. I focus on the second part … probably more than I should. The truth is I stop off here *most* nights, before heading out into the nightmares. I sit on the dirt and I stare at the door. I won't always come, mooning like this. I want Alice to move on and one day I'll do the same. Once the kids in here are safe enough – when the worst of the monsters are gone – there'll be other places. Other things. I've got eternity in store – this is just the beginning for me, by definition. But right now I want to be here, at the Rocket. I almost never go any closer. Being so near yet so far is too much of a tease. I generally have more self-control than to actually go inside … but tonight's the exception.

Five steps and I'm standing right in front of the hatch door. The Rocket isn't exactly huge – I'm guessing it was a little kid that dreamt it. Everything's on a slightly smaller scale, so climbing through the hatch is always tricky. My wings are the problem, but I'm slowly getting the hang of how to control them.

Inside there's still a bit of a spaceship feel about the place, though that's changing. Little personal touches are growing day by day – the drawings, some knick-knacks, a bed. Kell's already here, just like she always is at this time of night. Right now she's busy sketching something onto the wall, mostly in charcoal. She doesn't turn around, but she knows that I'm here. She knows *why* I'm here. I've weakened before.

I stand in a corner, not saying a word. Alice must be close – I can't see her or feel her, but my heart's racing. I close my eyes and imagine her instead. I imagine her growing up and making friends and seeing the world and falling in love and finding her way. No, I don't imagine it, I *hope* it. Talk about an about-face on *that* front.

Kell must have turned around and seen me standing here with my eyes closed. She must think I look ridiculous, because I hear her say, 'Pathetic.' I don't care that she's probably right. I don't care *what* she thinks about how I look. Actually, I don't care what *anyone* thinks about all that anymore. I smile to myself; Ivan's 'lighten-up' campaign might actually be working.

ALICE

Marcus walked me home again today, which is sort of becoming our thing. After we visit whoever's next on our list, he strolls with me all the way to my front door, comes inside to say a quick hi to Dad, and then ends up staying for dinner. He says it's because his nanna's a lousy cook, but we both know that's not the real reason.

Tonight when we got inside Dad was out back feeding your sort-of-pet kookaburra. He's making an effort, and Marcus is helping.

'I'll go get changed,' I said to Marcus as I headed to our room. Although, I suppose it's finally *my* room now, as opposed to yours and mine. I pushed our beds together to make it a double, and Marcus helped me paint the walls this pale green that I'm kind of regretting. We're going to paint it again once I pick something new, but I'm still deciding.

I'm working out what my personal style is, you know? It's a work in progress.

It was getting late, so I hurried to change out of my school clothes. Not the infamous dress, if that's what you're thinking. These days I wear a skirt and top in more or less the right colours. It sets me apart a bit but that's okay. I'll never really 'blend' in this town, so I might as well embrace it.

I pulled on a comfy tracksuit and picked up my journal. Sitting at the desk, I tried to decide what to write about. Was it too soon to declare some progress with Mrs Connor? Should I mention that Dad made small talk over breakfast, which was kind of a really big deal?

But then I heard something behind me. I spun around and there she was, suspended in mid-air again. They did a pretty good job of lining things up – their camp, my room – but the furniture still doesn't mirror exactly. Whenever Kell sits on the bed in that world, she looks downright gravity-defying in this one.

'What, did I scare you?' said Kell, paying me out.

'Yeah, I'm terrified.'

Kell just rolled her eyes, exactly like I do. We've got stuff like that in common, funnily enough. In fact, crazy as it sounds, we're kind of becoming sort-of-almost friends. God, wouldn't Dr Ben have a field day with that? I mean, me *literally* 'learning to like myself'? Talk about vomit-worthy. It's true, though, I *do* like her. She's got her issues, sure, but she's not a monster or anything. Well, not unless you count her being *monstrously* judgemental when it comes to fashion choices. It took her all of about two seconds to notice my outfit. She gave it an exaggerated once-over, then said, 'Really?' I just shrugged.

'It's all that fitted.' Which was basically true. After I got back, things changed for me. I don't just pick at my food anymore, trying to deny even the simple pleasures. I eat slowly. I appreciate every mouthful … and I'm packing on the kilos because of it. Seriously, these days I'm sporting some major healthy roundness instead of the punishment thin. I rather like it, to be honest. The filled-in cheeks, the hint at some curves. It suits me. It's the look of a girl who's comfortable in her own skin.

'What's it even *made* of?' said Kell, leaning in for a closer look at my trackie, but still keeping her distance. Because the one thing we *never* do is touch. Sometimes I wonder what Kell told the others about that. Whether she lied and said that we'd tried, but the magic was gone. Bullshit of course. The truth is Kell and I have *no idea* what would happen if we touched again because, since that night back at the Emu, we haven't done it.

It's not something we ever talked about. There was never any 'pros and cons' discussion, we just avoid contact. Keep a buffer, you know? It started that first time we met up again, almost six months ago.

It was a Tuesday, my second Tuesday since swapping back, and I was aching with bruises. Everything hurt, but that wasn't my main problem. No, my *main* problem was Kell. You see, I'd waited at Dumbo's Peak every night for over a week, first by myself and then with Marcus, but she *still* hadn't showed. That's when the doubts set in. I worried that the plan I'd laid out back inside the Emu was a bust. That Kell had heard me wrong about when and where to meet. Or that she and the others were dead. Or that when she said, 'We'll have to see about that,' she really meant 'No': that she'd chosen *not* to come.

And here's the thing: *I'd given her that choice.* Hell, I'd kept my plan a secret from Lux precisely so that she could have it. So Kell could decide for herself whether or not to help, without all the pressure. Because it had to be her call, like with Lux, when he put the gun down. Because you can't force someone to 'do good' any more than you can force them into the opposite. Because there's always a choice … and I'd gambled that a version of me would make the right one.

The actual plan itself was never much; just an idea, really. The notion that if Kell and I worked together, we could help. That maybe I could get her the code to the Lookout, and we'd take it from there. *That if the two of us communicated, lives could be saved.* Radical concept, I know, and yet I'd blown it. *Kell wasn't coming.* But I was wrong. On the ninth day she was right there waiting. A world away, I'd finally come through.

We stayed at Dumbo's Peak until dawn, that Tuesday night. Kell and I talked for hours while Marcus just sat there, watching me chat to thin air, but trusting it anyway. Questions, theories, apologies – we covered the lot. And by sunrise Kell had agreed to help. Or rather, we'd agreed to help each other. That was almost six months ago, and Kell and I have met up most nights since. But we always keep our distance, careful not to touch. Even though Kell would probably love the chance to swap into my world once in a while, for a meal and a shower. Even though I would *definitely* love the chance to swap into her world, for Lux.

But it's not about what we want.

'So, everyone's safe inside then?' I said, trying to distract myself. Kell gave me a 'dumb question' look, and fair enough too. They're always safe in the Lookout by now, I know that. But sometimes I still like hearing it.

The Lookout's just outside my window, except that it isn't. Except that it's a world away. I've worked out the exact spot where it must be, right on top of the letterbox. I can't see it, but I can imagine it. And over the months I've hounded Kell for details. Tidbits of information to help me form a mental image. Like the patch of green that Ivan planted along the back wall. And the annex made from bedsheets for afternoon shade. *And the bullet marks from the attack two months back.* It was a bad attack, apparently, but everyone survived. The monsters might have breached the fence but they couldn't get into the panic room. Thank heavens for Mrs Bell and her paranoia – she clearly paid top dollar.

Not that there's much point buying yourself a state-of-the-art panic room if you're going to get loose with the door code. It only took Marcus four visits, twelve cups of tea, and a packet of Monte Carlo biscuits to charm it out of her. The boy really does have a way with people. In fact, I'd say he's getting more and more of the old Marcus back.

He'll never be *quite* the same – *none* of us will – but he's a lot closer to his former self than he is to that boy with the crowbar.

'And how's *my* old gang?' I asked, just to piss Kell off.

'Peachy,' she said, not taking the bait. 'Dunno says hi.' I got Kell to tell Dunno a while back that her real name's Lauren, but the kid insists on sticking with Dunno. She says she's not the same girl as some 'other version' and, hey, who could possibly argue?

'And the others? Everyone else?'

'Fine,' said Kell. *Fine.* Just one little word, but I'll take it. If I've had a bad day, which still happens often enough, hearing that they're 'fine' always helps.

Part of it's the new faces – more kids, safe for now – and part of it is the old ones. You see, the townsfolk dream of the dead more calmly now. From the descriptions that Kell gives me, I'd say there are more and more versions of the kids you killed who've found their way into the fold. Not the *same* kids, obviously. I'm not suggesting that the dead have been replaced or 'live on' or anything easy and cheesy. I guess I just like the idea of infinite, unknowable possibilities. I like it a lot better than my closed-off 'no reason, no fairness, no God' mantra of before.

'Anyone new?' I asked, like I do every night.

'Just one,' said Kell. 'A kid calling herself Polly. She insists it's her actual name.'

We used to think that remembering your dream or your name was a total exception: that it was only the rare few who did. But plenty of kids know exactly who they are these days, so maybe we were wrong. Or maybe we were right and things are just changing. Either way, I don't know a Polly. Maybe she's too young for me to recognise her around town. Too young, even, for her to recognise me? I like that idea; that she's part of a brand new, fresh generation.

'And Lux?' I said, because I couldn't help asking.

'Got himself knifed a bit,' said Kell with a shrug. The Hollywood Blonde, perhaps, or one of her lackeys? The who or what didn't matter – what mattered was that Lux had been hurt, *again*.

Lux is the only one who goes out at night anymore. Ivan hates it and I hate it more, but Lux just won't budge on the subject. According to Kell he says that we can't just *ignore* the nightmares or the monsters, and then he plays the immortal card, which makes it hard to argue.

'Bad?' I asked, trying to pretend it didn't kill me that he was hurt and I was elsewhere. That I couldn't patch him up or hold him in my arms or scold him to *please be more careful*.

'He'll live,' said Kell, giving me nothing. Then, 'I've got five for you today.' She fished a scrap of paper out of her camo pants. Paper's hard to come by so Lux re-uses the same piece, which has almost no white left on it. It took Kell a moment to find the new notes, crammed between all the old crossed-out ones.

'Skipping rope?' she said, squinting at Lux's tiny scrawl. *Skipping rope.* Two words was all it took for me to know that the nightmare belonged to Sally Dawson, whose sister died that day. I made a mental note to tell Marcus – I figured maybe we could go and see her tomorrow, after we tried again with Mrs Cooper.

Anger is almost always their first reaction when they see me on their doorstep. But I don't run away from it anymore; I let them get it all out. After that, if and when they're ready, I talk. Nobody in our town ever really talked about what happened, especially not with me, but that's what I do. I tell them about Merryview and the cuts and the punishment walks and the mail on my doorstep. I tell them about hating myself and tempting fate and dying my hair and looking for answers and being *goddamn terrified* of turning out like you.

And sometimes – not always but sometimes – they talk back. They yell or they whisper, they cry or don't, they pace or stay weirdly still. I let them ask their questions and I answer everything – absolutely everything. Even if I'm not sure, or it makes me look bad, or it makes them feel worse, I give them an answer. And you know what? Usually *that* helps too. Maybe it's because *any* answer is better than none. Then again, maybe they really do just need someone to talk to. Someone who isn't pretending it didn't happen or that it won't always hurt or that it makes any sense, even years later.

I can't take their pain away. I can't magically fix it so that they start dreaming of fluffy bunnies. I can try, though, and sometimes that's enough. It's a start.

According to Kell, things in her world are slowly getting better. The nightmares aren't as bad as they used to be, so maybe it's even progress.

I don't do it alone. Marcus is always there with me. He says he's concerned for my safety, but it's more than that. He's part of it too now. Hell, maybe he was *always* part of it. Besides, it helps for people to see that Marcus and I are friends. For them to understand that he forgave me, even after what my sister did to his, and that I forgave him, even after what he did to me.

The scar's actually quite impressive – it runs from my nose to my chin, puckering the top lip slightly. This might sound a bit messed up, but I actually rather *like* it. That's not some throwback to the self-destructive me of old. I like it because it *literally* marked the start of something new.

The morning after Marcus turned himself in I dragged myself down to the station. I took Sergeant Collins aside and said, 'It was an accident. I slipped.' Collins was having none of it. He went on and on about 'consequences' and 'violence not being the answer'. I begged him to not lay charges. To give Marcus a second chance. *To just let me forgive him instead.*

Something about me standing there all beaten up, crying my heart out, must have won Collins over. He started shuffling papers around, getting emotional too. Eventually he said, 'Fine, have it your way. Just make sure you never slip again, okay, Alice?'

After that, people took notice. Hell, half the town had probably fantasised about hurting me, but seeing it for real? Seeing my face all broken and swollen? Violence just isn't in everyone. We might *think* it is. We might imagine it *could* be, but the ugly truth of hurting another? It never really helps. It doesn't scratch the itch or even the score or make things better.

And the fact that the cut left a scar? It means that I'm different. Different to the way *you* looked, but also different to the me who was so hell-bent on destruction. I know, I know, it's not about difference on the outside it's about difference on the inside blah blah blah. Well, whatever. No one's perfect. I *like* the new me.

Marcus takes a less philosophical view, of course. He feels awful about my scar, or rather, what caused it. At least once a week, when I'm least expecting it, he apologises all over again. I've tried to reassure him that it's okay, but you know what? He did the deed. In a moment of weakness he lashed out and hurt someone in a way that he can never take back. That's *his* thing to get over. That's *his* shame to atone for.

Anyway, after 'skipping rope', Kell had four more notes for me. I didn't know what they meant, not yet, but I still wrote them down. It's a small town; with enough details Marcus and I can usually guess who dreamt up each horror. It helps us work out who's still hurting the most, so we can add them to our list.

And then, after Kell had delivered the notes, it was my turn. I used to just hold up printouts or pictures in books, but that was too much detail. Now I draw instead. I study the 'good eats' and sketch them as simply as I can, for Kell to copy. Given the paper shortage, she's taken to drawing straight onto the walls. Plants mostly, with the occasional grub or nut. A growing mural of what you can live on out bush. Because here's the thing – Kell and the others don't just rely on the dreams and nightmares for food anymore. *They also rely on the land.* On the endless 'beyond' that can keep you alive, if you know what to look for. That's where *I* come in; researching what's edible, like you with your survival printouts. Helping Kell draw it on walls a world away.

I know, I know – drawing was *your* hidden talent, but thanks to some practice, I'm actually not half bad. And guess what? Having that in common with you doesn't bother me like maybe once it would have.

When Kell had finished adding a bush yam to her wall, it was time to go. I hate our goodbyes. Not because I'm sentimental. It's because I always waver the most in our 'see you soon' moments. I start wishing that I could just reach out and touch Kell's hand. That I could try and swap back, to Lux. Do what *I* wanted, what would make *me* happy.

But like I said, it's not just about me. There are other people to think of now, and Kell and I are trying to do right by them. To invest in something bigger than ourselves, you know? Dumb question – of course you wouldn't.

The point is, what if I *did* go to Lux and got stuck in his world forever? It's not as if we understand how things work on that front. There's no manual, no rulebook. What if the crazy force that allowed Kell and me to swap went away? What if it simply ran out and left us stranded? I'm not much good at leading a gang of kids, and Kell would be downright *lousy* at helping the townsfolk deal with what happened. And so we stay put. We don't take any chances.

Besides, sometimes you've got to deal with the problems in front of you. Work on the issues in your own world, you know? Sometimes skipping out is like running away.

So Kell and I said goodbye for another night. Well, sort of. Our goodbyes never involve any use of the actual word. I don't know why: too serious, I guess. Usually it's just some pay-out or joke that heralds her departure. Tonight she gave me a flick of her wrist then helpfully provided the translation: 'pathetic'. Ivan's teaching her the language as best he can without claws, but he insists on covering all the insults first. And that was it. On the touching note of 'pathetic', Kell turned to leave. But then she stopped. She stood with her back to me; she sighed.

'There,' said Kell, pointing right at me, 'and there,' pointing to the corner of my room. And then she shook her head and left.

I stared at the spot where she'd pointed, my heart racing. Kell didn't have to explain, to expand. *Lux was here. He was standing in that corner, albeit a world away.* I couldn't see him and he couldn't see me, but thanks to Kell we at least knew where to look. Where to imagine.

It's not always the case. Lux normally stays away, or if he *does* come, then Kell doesn't tell me. Our moments together – if that's what you'd call them – are rare. And they happen less and less, which is probably healthy. For the best, et cetera. But I'm not perfect, and neither are endings. Saying goodbye isn't always tidy and flawless and clean. I'm not a goddamn pillar of self-restraint. And so tonight when Lux showed up, I wasn't complaining.

I stared at his empty corner, staying perfectly still. I imagined him walking towards me. Standing right in front of me, kissing the air of my mouth. Breathing in the nothingness of my neck. Reaching out and touching me, touching into me, through me. Inching forward until our bodies overlapped, sharing the same space. Him literally inside me, and me inside him too, infinitely connected.

I won't pretend that I could actually *feel* him. I know there's no 'mysterious connection', no invisible thread any more than I have – or had – with you. But I talked to him anyway, mostly in whispers. Not that he heard me or will ever know what I said.

It doesn't have to be that way. We could cheat. We could pass messages through Kell, like sneaky kids in a classroom. Kell the middleman, delivering all our 'he said, she said' longings. But we don't. Back at the start I didn't and he didn't either and pretty soon that just became our way. I guess neither one of us wanted to be the one to cave. To swap our proper in-the-flesh goodbye for some cheap tease. *Some cheap tease a bit like tonight was.*

Deep down I already know that my moments with Lux – or whatever they are – will have to stop. That sooner or later we'll both need to do that impossible thing: move on. Because you can't live in the past, right? You can't obsess forever over someone who's gone.

But tonight, for maybe one of the last times, I savoured the moment. I closed my eyes and indulged in the classics of loss. Thoughts like 'I love you' and 'I miss you' and 'it's not fair' and 'what I wouldn't give to see you again, just one more time'. And then, in a lot less time than it used to take, I pulled myself together. I wiped my eyes and refocused on the now, on my actual life.

Tonight my 'actual life' involved football. When I eventually went back out into the lounge room Marcus and Dad were watching the game, which is becoming their thing. Dad never says much – just the occasional 'nice pass' or whatever, but it's a start. It's a shitload better than how things *used* to be.

I cooked dinner – chops with chips – that we ate in front of the TV. Marcus waited for Dad to fall asleep on the couch, and then he went home. He only hangs around for my sake. It's better between Dad and me when he's here. Less pressure. Less silence, you know?

I'm not saying it'll ever be easy and carefree between Marcus and me. My sister killed his sister. He almost killed me, or at least he almost tried to. But I don't think either of us is really the *type* for easy and carefree anymore. Not yet, anyway. And besides, we understand one another. We share the same goals, the same pain. It's raw, but it's friendship.

Once Marcus was gone I squirted some dishwashing liquid into the pan, so that the bubbles could work on the grime overnight. Then I went to write in my journal. Not the journal I keep about the nightmares that Kell describes, so I can follow up on who's still hurting. This journal – *the one I've been writing to you.*

So here we are, then. I guess that more or less brings you up to date. Right now I'm sitting at our desk – the one with two sets of initials scratched into the paint and a rainbow stain where your textas leaked. It's taken me a long time to write this to you, but I'm done now. This is the end of our story. After I've finished tonight's entry I'll pack this journal away for good, along with the rest of 'you'.

Marcus and I have collected up everything – the backpack, your running-away printouts, Dad's boots. I even got your Scribble Book back from down at the station. Sergeant Collins was reluctant to hand it over at first, until I explained what I had planned. When I told him that I was going to get rid of it all, no fuss, no glory, he thought it was a sensible idea. And so yes, I've even got the very last picture you drew of Lux, which was always at the heart of it.

It's not everything you ever owned, of course. I packed up most of your things last month and gave them to charity. Some of your stuff is still hanging around the house too. It's not like I purged every reminder, like you did when Mum left. But the big-ticket items – the things that really matter – they're ready to go.

Marcus and I debated all kinds of possible fates for them, but in the end the answer was obvious. *The half-house.* In the morning, before first light, Marcus and I are going to put your things right back under the floorboards. We're going to bury them in the same secret spot where you once kept your running-away bag, alongside Dad's gun. Your artefacts won't be pondered over in some macabre but trendy exhibition, or sold on the internet to rubberneckers, or given another second of undeserved glory. Instead they'll be buried, not far from the children you killed.

Maybe a generation from now someone will find our little stash. Maybe they'll read this journal and decide that your twin sister really was bonkers after all. But guess what? I don't care. I'm not paranoid anymore about people thinking I'm crazy. Or more specifically, *that I'm crazy like you*.

Because here's the thing, dear sister – it's not about *you* anymore. It's not about whether I'm 'like you' or 'not like you' or any of that You-You-You drama. The world doesn't revolve around one disturbed girl, no matter how low she sank to make an impression. Life is *more* than that. It's blissful and rubbish and crappy and kind and infinite worlds of emotion. And you know what? So are people. We've all got good in us and bad in us, and miles of murky greyness. I suppose the difference is what you choose to focus on. Whether it's on the gutter, or on the stars, or just on your miserable self.

And so when I take this journal to the half-house tomorrow, it won't be as your sister – it will be as the stand-alone me. A definite work in progress. A girl who sometimes gets it right and sometimes gets it wrong, but mostly hits the human in-between.

And you know what else? As I walk there for the first time since that terrible night … *I will not count a single goddamn step along the way.*

ACKNOWLEDGEMENTS

Thank you to Susannah Chambers, who backed this story and whose incredible talents helped to make it so much stronger.

Thank you to Sophie Splatt and Eva Mills, who guided this story through to the end with unwavering insight and skill.

Thank you to Clare Keighery and Theresa Bray for going above and beyond, as well as everyone else in the wonderful Allen & Unwin team.

Thank you to Mum and Dad, who gave me their complete support when it came to writing this book ... just like they've always done, with everything.

Thank you to Adam, Sian, Mark, Sarah, Dave, Greg and Marie for the endless encouragement (and patience) ... and to Harrison, Austin and Ethan for the smiles.

Thank you to Joanna Houghton, Kate Armstrong-Smith and Charlotte DeFreyne – trusted readers and dear friends, who always took the time and never doubted.

Thank you to Penny Bissett, for all the loving care.

Thank you to everyone near and dear to me who's accepted 'I have to write' as a legitimate excuse year after year.

And thank you to 'my boys', for more than I could ever put into words. The three of you are my whole world and my love for you is bigger than universes.

ABOUT THE AUTHOR

Kathryn Barker was born in Canberra, but growing up involved plenty of travel. She started primary school in Tokyo (the only kid with a sandwich in her lunchbox) and finished high school in the woods outside Olympia, Washington State, USA (aka that rainy place where *Twilight* was set). In the years that followed she went to university, became a lawyer, changed her mind, re-trained as a film producer and worked in television. Kathryn currently lives in Sydney with her family. *In the Skin of a Monster* is her first novel.